THE HOUND OF DEATH
AND OTHER STORIES

THE
HOUND OF DEATH

AND OTHER STORIES

By

AGATHA CHRISTIE

ODHAMS PRESS LIMITED
LONDON, W.C.2

CONTENTS

THE HOUND OF DEATH

I

IT was from William P. Ryan, American newspaper correspondent, that I first heard of the affair. I was dining with him in London on the eve of his return to New York and happened to mention that on the morrow I was going down to Folbridge.

He looked up and said sharply: "Folbridge, Cornwall?"

Now only about one person in a thousand knows that there is a Folbridge in Cornwall. They always take it for granted that the Folbridge, Hampshire, is meant. So Ryan's knowledge aroused my curiosity.

"Yes," I said. "Do you know it?"

He merely replied that he was darned. He then asked if I happened to know a house called Trearne down there.

My interest increased.

"Very well indeed. In fact, it's to Trearne I'm going. It's my sister's house."

"Well," said William P. Ryan. "If that doesn't beat the band!"

I suggested that he should cease making cryptic remarks and explain himself.

"Well," he said. "To do that I shall have to go back to an experience of mine at the beginning of the war."

I sighed. The events which I am relating took place in 1921. To be reminded of the war was the last thing any man wanted. We were, thank God, beginning to forget. . . . Besides, William P. Ryan on his war experiences was apt, as I knew, to be unbelievably long-winded.

7

But there was no stopping him now.

" At the start of the war, as I dare say you know, I was in Belgium for my paper—moving about some. Well, there's a little village—I'll call it X. A one horse place if there ever was one, but there's quite a big convent there. Nuns in white what do you call 'em—I don't know the name of the order. Anyway, it doesn't matter. Well, this little burgh was right in the way of the German advance. The Uhlans arrived——"

I shifted uneasily. William P. Ryan lifted a hand reassuringly.

" It's all right," he said.   " This isn't a German atrocity story.   It might have been, perhaps, but it isn't. As a matter of fact, the boot's on the other leg. The Huns made for that convent—they got there and the whole thing blew up."

" Oh!" I said, rather startled.

" Odd business, wasn't it?   Of course, off-hand, I should say the Huns had been celebrating and had monkeyed round with their own explosives.   But it seems they hadn't anything of that kind with them. They weren't the high explosive johnnies. Well, then, I ask you, what should a pack of nuns know about high explosive? Some nuns, I should say!"

" It is odd," I agreed.

" I was interested in hearing the peasants' account of the matter. They'd got it all cut and dried. According to them it was a slap-up one hundred per cent. efficient first-class modern miracle. It seems one of the nuns had got something of a reputation—a budding saint—went into trances and saw visions. And according to them she worked the stunt. She called down the lightning to blast the impious Hun—and it blasted him all right—and everything else within range. A pretty efficient miracle, that!

" I never really got at the truth of the matter—

hadn't time. But miracles were all the rage just then
—angels at Mons and all that. I wrote up the thing, put
in a bit of sob stuff, and pulled the religious stop out
well, and sent it to my paper. It went down very well
in the States. They were liking that kind of thing just
then.

" But (I don't know if you'll understand this) in
writing, I got kinder interested. I felt I'd like to know
what really had happened. There was nothing to see at
the spot itself. Two walls still left standing, and on one
of them was a black powder mark that was the exact
shape of a great hound. The peasants round about were
scared to death of that mark. They called it the Hound
of Death and they wouldn't pass that way after dark.

" Superstition's always interesting. I felt I'd like to
see the lady who worked the stunt. She hadn't perished,
it seemed. She'd gone to England with a batch of other
refugees. I took the trouble to trace her. I found she'd
been sent to Trearne, Folbridge, Cornwall."

I nodded.

" My sister took in a lot of Belgian refugees the beginning of the war. About twenty."

" Well, I always meant, if I had time, to look up
the lady. I wanted to hear her own account of the
disaster. Then, what with being busy and one thing and
another, it slipped my memory. Cornwall's a bit out of
the way anyhow. In fact, I'd forgotten the whole thing
till your mentioning Folbridge just now brought it
back."

" I must ask my sister," I said. " She may have
heard something about it. Of course, the Belgians have
all been repatriated long ago."

" Naturally. All the same, in case your sister does
know anything I'll be glad if you'd pass it on to me."

" Of course I will," I said heartily.

And that was that.

2

It was the second day after my arrival at Trearne that the story recurred to me. My sister and I were having tea on the terrace.

"Kitty," I said, "Didn't you have a nun among your Belgians?"

"You don't mean Sister Marie Angelique, do you?"

"Possibly I do," I said cautiously. "Tell me about her."

"Oh! my dear, she was the most uncanny creature. She's still here, you know."

"What? In the house?"

"No, no, in the village. Dr. Rose—you remember Dr. Rose?"

I shook my head.

"I remember an old man of about eighty-three."

"Dr. Laird. Oh! he died. Dr. Rose has only been here a few years. He's quite young and very keen on new ideas. He took the most enormous interest in Sister Marie Angelique. She has hallucinations and things, you know, and apparently is most frightfully interesting from a medical point of view. Poor thing, she'd nowhere to go—and really was in my opinion quite potty —only impressive, if you know what I mean—well, as I say, she'd nowhere to go, and Dr. Rose very kindly fixed her up in the village. I believe he's writing a monograph or whatever it is that doctors write, about her."

She paused and then said.

"But what do you know about her?"

"I heard a rather curious story."

I passed on the story as I had received it from Ryan. Kitty was very much interested.

" She looks the sort of person who could blast you—
if you know what I mean," she said.

" I really think," I said, my curiosity heightened,
" that I must see this young woman."

" Do. I'd like to know what you think of her. Go
and see Dr. Rose first. Why not walk down to the village
after tea?"

I accepted the suggestion.

I found Dr. Rose at home and introduced myself. He
seemed a pleasant young man, yet there was something
about his personality that rather repelled me. It was
too forceful to be altogether agreeable.

The moment I mentioned Sister Marie Angelique he
stiffened to attention. He was evidently keenly interested. I gave him Ryan's account of the matter.

" Ah!" he said thoughtfully. " That explains a great
deal."

He looked up quickly at me and went on.

" The case is really an extraordinarily interesting one.
The woman arrived here having evidently suffered some
severe mental shock. She was in a state of great mental
excitement also. She was given to hallucinations of a
most startling character. Her personality is most unusual. Perhaps you would like to come with me and
call upon her. She is really well worth seeing."

I agreed readily.

We set out together. Our objective was a small cottage
on the outskirts of the village. Folbridge is a most
picturesque place. It lies in the mouth of the river
Fol mostly on the east bank, the west bank is too pre-
cipitous for building, though a few cottages do cling to
the cliffside there. The doctor's own cottage was perched
on the extreme edge of the cliff on the west side. From
it you looked down on the big waves lashing against the
black rocks.

The little cottage to which we were now proceeding lay inland out of sight of the sea.

" The district nurse lives here," explained Dr. Rose. " I have arranged for Sister Marie Angelique to board with her. It is just as well that she should be under skilled supervision."

" Is she quite normal in her manner?" I asked curiously.

" You can judge for yourself in a minute," he replied, smiling.

The district nurse, a dumpy pleasant little body, was just setting out on her bicycle when we arrived.

" Good-evening, nurse, how's your patient?" called out the doctor.

" She's much as usual, doctor. Just sitting there with her hands folded and her mind far away. Often enough she'll not answer when I speak to her, though for the matter of that it's little enough English she understands even now."

Rose nodded, and as the nurse bicycled away, he went up to the cottage door, rapped sharply and entered.

Sister Marie Angelique was lying in a long chair near the window. She turned her head as we entered.

It was a strange face—pale, transparent looking, with enormous eyes. There seemed to be an infinitude of tragedy in those eyes.

" Good-evening, my sister," said the doctor in French.

" Good-evening, M. le docteur."

" Permit me to introduce a friend, Mr. Anstruther."

I bowed and she inclined her head with a faint smile.

" And how are you to-day?" inquired the doctor, sitting down beside her.

" I am much the same as usual." She paused and then went on. " Nothing seems real to me. Are they days that pass—or months—or years? I hardly know. Only my dreams seem real to me."

"You still dream a lot, then?"

"Always—always—and, you understand?—the dreams seem more real than life."

"You dream of your own country—of Belgium?"

She shook her head.

"No. I dream of a country that never existed—never. But you know this, M. le docteur. I have told you many times." She stopped and then said abruptly: "But perhaps this gentleman is also a doctor—a doctor perhaps for the diseases of the brain?"

"No, no." Rose was reassuring, but as he smiled I noticed how extraordinarily pointed his canine teeth were, and it occurred to me that there was something wolf-like about the man. He went on:

"I thought you might be interested to meet Mr. Anstruther. He knows something of Belgium. He has lately been hearing news of your convent."

Her eyes turned to me. A faint flush crept into her cheeks.

"It's nothing, really," I hastened to explain. "But I was dining the other evening with a friend who was describing the ruined walls of the convent to me."

"So it was ruined!"

It was a soft exclamation, uttered more to herself than to us. Then looking at me once more she asked hesitatingly: "Tell me, Monsieur, did your friend say how—in what way—it was ruined?"

"It was blown up," I said, and added: "The peasants are afraid to pass that way at night."

"Why are they afraid?"

"Because of a black mark on a ruined wall. They have a superstitious fear of it."

She leaned froward.

H.D.   B

" Tell me, Monsieur—quick—quick—tell me! What is that mark like?"

" It has the shape of a huge hound," I answered. " The peasants call it the Hound of Death."

" Ah!"

A shrill cry burst from her lips.

" It is true then—it is true. All that I remember is true. It is not some black nightmare. It happened! It happened!"

" What happened, my sister?" asked the doctor in a low voice.

She turned to him eagerly.

" *I remembered*. There on the steps, I remembered. I remembered the way of it. I used the power as we used to use it. I stood on the altar steps and I bade them to come no farther. I told them to depart in peace. They would not listen, they came on although I warned them. And so——" she leaned forward and made a curious gesture. " And so I loosed the Hound of Death on them. . . ."

She lay back on her chair shivering all over, her eyes closed.

The doctor rose, fetched a glass from a cupboard, half-filled it with water, added a drop or two from a little bottle which he produced from his pocket, then took the glass to her.

" Drink this," he said authoritatively.

She obeyed—mechanically as it seemed. Her eyes looked far away as though they contemplated some inner vision of her own.

" But then it is all true," she said. " Everything. The City of the Circles, the People of the Crystal— everything. It is all true."

" It would seem so," said Rose.

His voice was low and soothing, clearly designed to encourage and not to disturb her train of thought.

" Tell me about the City," he said. " The City of Circles, I think you said?"

She answered absently and mechanically.

" Yes—there were three circles. The first circle for the chosen, the second for the priestesses and the outer circle for the priests."

" And in the centre?"

She drew her breath sharply and her voice sank to a tone of indescribable awe.

" The House of the Crystal. . . ."

As she breathed the words, her right hand went to her forehead and her finger traced some figure there.

Her figure seemed to grow more rigid, her eyes closed, she swayed a little—then suddenly she sat upright with a jerk, as though she had suddenly awakened.

" What is it?" she said confusedly. " What have I been saying?"

" It is nothing," said Rose. " You are tired. You want to rest. We will leave you."

She seemed a little dazed as we took our departure.

" Well," said Rose when we were outside. " What do you think of it?"

He shot a sharp glance sideways at me.

" I suppose her mind must be totally unhinged," I said slowly.

" It struck you like that?"

" No—as a matter of fact, she was—well, curiously convincing. When listening to her I had the impression that she actually had done what she claimed to do— worked a kind of gigantic miracle. Her belief that she did so seems genuine enough. That is why——"

" That is why you say her mind must be unhinged. Quite so. But now approach the matter from another angle. Supposing that she did actually work that miracle —supposing that she did, personally, destroy a building and several hundred human beings."

" By the mere exercise of will?" I said with a smile.

" I should not put it quite like that. You will agree that one person could destroy a multitude by touching a switch which controlled a system of mines."

" Yes, but that is mechanical."

" True, that is mechanical, but it is, in essence, the harnessing and controlling of natural forces. The thunderstorm and the power house are, fundamentally, the same thing."

" Yes, but to control the thunderstorm we have to use mechanical means."

Rose smiled.

" I am going off at a tangent now. There is a substance called wintergreen. It occurs in nature in vegetable form. It can also be built up by man synthetically and chemically in the laboratory."

" Well?"

" My point is that there are often two ways of arriving at the same result. Ours is, admittedly, the synthetic way. There might be another. The extraordinary results arrived at by Indian fakirs, for instance, cannot be explained away in any easy fashion. The things we call supernatural are not necessarily supernatural at all. An electric flashlight would be supernatural to a savage. The supernatural is only the natural of which the laws are not yet understood."

" You mean?" I asked, fascinated.

" That I cannot entirely dismiss the possibility that a human being *might* be able to tap some vast destructive force and use it to further his or her ends. The means by which this was accomplished might seem to us supernatural—but would not be so in reality."

I stared at him.

He laughed.

" It's a speculation, that's all," he said lightly.

" Tell me, did you notice a gesture she made when she mentioned the House of the Crystal?"

" She put her hand to her forehead."

" Exactly. And traced a circle there. Very much as a Catholic makes the sign of the cross. Now, I will tell you something rather interesting, Mr. Anstruther. The word crystal having occurred so often in my patient's rambling, I tried an experiment. I borrowed a crystal from someone and produced it unexpectedly one day to test my patient's reaction to it."

" Well?"

" Well, the result was very curious and suggestive. Her whole body stiffened. She stared at it as though unable to believe her eyes. Then she slid to her knees in front of it, murmured a few words—and fainted."

" What were the few words?"

" Very curious ones. She said: ' *The Crystal! Then the Faith still lives!*' "

" Extraordinary !"

" Suggestive, is it not? Now the next curious thing. When she came round from her faint she had forgotten the whole thing. I showed her the crystal and asked her if she knew what it was. She replied that she supposed it was a crystal such as fortune tellers used. I asked her if she had ever seen one before? She replied: ' Never, M. le docteur.' But I saw a puzzled look in her eyes. ' What troubles you, my sister?' I asked. She replied: ' Because it is so strange. I have never seen a crystal before and yet—it seems to me that I know it well. There is something—if only I could remember. . . .' The effort at memory was obviously so distressing to her that I forbade her to think any more. That was two weeks ago. I have purposely been biding my time. To-morrow, I shall proceed to a further experiment."

" With the crystal?"

" With the crystal. I shall get her to gaze into it. I think the result ought to be interesting."

" What do you expect to get hold of?" I asked curiously.

The words were idle ones but they had an unlooked-for result. Rose stiffened, flushed, and his manner when he spoke had changed insensibly. It was more formal, more professional.

" Light on certain mental disorders imperfectly understood. Sister Marie Angelique is a most interesting study."

So Rose's interest was purely professional? I wondered.

" Do you mind if I come along too?" I asked.

It may have been my fancy, but I thought he hesitated before he replied. I had a sudden intuition that he did not want me.

" Certainly. I can see no objection."

He added:

" I suppose you're not going to be down here very long?"

" Only till the day after to-morrow."

I fancied that the answer pleased him. His brow cleared and he began talking of some recent experiments carried out on guinea pigs.

3

I met the doctor by appointment the following afternoon, and we went together to Sister Marie Angelique. To-day the doctor was all geniality. He was anxious, I thought, to efface the impression he had made the day before.

" You must not take what I said too seriously," he observed, laughing. " I shouldn't like you to believe me a dabbler in occult sciences. The worst of me is I have an infernal weakness for making out a case."

" Really?"

" Yes, and the more fantastic it is, the better I like it."

He laughed as a man laughs at an amusing weakness.

When we arrived at the cottage, the district nurse had something she wanted to consult Rose about, so I was left with Sister Marie Angelique.

I saw her scrutinising me closely. Presently she spoke.

" The good nurse here, she tells me that you are the brother of the kind lady at the big house where I was brought when I came from Belgium?"

" Yes," I said.

" She was very kind to me. She is good."

She was silent, as though following out some train of thought. Then she said:

" M. le docteur, he too is a good man?"

I was a little embarrassed.

" Why, yes. I mean—I think so."

" Ah!" She paused and then said: " Certainly he has been very kind to me."

" I'm sure he has."

She looked up at me sharply.

" Monsieur—you—you who speak to me now—do you believe that I am mad?"

" Why, my sister, such an idea never——"

She shook her head slowly—interrupting my protest.

" Am I mad? I do not know—the things I remember —the things I forget . . ."

She sighed, and at that moment Rose entered the room.

He greeted her cheerily and explained what he wanted her to do.

" Certain people, you see, have a gift for seeing things in a crystal. I fancy you might have such a gift, my sister."

She looked distressed.

" No, no, I cannot do that. To try to read the future—that is sinful."

Rose was taken aback. It was the nun's point of view for which he had not allowed. He changed his ground cleverly.

" One should not look into the future. You are quite right. But to look into the past—that is different."

" The past?"

" Yes—there are many strange things in the past. Flashes come back to one—they are seen for a moment —then gone again. Do not seek to see anything in the crystal since that it not allowed you. Just take it in your hands—so. Look into it—look deep. Yes—deeper —deeper still. You remember, do you not? You remember. You hear me speaking to you. You can answer my questions. Can you not hear me?"

Sister Marie Angelique had taken the crystal as bidden, handling it with a curious reverence. Then, as she gazed into it, her eyes became blank and unseeing, her head drooped. She seemed to sleep.

Gently the doctor took the crystal from her and put it

on the table. He raised the corner of her eyelid. Then he came and sat by me.

" We must wait till she wakes. It won't be long, I fancy."

He was right. At the end of five minutes, Sister Marie Angelique stirred. Her eyes opened dreamily.

" Where am I? "

" You are here—at home. You have had a little sleep. You have dreamt, have you not? "

She nodded.

" Yes, I have dreamt."

" You have dreamt of the Crystal? "

" Yes."

" Tell us about it."

" You will think me mad, M. le docteur. For see you, in my dream, the Crystal was a holy emblem. I even figured to myself a second Christ, a Teacher of the Crystal who died for his faith, his followers hunted down —persecuted. . . . But the faith endured."

" The faith endured? "

" Yes—for fifteen thousand full moons—I mean, for fifteen thousand years."

" How long was a full moon? "

" Thirteen ordinary moons. Yes, it was in the fifteenth thousand full moon—of course, I was a Priestess of the Fifth Sign in the House of the Crystal. It was in the first days of the coming of the Sixth Sign . . ."

Her brows drew together, a look of fear passed over her head.

" Too soon," she murmured. " Too soon. A mistake. . . . Ah! yes, I remember! The Sixth Sign! "

She half sprang to her feet, then dropped back, passing her hand over her face and murmuring:

" But what am I saying? I am raving. These things never happened."

" Now don't distress yourself."

But she was looking at him in anguished perplexity.

" M. le docteur, I do not understand. Why should I have these dreams—these fancies? I was only sixteen when I entered the religious life. I have never travelled. Yet I dream of cities, of strange people, of strange customs. Why?" She pressed both hands to her head.

" Have you ever been hypnotised, my sister? Or been in a state of trance?"

" I have never been hypnotised, M. le docteur. For the other, when at prayer in the chapel, my spirit has often been caught up from my body, and I have been as one dead for many hours. It was undoubtedly a blessed state, the Reverend Mother said—a state of grace. Ah! yes," she caught her breath. " *I remember, we too called it a state of grace.*"

" I would like to try an experiment, my sister." Rose spoke in a matter-of-fact voice. " It may dispel those painful half-recollections. I will ask you to gaze once more in the crystal. I will then say a certain word to you. You will answer with another. We will continue in this way until you become tired. Concentrate your thoughts on the crystal, not upon the words."

As I once more unwrapped the crystal and gave it into Sister Marie Angelique's hands, I noticed the reverent way her hands touched it. Reposing on the black velvet, it lay between her slim palms. Her wonderful deep eyes gazed into it. There was a short silence, and then the doctor said: " *Hound.*"

Immediately Sister Marie Angelique answered " *Death.*"

4

I do not propose to give a full account of the experiment. Many unimportant and meaningless words were purposely introduced by the doctor. Other words he repeated several times, sometimes getting the same answer to them, sometimes a different one.

That evening in the doctor's little cottage on the cliffs we discussed the result of the experiment.

He cleared his throat, and drew his note-book closer to him.

" These results are very interesting—very curious. In answer to the words ' Sixth Sign,' we get variously *Destruction, Purple, Hound, Power*, then again *Destruction*, and finally *Power*.   Later, as you may have noticed, I reversed the method, with the following results.   In answer to *Destruction*, I get *Hound*; to *Purple, Power*; to *Hound, Death* again, and to *Power, Hound*. That all holds together, but on a second repetition of *Destruction*, I get *Sea*, which appears utterly irrelevant.   To the words ' Fifth Sign,' I get *Blue, Thoughts, Bird, Blue* again, and finally the rather suggestive phrase *Opening of mind to mind*. From the fact that ' Fourth Sign ' elicits the word *Yellow*, and later *Light*, and that ' First Sign ' is answered by *Blood*, I deduce that each Sign had a particular colour, and possibly a particular symbol, that of the Fifth Sign being a *bird*, and that of the Sixth a *hound*. However, I surmise that the Fifth Sign represented what is familiarly known as telepathy—the opening of mind to mind. The Sixth Sign undoubtedly stands for the Power of Destruction."

" What is the meaning of *Sea*?"

" That I confess I cannot explain.   I introduced the

word later and got the ordinary answer of *Boat*. To
Seventh Sign I got first *Life*, the second time *Love*. To
Eighth Sign, I got the answer *None*. I take it there-
fore that Seven was the sum and number of the signs."

" But the Seventh was not achieved," I said on a
sudden inspiration. " Since through the Sixth came
Destruction!"

" Ah! You think so? But we are taking these—mad
ramblings very seriously. They are really only interesting from a medical point of view."

" Surely they will attract the attention of psychic in-
vestigators."

The doctor's eyes narrowed. " My dear sir, I have
no intention of making them public."

" Then your interest?"

" Is purely personal. I shall make notes on the case,
of course."

" I see." But for the first time I felt, like the blind
man, that I didn't see at all. I rose to my feet.

" Well, I'll wish you good-night, doctor. I'm off
to town again to-morrow."

" Ah!" I fancied there was satisfaction, relief perhaps, behind the exclamation.

" I wish you good luck with your investigations," I
continued lightly. " Don't loose the Hound of Death
on me next time we meet!"

His hand was in mine as I spoke, and I felt the start
it gave. He recovered himself quickly. His lips drew
back from his long pointed teeth in a smile.

" For a man who loved power, what a power that
would be!" he said. " To hold every human being's
life in the hollow of your hand!"

And his smile broadened.

5

That was the end of my direct connection with the affair.

Later, the doctor's note-book and diary came into my hands. I will reproduce the few scanty entries in it here, though you will understand that it did not really come into my possession until some time afterwards.

Aug. 5th. Have discovered that by " the Chosen," Sister M.A. means those who reproduced the race. Apparently they were held in the highest honour, and exalted above the Priesthood. Contrast this with early Christians.

Aug. 7th. Persuaded Sister M.A. to let me hypnotise her. Succeeded in inducing hypnotic sleep and trance, but no *rapport* established.

Aug. 9th. Have there been civilisations in the past to which ours is as nothing? Strange if it should be so, and I the only man with the clue to it. . . .

Aug 12th. Sister M.A. not at all amenable to suggestion when hypnotised. Yet state of trance easily induced. Cannot understand it.

Aug. 13th. Sister M.A. mentioned to-day that in " state of grace " the " gate must be closed, lest another should command the body." Interesting—but baffling.

Aug. 18th. So the First Sign is none other than . . . (*words erased here*) . . . then how many centuries will it take to reach the Sixth? But if there should be a short-cut to Power . . .

Aug. 20th. Have arranged for M.A. to come here with Nurse. Have told her it is necessary to keep patient under morphia. Am I mad? Or shall I be the Superman, with the Power of Death in my hands?

(*Here the entries cease*)

6

It was, I think, on August 29th that I received the letter. It was directed to me, care of my sister-in-law, in a sloping foreign handwriting. I opened it with some curiosity. It ran as follows:

" CHER MONSIEUR,—I have seen you but twice, but I have felt that I could trust you. Whether my dreams are real or not, they have grown clearer of late. . . . And, Monsieur, one thing at all events, the Hound of Death is no dream. . . . In the days I told you of (whether they are real or not, I do not know) He Who was Guardian of the Crystal revealed the Sixth Sign to the People too soon. . . . Evil entered into their hearts. They had the power to slay at will—and they slew without justice—in anger. They were drunk with the lust of Power. When we saw this, We who were yet pure, we knew that once again we should not complete the Circle and come to the Sign of Everlasting Life. He who would have been the next Guardian of the Crystal was bidden to act. That the old might die, and the new, after endless ages, might come again, *he loosed the Hound of Death upon the sea* (being careful not to close the circle). and the sea rose up in the shape of a Hound and swallowed the land utterly. . . .

" Once before I remembered this—*on the altar steps in Belgium*. . . .

" The Dr. Rose, he is of the Brotherhood. He knows the First Sign, and the form of the Second, though its meaning is hidden to all save a chosen few. *He would learn of me the Sixth*. I have withstood him so far— but I grow weak. Monsieur, it is not well that a man should come to power before his time. Many centuries

must go by ere the world is ready to have the power of
death delivered into its hand. . . . I beseech of you,
Monsieur, you who love goodness and truth, to help
me . . . before it is too late.

"Your sister in Christ,
"MARIE ANGELIQUE."

I let the paper fall. The solid earth beneath me
seemed a little less solid than usual. Then I began to
rally. The poor woman's belief, genuine enough, had
almost affected *me*! One thing was clear. Dr. Rose, in
his zeal for a case, was grossly abusing his professional
standing. I would run down and——

Suddenly I noticed a letter from Kitty amongst my
other correspondence. I tore it open.

" Such an awful thing has happened," I read. " You
remember Dr. Rose's little cottage on the cliff? It was
swept away by a landslide last night, and the doctor
and that poor nun, Sister Marie Angelique, were killed.
The *débris* on the beach is too awful—all piled up in a
fantastic mass—from a distance it looks like a great
hound. . . ."

The letter dropped from my hand.

The other facts may be coincidence. A Mr. Rose,
whom I discovered to be a wealthy relative of the
doctor's, died suddenly that same night—it was said
struck by lightning. As far as was known no thunderstorm had occurred in the neighbourhood, but one or
two people declared they had heard one peal of thunder.
He had an electric burn on him " of a curious shape."
His will left everything to his nephew, Dr. Rose.

Now, supposing that Dr. Rose succeeded in obtaining
the secret of the Sixth Sign from Sister Marie Angelique.
I had always felt him to be an unscrupulous man—he

would not shrink at taking his uncle's life if he were sure it could not be brought home to him. But one sentence of Sister Marie Angelique's letter rings in my brain: ". . . being careful not to close the Circle. . . ." Dr. Rose did not exercise that care—was perhaps unaware of the steps to take, or even of the need for them. So the Force he employed returned, completing its circuit. . . .

But of course it is all nonsense! Everything can be accounted for quite naturally. That the doctor believed in Sister Marie Angelique's hallucinations merely proves that *his* mind, too, was slightly unbalanced.

Yet sometimes I dream of a continent under the seas where men once lived and attained to a degree of civilisation far ahead of ours. . . .

Or did Sister Marie Angelique remember *backwards*— as some say is possible—and is this City of the Circles in the future and not the past?

Nonsense—of course the whole thing was mere hallucination!

THE RED SIGNAL

"NO, but how too thrilling," said pretty Mrs. Eversleigh, opening her lovely, but slightly vacant, blue eyes very wide. "They always say women have a sixth sense; do you think it's true, Sir Alington?"

The famous alienist smiled sardonically. He had an unbounded contempt for the foolish pretty type, such as his fellow guest. Alington West was the supreme authority on mental disease, and he was fully alive to his own position and importance. A slightly pompous man of full figure.

"A great deal of nonsense is talked, I know that, Mrs. Eversleigh. What does the term mean—a sixth sense?"

"You scientific men are always so severe. And it really is extraordinary the way one seems to positively know things sometimes—just know them, feel them, I mean—quite uncanny—it really is. Claire knows what I mean, don't you, Claire?"

She appealed to her hostess with a slight pout, and a tilted shoulder.

Claire Trent did not reply at once. It was a small dinner party, she and her husband, Violet Eversleigh, Sir Alington West, and his nephew Dermot West, who was an old friend of Jack Trent's. Jack Trent himself, a somewhat heavy florid man, with a good-humoured smile, and a pleasant lazy laugh, took up the thread.

"Bunkum, Violet! Your best friend is killed in a railway accident. Straight away you remember that you dreamt of a black cat last Tuesday—marvellous, you felt all along that something was going to happen!"

"Oh, no, Jack, you're mixing up premonitions with

intuition now. Come, now, Sir Alington, you must admit
that premonitions are real?"

" To a certain extent, perhaps," admitted the
physician cautiously. " But coincidence accounts for a
good deal, and then there is the invariable tendency to
make the most of a story afterwards—you've always
got to take that into account."

" I don't think there is any such thing as premonition," said Claire Trent, rather abruptly. " Or intuition,
or a sixth sense, or any of the things we talk about so
glibly. We go through life like a train rushing through
the darkness to an unknown destination."

" That's hardly a good simile, Mrs. Trent," said
Dermot West, lifting his head for the first time and taking
part in the discussion. There was a curious glitter in the
clear grey eyes that shone out rather oddly from the
deeply tanned face. " You've forgotten the signals, you
see."

" The signals?"

" Yes, green if it's all right, and red—for danger!"

" Red—for danger—how thrilling!" breathed Violet
Eversleigh.

Dermot turned from her rather impatiently.

" That's just a way of describing it, of course. Danger
ahead! The red signal! Look out!"

Trent stared at him curiously.

" You speak as though it were an actual experience,
Dermot, old boy."

" So it is—has been, I mean."

" Give us the yarn."

" I can give you one instance. Out in Mesopotamia—
just after the Armistice, I came into my tent one evening
with the feeling strong upon me. Danger! Look out!
Hadn't the ghost of a notion what it was all about. I
made a round of the camp, fussed unnecessarily, took
all precautions against an attack by hostile Arabs. Then

I went back to my tent. As soon as I got inside, the
feeling popped up again stronger than ever. Danger!
In the end, I took a blanket outside, rolled myself up
in it and slept there.''

" Well?"

" The next morning, when I went inside the tent, first
thing I saw was a great knife arrangement—about half
a yard long—struck down through my bunk, just where
I would have lain. I soon found out about it—one of the
Arab servants. His son had been shot as a spy. What
have you got to say to that, Uncle Alington, as an
example of what I call the red signal?"

The specialist smiled non-committally.

" A very interesting story, my dear Dermot."

" But not one that you accept unreservedly?"

" Yes, yes, I have no doubt but that you had the
premonition of danger, just as you state. But it is the
origin of the premonition I dispute. According to you,
it came from without, impressed by some outside source
upon your mentality. But nowadays we find that nearly
everything comes from within—from our subconscious
self."

" Good old subconscious," cried Jack Trent. " It's
the jack-of-all-trades nowadays."

Sir Alington continued without heeding the interruption.

" I suggest that by some glance or look this Arab had
betrayed himself. Your conscious self did not notice or
remember, but with your subconscious self it was otherwise. The subconscious never forgets. We believe, too,
that it can reason and deduce quite independently of
the higher or conscious will. Your subconscious self,
then, believed that an attempt might be made to assassin-
ate you, and succeeded in forcing its fear upon your
conscious realisation."

"That sounds very convincing, I admit," said Dermot, smiling.

"But not nearly so exciting," pouted Mrs. Eversleigh.

"It is also possible that you may have been sub-consciously aware of the hate felt by the man towards you. What in old days used to be called telepathy certainly exists, though the conditions governing it are very little understood."

"Have there been any other instances?" asked Claire of Dermot.

"Oh! yes, but nothing very pictorial—and I suppose they could all be explained under the heading of coincidence. I refused an invitation to a country house once, for no other reason than the hoisting of the ' red signal.' The place was burnt out during the week. By the way, Uncle Alington, where does the subconscious come in there?"

"I'm afraid it doesn't," said Sir Alington, smiling.

"But you've got an equally good explanation. Come, now. No need to be tactful with near relatives."

"Well, then, nephew, I venture to suggest that you refused the invitation for the ordinary reason that you didn't much want to go, and that after the fire, you suggested to yourself that you had had a warning of danger, which explanation you now believe implicitly."

"It's hopeless," laughed Dermot. "It's heads you win, tails I lose."

"Never mind, Mr. West," cried Violet Eversleigh. "I believe in your Red Signal implicitly. Is the time in Mesopotamia the last time you had it?"

"Yes—until——"

"I beg your pardon?"

"Nothing."

Dermot sat silent. The words which had nearly left his lips were: "Yes, *until to-night.*" They had come quite unbidden to his lips, voicing a thought which had

as yet not been consciously realised, but he was aware
at once that they were true. The Red Signal was looming
up out of the darkness. Danger! Danger close at
hand!

But why? What conceivable danger could there be
here? Here in the house of his friends? At least—well,
yes, there was that kind of danger. He looked at Claire
Trent—her whiteness, her slenderness, the exquisite
droop of her golden head. But that danger had been
there for some time—it was never likely to get acute.
For Jack Trent was his best friend, and more than his
best friend, the man who had saved his life in Flanders
and been recommended for the V.C. for doing so. A
good fellow, Jack, one of the best. Damned bad luck
that he should have fallen in love with Jack's wife. He'd
get over it some day, he supposed. A thing couldn't go
on hurting like this for ever. One could starve it out—
that was it, starve it out. It was not as though she would
ever guess—and if she did guess, there was no danger
of her caring. A statue, a beautiful statue, a thing of
gold and ivory and pale pink coral . . . a toy for a king,
not a real woman. . . .

Claire . . . the very thought of her name, uttered
silently, hurt him. . . . He must get over it. He'd cared
for women before. . . . " But not like this!" said something. " Not like this." Well, there it was. No danger
there—heartache, yes, but not danger. Not the danger
of the Red Signal. That was for something else.

He looked round the table and it struck him for the
first time that it was rather an unusual little gathering.
His uncle, for instance, seldom dined out in this small,
informal way. It was not as though the Trents were old
friends; until this evening Dermot had not been aware
that he knew them at all.

To be sure, there was an excuse. A rather notorious
medium was coming after dinner to give a *séance*. Sir

Alington professed to be mildly interested in spiritualism. Yes, that was an excuse, certainly.

The word forced itself on his notice. An *excuse*. Was the *séance* just an excuse to make the specialist's presence at dinner natural? If so, what was the real object of his being here? A host of details came rushing into Dermot's mind, trifles unnoticed at the time, or, as his uncle would have said, unnoticed by the conscious mind.

The great physician had looked oddly, very oddly, at Claire more than once. He seemed to be watching her. She was uneasy under his scrutiny. She made little twitching motions with her hands. She was nervous, horribly nervous, and was it, could it be, *frightened*? Why was she frightened?

With a jerk, he came back to the conversation round the table. Mrs. Eversleigh had got the great man talking upon his own subject.

" My dear lady," he was saying, " what *is* madness? I can assure you that the more we study the subject, the more difficult we find it to pronounce. We all practise a certain amount of self-deception, and when we carry it so far as to believe we are the Czar of Russia, we are shut up or restrained. But there is a long road before we reach that point. At what particular spot on it shall we erect a post and say ' On this side sanity, on the other madness '? It can't be done, you know. And I will tell you this, if the man suffering from a delusion happened to hold his tongue about it, in all probability we should never be able to distinguish him from a normal individual. The extraordinary sanity of the insane is a most interesting subject."

Sir Alington sipped his wine with appreciation, and beamed upon the company.

" I've always heard they are very cunning," remarked Mrs. Eversleigh. " Loonies, I mean."

" Remarkably so. And suppression of one's particular

delusion has a disastrous effect very often. All suppressions are dangerous, as psycho-analysis has taught us. The man who has a harmless eccentricity, and can indulge it as such, seldom goes over the border line. But the man "—he paused—" or woman who is to all appearance perfectly normal, may be in reality a poignant source of danger to the community."

His gaze travelled gently down the table to Claire, and then back again. He sipped his wine once more.

A horrible fear shook Dermot. Was *that* what he meant? Was *that* what he was driving at? Impossible, but——

" And all from suppressing oneself," sighed Mrs. Eversleigh. " I quite see that one should be very careful always to—to express one's personality. The dangers of the other are frightful."

" My dear Mrs. Eversleigh," expostulated the physician. " You have quite misunderstood me. The cause of the mischief is in the physical matter of the brain—sometimes arising from some outward agency such as a blow; sometimes, alas, congenital."

" Heredity is so sad," sighed the lady vaguely. " Consumption and all that."

" Tuberculosis is not hereditary," said Sir Alington drily.

" Isn't it? I always thought it was. But madness is! How dreadful. What else?"

" Gout," said Sir Alington, smiling. " And colour blindness—the latter is rather interesting. It is transmitted direct to males, but is latent in females. So, while there are many colour blind men, for a woman to be colour blind, it must have been latent in her mother as well as present in her father—rather an unusual state of things to occur. That is what is called sex limited heredity."

" How interesting. But madness is not like that, is it?"

" Madness can be handed down to men or women equally," said the physician gravely.

Claire rose suddenly, pushing back her chair so abruptly that it overturned and fell to the ground. She was very pale and the nervous motions of her fingers were very apparent.

" You—you will not be long, will you?" she begged. " Mrs. Thompson will be here in a few minutes now."

" One glass of port, and I will be with you, for one," declared Sir Alington. " To see this wonderful Mrs. Thompson's performance is what I have come for, is it not? Ha, ha! Not that I needed any inducement." He bowed.

Claire gave a faint smile of acknowledgment and passed out of the room, her hand on Mrs. Eversleigh's shoulder.

" Afraid I've been talking shop," remarked the physician as he resumed his seat. " Forgive me, my dear fellow."

" Not at all," said Trent perfunctorily.

He looked strained and worried. For the first time, Dermot felt an outsider in the company of his friend. Between these two was a secret that even an old friend might not share. And yet the whole thing was fantastic and incredible. What had he to go upon? Nothing but a couple of glances and a woman's nervousness.

They lingered over their wine but a very short time, and arrived up in the drawing-room just as Mrs. Thompson was announced.

The medium was a plump middle-aged woman, atrociously dressed in magenta velvet, with a loud rather common voice.

" Hope I'm not late, Mrs. Trent," she said cheerily. " You did say nine o'clock, didn't you?"

"You are quite punctual, Mrs. Thompson," said Claire in her sweet, slightly husky voice. "This is our little circle."

No further introductions were made, as was evidently the custom. The medium swept them all with a shrewd, penetrating eye.

"I hope we shall get some good results," she remarked briskly. "I can't tell you how I hate it when I go out and I can't give satisfaction, so to speak. It just makes me mad. But I think Shiromako (my Japanese control, you know) will be able to get through all right to-night. I'm feeling ever so fit, and I refused the welsh rabbit, fond of toasted cheese though I am."

Dermot listened, half-amused, half-disgusted. How prosaic the whole thing was! And yet, was he not judging foolishly? Everything, after all, was natural— the powers claimed by mediums were natural powers, as yet imperfectly understood. A great surgeon might be wary of indigestion on the eve of a delicate operation. Why not Mrs. Thompson?

Chairs were arranged in a circle, lights so that they could conveniently be raised or lowered. Dermot noticed that there was no question of *tests*, or of Sir Alington satisfying himself as to the conditions of the *séance*. No, this business of Mrs. Thompson was only a blind. Sir Alington was here for quite another purpose. Claire's mother, Dermot remembered, had died abroad. There had been some mystery about her. . . . Hereditary. . . .

With a jerk he forced his mind back to the surroundings of the moment.

Everyone took their places, and the lights were turned out, all but a small red-shaded one on a far table.

For a while nothing was heard but the low even breathing of the medium. Gradually it grew more and more stertorous. Then, with a suddenness that made

Dermot jump, a loud rap came from the far end of the room. It was repeated from the other side. Then a perfect crescendo of raps was heard. They died away, and a sudden high peal of mocking laughter rang through the room. Then silence, broken by a voice utterly unlike that of Mrs. Thompson, a high-pitched, quaintly inflected voice.

" I am here, gentlemen," it said. " Yess, I am here. You wish ask me things?"

" Who are you? Shiromako?"

" Yess. I Shiromako. I pass over long time ago. I work. I very happy."

Further details of Shiromako's life followed. It was all very flat and uninteresting, and Dermot had heard it often before. Everyone was happy, very happy. Messages were given from vaguely described relatives, the description being so loosely worded as to fit almost any contingency. An elderly lady, the mother of someone present, held the floor for some time, imparting copy book maxims with an air of refreshing novelty hardly borne out by her subject matter.

" Someone else want to get through now," announced Shiromako. " Got a very important message for one of the gentlemen."

There was a pause, and then a new voice spoke, prefacing its remarks with an evil demoniacal chuckle.

" Ha, ha! Ha, ha, ha! Better not go home. Better not go home. Take my advice."

" Who are you speaking to?" asked Trent.

" One of you three. I shouldn't go home if I were him. Danger! Blood! Not very much blood—quite enough. No, don't go home." The voice grew fainter. " *Don't go home!*"

It died away completely. Dermot felt his blood tingling. He was convinced that the warning was meant for him. Somehow or other, there was danger abroad to-night.

There was a sigh from the medium, and then a groan. She was coming round. The lights were turned on, and presently she sat upright, her eyes blinking a little.

" Go off well, my dear? I hope so."

" Very good indeed, thank you, Mrs. Thompson."

" Shiromako, I suppose?"

" Yes, and others."

Mrs. Thompson yawned.

" I'm dead beat. Absolutely down and out. Does fairly take it out of you. Well, I'm glad it was a success. I was a bit afraid it mightn't be—afraid something disagreeable might happen. There's a queer feel about this room to-night."

She glanced over each ample shoulder in turn, and then shrugged them uncomfortably.

" I don't like it," she said. " Any sudden deaths among any of you people lately?"

" What do you mean—among us?"

" Near relatives—dear friends? No? Well, if I wanted to be melodramatic, I'd say that there was death in the air to-night. There, it's only my nonsense. Goodbye, Mrs. Trent. I'm glad you've been satisfied."

Mrs. Thompson in her magenta velvet gown went out.

" I hope you've been interested, Sir Alington," murmured Claire.

" A most interesting evening, my dear lady. Many thanks for the opportunity. Let me wish you good-night. You are all going on to a dance, are you not?"

" Won't you come with us?"

" No, no. I make it a rule to be in bed by half-past eleven. Good-night. Good-night, Mrs. Eversleigh. Ah! Dermot, I rather want to have a word with you. Can you come with me now? You can rejoin the others at the Grafton Galleries."

"Certainly, uncle. I'll meet you there then, Trent."

Very few words were exchanged between uncle and nephew during the short drive to Harley Street. Sir Alington made a semi-apology for dragging Dermot away, and assured him that he would only detain him a few minutes.

"Shall I keep the car for you, my boy?" he asked, as they alighted.

"Oh, don't bother, uncle. I'll pick up a taxi."

"Very good. I don't like to keep Charlson up later than I can help. Good-night, Charlson. Now where the devil did I put my key?"

The car glided away as Sir Alington stood on the steps vainly searching his pockets.

"Must have left it in my other coat," he said at length. "Ring the bell, will you? Johnson is still up, I dare say."

The imperturbable Johnson did indeed open the door within sixty seconds.

"Mislaid my key, Johnson," explained Sir Alington. "Bring a couple of whiskies and sodas into the library, will you?"

"Very good, Sir Alington."

The physician strode on into the library and turned on the lights. He motioned to Dermot to close the door behind him after entering.

"I won't keep you long, Dermot, but there's just something I want to say to you. Is it my fancy, or have you a certain—*tendresse*, shall we say, for Mrs. Jack Trent?"

The blood rushed to Dermot's face.

"Jack Trent is my best friend."

"Pardon me, but that is hardly answering my question. I dare say that you consider my views on divorce and such matters highly puritanical, but I must remind you that you are my only near relative and that you are my heir."

"There is no qestion of a divorce," said Dermot angrily.

"There certainly is not, for a reason which I understand perhaps better than you do. That particular reason I cannot give you now, but I do wish to warn you. Claire Trent is not for you."

The young man faced his uncle's gaze steadily.

"I do understand—and permit me to say, perhaps better than you think. I know the reason for your presence at dinner to-night."

"Eh?" The physician was clearly startled. "How did you know that?"

"Call it a guess, sir. I am right, am I not, when I say that you were there in your—professional capacity."

Sir Alington strode up and down.

"You are quite right, Dermot. I could not, of course, have told you so myself, though I am afraid it will soon be common property."

Dermot's heart contracted.

"You mean that you have—made up your mind?"

"Yes, there is insanity in the family—on the mother's side. A sad case—a very sad case."

"I can't believe it, sir."

"I dare say not. To the layman there are few if any signs apparent."

"And to the expert?"

"The evidence is conclusive. In such a case, the patient must be placed under restraint as soon as possible."

"My God!" breathed Dermot. "But you can't shut anyone up for nothing at all."

"My dear Dermot! Cases are only placed under restraint when their being at large would result in danger to the community."

" Danger?"

" Very grave danger. In all probability a peculiar form of homicidal mania. It was so in the mother's case."

Dermot turned away with a groan, burying his face in his hands. Claire—white and golden Claire!

" In the circumstances," continued the physician comfortably, " I felt it incumbent on me to warn you."

" Claire," murmured Dermot. " My poor Claire."

" Yes, indeed, we must all pity her."

Suddenly Dermot raised his head.

" I don't believe it."

" What?"

" I say I don't believe it. Doctors make mistakes. Everyone knows that. And they're always keen on their own speciality."

" My dear Dermot," cried Sir Alington angrily.

" I tell you I don't believe it—and anyway, even if it is so, I don't care. I love Claire. If she will come with me, I shall take her away—far away—out of the reach of meddling physicians. I shall guard her, care for her, shelter her with my love."

" You will do nothing of the sort. Are you mad?"

Dermot laughed scornfully.

" *You* would say so, I dare say."

" Understand me, Dermot." Sir Alington's face was red with suppressed passion. " If you do this thing— this shameful thing—it is the end. I shall withdraw the allowance I am now making you, and I shall make a new will leaving all I possess to various hospitals."

" Do as you please with your damned money," said Dermot in a low voice. " I shall have the woman I love."

" A woman who——"

" Say a word against her, and, by God! I'll kill you!" cried Dermot.

A slight chink of glasses made them both swing round. Unheard by them in the heat of their argument, Johnson had entered with a tray of glasses. His face was the imperturbable one of the good servant, but Dermot wondered how much he had overheard.

" That'll do, Johnson," said Sir Alington curtly. " You can go to bed."

" Thank you, sir. Good-night, sir."

Johnson withdrew.

The two men looked at each other. The momentary interruption had calmed the storm.

" Uncle," said Dermot. " I shouldn't have spoken to you as I did. I can quite see that from your point of view you are perfectly right. But I have loved Claire Trent for a long time. The fact that Jack Trent is my best friend has hitherto stood in the way of my ever speaking of love to Claire herself. But in these circumstances that fact no longer counts. The idea that any monetary conditions can deter me is absurd. I think we've both said all there is to be said. Good-night."

" Dermot——"

" It is really no good arguing further. Good-night, Uncle Alington. I'm sorry, but there it is."

He went out quickly, shutting the door behind him. The hall was in darkness. He passed through it, opened the front door and emerged into the street, banging the door behind him.

A taxi had just deposited a fare at a house farther along the street and Dermot hailed it, and drove to the Grafton Galleries.

In the door of the ballroom he stood for a minute bewildered, his head spinning. The raucous jazz music, the smiling women—it was as though he had stepped into another world.

Had he dreamt it all ? Impossible that that grim conversation with his uncle should have really taken place.

There was Claire floating past, like a lily in her white and silver gown that fitted sheathlike to her slenderness. She smiled at him, her face calm and serene. Surely it was all a dream.

The dance had stopped. Presently she was near him, smiling up into his face. As in a dream he asked her to dance. She was in his arms now, the raucous melodies had begun again.

He felt her flag a little.

" Tired? Do you want to stop?"

" If you don't mind. Can we go somewhere where we can talk. There is something I want to say to you."

Not a dream. He came back to earth with a bump. Could he ever have thought her face calm and serene? It was haunted with anxiety, with dread. How much did she know?

He found a quiet corner, and they sat down side by side.

" Well," he said, assuming a lightness he did not feel. " You said you had something you wanted to say to me?"

" Yes." Her eyes were cast down. She was playing nervously with the tassel of her gown. " It's difficult—rather."

" Tell me, Claire."

" It's just this. I want you to—to go away for a time."

He was astonished. Whatever he had expected, it was not this.

" You want me to go away? Why?"

" It's best to be honest, isn't it? I—I know that you are a—a gentleman and my friend. I want you to go away because I—I have let myself get fond of you."

" Claire."

Her words left him dumb—tongue-tied.

" Please do not think that I am conceited enough to

fancy that you—that you would ever be likely to fall in love with me. It is only that—I am not very happy—and—oh! I would rather you went away."

" Claire, don't you know that I have cared—cared damnably—ever since I met you?"

She lifted startled eyes to his face.

" You cared? You have cared a long time?"

" Since the beginning."

" Oh!" she cried. "Why didn't you tell me? Then? When I could have come to you! Why tell me now when it's too late. No, I'm mad—I don't know what I'm saying. I could never have come to you."

" Claire, what did you mean when you said ' now that it's too late?' Is it—is it because of my uncle? What he knows? What he thinks?"

She nodded dumbly, the tears running down her face.

" Listen, Claire, you're not to believe all that. You're not to think about it. Instead, you will come away with me. We'll go to the South Seas, to islands like green jewels. You will be happy there, and I will look after you—keep you safe for always."

His arms went round her. He drew her to him, felt her tremble at his touch. Then suddenly she wrenched herself free.

" Oh, no, please. Can't you see? I couldn't now. It would be ugly—ugly—ugly. All along I've wanted to be good—and now—it would be ugly as well."

He hesitated, baffled by her words. She looked at him appealingly.

" Please," she said. " I want to be good. . . ."

Without a word, Dermot got up and left her. For the moment he was touched and racked by her words beyond argument. He went for his hat and coat, running into Trent as he did so.

" Hallo, Dermot, you're off early."

" Yes, I'm not in the mood for dancing to-night."

"It's a rotten night," said Trent gloomily. "But you haven't got my worries."

Dermot had a sudden panic that Trent might be going to confide in him. Not that—anything but that!

"Well, so long," he said hurriedly. "I'm off home."

"Home, eh? What about the warning of the spirits?"

"I'll risk that. Good-night, Jack."

Dermot's flat was not far away. He walked there, feeling the need of the cool night air to calm his fevered brain.

He let himself in with his key and switched on the light in the bedroom.

And all at once, for the second time that night, the feeling that he had designated by the title of the Red Signal surged over him. So overpowering was it that for the moment it swept even Claire from his mind.

Danger! He was in danger. At this very moment, in this very room, he was in danger.

He tried in vain to ridicule himself free of the fear. Perhaps his efforts were secretly half-hearted. So far, the Red Signal had given him timely warning which had enabled him to avoid disaster. Smiling a little at his own superstition, he made a careful tour of the flat. It was possible that some malefactor had got in and was lying concealed there. But his search revealed nothing. His man, Milson, was away, and the flat was absolutely empty.

He returned to his bedroom and undressed slowly, frowning to himself. The sense of danger was acute as ever. He went to a drawer to get out a handkerchief, and suddenly stood stock still. There was an unfamiliar lump in the middle of the drawer—something hard.

His quick nervous fingers tore aside the handkerchiefs and took out the object concealed beneath them. It was a revolver.

With the utmost astonishment Dermot examined it

keenly. It was of a somewhat unfamiliar pattern, and one shot had been fired from it lately. Beyond that, he could make nothing of it. Someone had placed it in that drawer that very evening. It had not been there when he dressed for dinner—he was sure of that.

He was about to replace it in the drawer, when he was startled by a bell ringing. It rang again and again, sounding unusually loud in the quietness of the empty flat.

Who could it be coming to the front door at this hour? And only one answer came to the question—an answer instinctive and persistent.

" Danger—danger—danger. . . ."

Led by some instinct for which he did not account, Dermot switched off his light, slipped on an overcoat that lay across a chair, and opened the hall door.

Two men stood outside. Beyond them Dermot caught sight of a blue uniform. A policeman!

" Mr. West?" asked the foremost of the two men.

It seemed to Dermot that ages elapsed before he answered. In reality it was only a few seconds before he replied in a very fair imitation of his man's expressionless voice :

" Mr. West hasn't come in yet. What do you want with him at this time of night?"

" Hasn't come in yet, eh? Very well, then, I think we'd better come in and wait for him."

" No, you don't."

" See here, my man, my name is Inspector Verall of Scotland Yard, and I've got a warrant for the arrest of your master. You can see it if you like."

Dermot perused the proffered paper, or pretended to do so, asking in a dazed voice :

" What for? What's he done?"

" Murder. Sir Alington West of Harley Street."

His brain in a whirl, Dermot fell back before his redoubtable visitors. He went into the sitting-room and switched on the light. The inspector followed him.

" Have a search round," he directed the other man. Then he turned to Dermot.

" You stay here, my man. No slipping off to warn your master. What's your name, by the way?"

" Milson, sir."

" What time do you expect your master in, Milson?"

" I don't know, sir, he was going to a dance, I believe. At the Grafton Galleries."

" He left there just under an hour ago. Sure he's not been back here?"

" I don't think so, sir. I fancy I should have heard him come in."

At this moment the second man came in from the adjoining room. In his hand he carried the revolver. He took it across to the inspector in some excitement. An expression of satisfaction flitted across the latter's face.

" That settles it," he remarked. " Must have slipped in and out without your hearing him. He's hooked it by now. I'd better be off. Cawley, you stay here, in case he should come back again, and you can keep an eye on this fellow. He may know more about his master than he pretends."

The inspector bustled off. Dermot endeavoured to get at the details of the affair from Cawley, who was quite ready to be talkative.

" Pretty clear case," he vouchsafed. " The murder was discovered almost immediately. Johnson, the man-servant, had only just gone up to bed when he fancied he heard a shot, and came down again. Found Sir Aling-ton dead, shot through the heart. He rang us up at once and we came along and heard his story."

" Which made it a pretty clear case?" ventured Dermot.

" Absolutely. This young West came in with his uncle and they were quarrelling when Johnson brought in the drinks. The old boy was threatening to make a new will, and your master was talking about shooting him. Not five minutes later the shot was heard. Oh! yes, clear enough. Silly young fool."

Clear enough indeed. Dermot's heart sank as he realised the overwhelming nature of the evidence against him. Danger indeed—horrible danger! And no way out save that of flight. He set his wits to work. Presently he suggested making a cup of tea. Cawley assented readily enough. He had already searched the flat and knew there was no back entrance.

Dermot was permitted to depart to the kitchen. Once there he put the kettle on, and chinked cups and saucers industriously. Then he stole swiftly to the window and lifted the sash. The flat was on the second floor, and outside the window was the small wire lift used by tradesmen which ran up and down on its steel cable.

Like a flash Dermot was outside the window and swinging himself down the wire rope. It cut into his hands, making them bleed, but he went on desperately.

A few minutes later he was emerging cautiously from the back of the block. Turning the corner, he cannoned into a figure standing by the sidewalk. To his utter amazement he recognised Jack Trent. Trent was fully alive to the perils of the situation.

" My God! Dermot! Quick, don't hang about here."

Taking him by the arm, he led him down a by-street, then down another. A lonely taxi was sighted and hailed and they jumped in, Trent giving the man his own address.

" Safest place for the moment. There we can decide what to do next to put those fools off the track. I came round here hoping to be able to warn you before the police got here, but I was too late."

"I didn't even know that you had heard of it. Jack, you don't believe——"

"Of course not, old fellow, not for one minute. I know you far too well. All the same, it's a nasty business for you. They came round asking questions—what time you got to the Grafton Galleries, when you left, etc. Dermot, who could have done the old boy in?"

"I can't imagine. Whoever did it put the revolver in my drawer, I suppose. Must have been watching us pretty closely."

"That *séance* business was damned funny. ' *Don't go home.*' Meant for poor old West. He did go home, and got shot."

"It applies to me too," said Dermot. "I went home and found a planted revolver and a police inspector."

"Well, I hope it doesn't get me too," said Trent. "Here we are."

He paid the taxi, opened the door with his latch-key, and guided Dermot up the dark stairs to his den, which was a small room on the first floor.

He threw open the door and Dermot walked in, whilst Trent switched on the light, and then came to join him.

"Pretty safe here for the time being," he remarked. " Now we can get our heads together and decide what is best to be done."

"I've made a fool of myself," said Dermot suddenly. " I ought to have faced it out. I see more clearly now. The whole thing's a plot. What the devil are you laughing at?"

For Trent was leaning back in his chair, shaking with unrestrained mirth. There was something horrible in the sound—something horrible, too, about the man altogether. There was a curious light in his eyes.

"A damned clever plot," he gasped out. " Dermot, my boy, you're done for."

He drew the telephone towards him.

" What are you going to do?" asked Dermot.

" Ring up Scotland Yard. Tell 'em their bird's here
—safe under lock and key. Yes, I locked the door when
I came in and the key's in my pocket. No good looking
at that other door behind me. That leads into Claire's
room, and she always locks it on her side. She's afraid
of me, you know. Been afraid of me a long time. She
always knows when I'm thinking about that knife—a
long sharp knife. No, you don't——"

Dermot had been about to make a rush at him, but
the other had suddenly produced an ugly-looking
revolver.

" That's the second of them," chuckled Trent. " I
put the first of them in your drawer—after shooting old
West with it—— What are you looking at over my
head? That door? It's no use, even if Claire was to
open it—and she might to *you*—I'd shoot you before you
got there. Not in the heart—not to kill, just wing you,
so that you couldn't get away. I'm a jolly good shot,
you know. I saved your life once. More fool I. No, no,
I want you hanged—yes, hanged. It isn't you I want
the knife for. It's Claire—pretty Claire, so white and
soft. Old West knew. That's what he was here for
to-night, to see if I was mad or not. He wanted to shut
me up—so that I shouldn't get at Claire with the knife.
I was very cunning. I took his latch-key and yours too.
I slipped away from the dance as soon as I got there.
I saw you come out from his house, and I went in. I
shot him and came away at once. Then I went to your
place and left the revolver. I was at the Grafton Galleries
again almost as soon as you were, and I put the latch-
key back in your coat pocket when I was saying good-
night to you. I don't mind telling you all this. There's
no one else to hear, and when you're being hanged I'd
like you to know I did it. . . . There's not a loophole
of escape. It makes me laugh. . . God, how it makes

me laugh! What are you thinking of? What the devil are you looking at?"

" I'm thinking of some words you quoted just now. You'd have done better, Trent, not to come home."

" What do you mean?"

" Look behind you?"

Trent spun round. In the doorway of the communicating room stood Claire—and Inspector Verall. . . .

Trent was quick. The revolver spoke just once—and found its mark. He fell forward across the table. The inspector sprang to his side, as Dermot stared at Claire in a dream. Thoughts flashed through his brain disjointedly. His uncle—their quarrel—the colossal misunderstanding—the divorce laws of England which would never free Claire from an insane husband—" we must all pity her "—the plot between her and Sir Alington which the cunning of Trent had seen through—her cry to him, " Ugly—ugly—ugly!" Yes, but now——

The inspector straightened up again.

" Dead," he said vexedly.

" Yes," Dermot heard himself saying, " he was always a good shot. . . ."

THE FOURTH MAN

CANON PARFITT panted a little. Running for trains was not much of a business for a man of his age. For one thing his figure was not what it was and with the loss of his slender silhouette went an increasing tendency to be short of breath. This tendency the Canon himself always referred to, with dignity, as " *My heart,* you know!"

He sank into the corner of the first-class carriage with a sigh of relief. The warmth of the heated carriage was most agreeable to him. Outside the snow was falling. Lucky to get a corner seat on a long night journey. Miserable business if you didn't. There ought to be a sleeper on this train.

The other three corners were already occupied, and noting this fact Canon Parfitt became aware that the man in the far corner was smiling at him in gentle recognition. He was a clean-shaven man with a quizzical face and hair just turning grey on the temples. His profession was so clearly the law that no one could have mistaken him for anything else for a moment. Sir George Durand was, indeed, a very famous lawyer.

" Well, Parfitt," he remarked genially, " you had a run for it, didn't you?"

" Very bad for my heart, I'm afraid," said the Canon. " Quite a coincidence meeting you, Sir George. Are you going far north?"

" Newcastle," said Sir George laconically. " By the way," he added, " do you know Dr. Campbell Clark?"

The man sitting on the same side of the carriage as the Canon inclined his head pleasantly.

" We met on the platform," continued the lawyer.
" Another coincidence."

Canon Parfitt looked at Dr. Campbell Clark with a
good deal of interest. It was a name of which he had
often heard. Dr. Clark was in the forefront as a physician
and mental specialist, and his last book, " The Problem
of the Unconscious Mind," had been the most discussed
book of the year.

Canon Parfitt saw a square jaw, very steady blue eyes
and reddish hair untouched by grey, but thinning
rapidly. And he received also the impression of a very
forceful personality.

By a perfectly natural association of ideas the Canon
looked across to the seat opposite him, half-expecting to
receive a glance of recognition there also, but the fourth
occupant of the carriage proved to be a total stranger—a
foreigner, the Canon fancied. He was a slight dark man,
rather insignificant in appearance. Huddled in a big
overcoat, he appeared to be fast asleep.

" Canon Parfitt of Bradchester?" inquired Dr. Campbell Clark in a pleasant voice.

The Canon looked flattered. Those " scientific sermons " of his had really made a great hit—especially
since the Press had taken them up. Well, that was what
the Church needed—good modern up-to-date stuff.

" I have read your book with great interest, Dr.
Campbell Clark," he said. " Though it's a bit technical
here and there for me to follow."

Durand broke in.

" Are you for talking or sleeping, Canon?" he asked.
" I'll confess at once that I suffer from insomnia and that
therefore I'm in favour of the former."

" Oh! certainly. By all means," said the Canon.
" I seldom sleep on these night journeys, and the book
I have with me is a very dull one."

" We are at any rate a representative gathering," re-

marked the doctor with a smile. " The Church, the
Law, the Medical Profession."

" Not much we couldn't give an opinion on between
us, eh?" laughed Durand. " The Church for the
spiritual view, myself for the purely worldly and legal
view, and you, doctor, with widest field of all, ranging
from the purely pathological to the—super-psycho-
logical! Between us three we should cover any ground
pretty completely, I fancy."

" Not so completely as you imagine, I think," said
Dr. Clark. " There's another point of view, you know,
that you left out, and that's rather an important one."

" Meaning?" queried the lawyer.

" The point of view of the Man in the Street."

" Is that so important? Isn't the Man in the Street
usually wrong?"

" Oh! almost always. But he has the thing that all
expert opinion must lack—the personal point of view.
In the end, you know, you can't get away from personal
relationships. I've found that in my profession. For
every patient who comes to me genuinely ill, at least five
come who have nothing whatever the matter with them
except an inability to live happily with the inmates of
the same house. They call it everything—from housemaid's knee to writer's cramp, but it's all the same
thing, the raw surface produced by mind rubbing against
mind."

" You have a lot of patients with ' nerves,' I suppose," the Canon remarked disparagingly. His own
nerves were excellent.

" Ah! and what do you mean by that?" The other
swung round on him, quick as a flash. " Nerves!
People use that word and laugh after it, just as you did.
' Nothing the matter with so and so,' they say. ' Just
nerves.' But, good God, man, you've got the crux of
everything there! You can get at a mere bodily ailment

and heal it. But at this day we know very little more
about the obscure causes of the hundred and one forms
of nervous disease than we did in—well, the reign of
Queen Elizabeth!''

" Dear me," said Canon Parfitt, a little bewildered by
this onslaught. "Is that so?"

" Mind you, it's a sign of grace," Dr. Campbell Clark
went on. " In the old days we considered man a simple
animal, body and soul—with stress laid on the former."

" Body, soul and spirit," corrected the clergyman
mildly.

" Spirit?" The doctor smiled oddly. " What do you
parsons mean exactly by spirit? You've never been
very clear about it, you know. All down the ages you've
funked an exact definition."

The Canon cleared his throat in preparation for speech,
but to his chagrin he was given no opportunity. The
doctor went on.

" Are we even sure the word is spirit—might it not be
spirits?"

" Spirits?" Sir George Durand questioned, his eyebrows raised quizzically.

" Yes." Campbell Clark's gaze transferred itself to
him. He leaned forward and tapped the other man
lightly on the breast. " Are you so sure," he said
gravely, " that there is only one occupant of this struc-
ture—for that is all it is, you know—this desirable
residence to be let furnished—for seven, twenty-one,
forty-one, seventy-one—whatever it may be!—years?
And in the end the tenant moves his things out—little by
little—and then goes out of the house altogether—and
down comes the house, a mass of ruin and decay. You're
the master of the house—we'll admit that, but aren't you
ever conscious of the presence of others—soft-footed
servants, hardly noticed, except for the work they do—
work that you're not conscious of having done? Or

friends—moods that take hold of you and make you, for the time being, a ' different man ' as the saying goes? You're the king of the castle, right enough, but be very sure the ' dirty rascal ' is there too."

" My dear Clark," drawled the lawyer. " You make me positively uncomfortable. Is my mind really a battle-ground of conflicting personalities? Is that Science's latest?"

It was the doctor's turn to shrug his shoulders.

" Your body is," he said drily. " If the body, why not the mind?"

" Very interesting," said Canon Parfitt. " Ah! Wonderful science—wonderful science."

And inwardly he thought to himself: " I can get a most arresting sermon out of that idea."

But Dr. Campbell Clark had leant back again in his seat, his momentary excitement spent.

" As a matter of fact," he remarked in a dry pro-fessional manner, " it is a case of dual personality that takes me to Newcastle to-night. Very interesting case. Neurotic subject, of course. But quite genuine."

" Dual personality," said Sir George Durand thought-fully. " It's not so very rare, I believe. There's loss of memory as well, isn't there? I know the matter cropped up in a case in the Probate Court the other day."

Dr. Clark nodded.

" The classic case, of course," he said, " was that of Felicie Bault. You may remember hearing of it?"

" Of course," said Canon Parfitt. " I remember read-ing about it in the papers—but quite a long time ago— seven years at least."

Dr. Campbell Clark nodded.

" That girl became one of the most famous figures in France. Scientists from all over the world came to see her. She had no less than four distinct personalities. They were known as Felicie 1, Felicie 2, Felicie 3, etc."

"Wasn't there some suggestion of deliberate trickery?" asked Sir George alertly.

"The personalities of Felicie 3 and Felicie 4 were a little open to doubt," admitted the doctor. "But the main facts remain. Felicie Bault was a Brittany peasant girl. She was the third of a family of five, the daughter of a drunken father and a mentally defective mother. In one of his drinking bouts the father strangled the mother and was, if I remember rightly, transported for life. Felicie was then five years of age. Some charitable people interested themselves in the children and Felicie was brought up and educated by an English maiden lady who had a kind of home for destitute children. She could make very little of Felicie, however. She describes the girl as abnormally slow and stupid, only taught to read and write with the greatest difficulty and clumsy with her hands. This lady, Miss Slater, tried to fit the girl for domestic service, and did indeed find her several places when she was of an age to take them. But she never stayed long anywhere owing to her stupidity and also her intense laziness."

The doctor paused for a minute, and the Canon, recrossing his legs, and arranging his travelling rug more closely round him, was suddenly aware that the man opposite him had moved very slightly. His eyes, which had formerly been shut, were now open, and something in them, something mocking and indefinable, startled the worthy Canon. It was as though the man were listening and gloating secretly over what he heard.

"There is a photograph taken of Felicie Bault at the age of seventeen," continued the doctor. "It shows her as a loutish peasant girl, heavy of build. There is nothing in that picture to indicate that she was soon to be one of the most famous persons in France.

"Five years later, when she was 22, Felicie Bault had a severe nervous illness, and on recovery the strange phenomena began to manifest themselves. The following are facts attested to by many eminent scientists. The personality called Felicie 1 was indistinguishable from the Felicie Bault of the last twenty-two years. Felicie 1 wrote French badly and haltingly, she spoke no foreign languages and was unable to play the piano. Felicie 2, on the contrary, spoke Italian fluently and German moderately. Her handwriting was quite dissimilar to that of Felicie 1, and she wrote fluent and expressive French. She could discuss politics and art and she was passionately fond of playing the piano. Felicie 3 had many points in common with Felicie 2. She was intelligent and apparently well educated, but in moral character she was a total contrast. She appeared, in fact, an utterly depraved creature—but depraved in a Parisian and not a provincial way. She knew all the Paris *argot*, and the expressions of the chic *demi monde*. Her language was filthy and she would rail against religion and so-called ' good people ' in the most blasphemous terms. Finally there was Felicie 4—a dreamy, almost half-witted creature, distinctly pious and professedly clairvoyant, but this fourth personality was very unsatisfactory and elusive and has been sometimes thought to be a deliberate trickery on the part of Felicie 3—a kind of joke played by her on a credulous public. I may say that (with the possible exception of Felicie 4) each personality was distinct and separate and had no knowledge of the others. Felicie 2 was undoubtedly the most predominant and would last sometimes for a fortnight at a time, then Felicie 1 would appear abruptly for a day or two. After that, perhaps, Felicie 3 or 4, but the two latter seldom remained in command for more than a few hours. Each change was accompanied by severe headache and heavy sleep, and in each case there was complete loss of memory of the other states, the personality in question taking up life where she had left it, unconscious of the passage of time."

" Remarkable," murmured the Canon. " Very remarkable. As yet we know next to nothing of the marvels of the universe."

" We know that there are some very astute impostors in it," remarked the lawyer drily.

" The case of Felicie Bault was investigated by lawyers as well as by doctors and scientists," said Dr. Campbell Clark quickly. " Maitre Quimbellier, you remember, made the most thorough investigation and confirmed the views of the scientists. And after all, why should it surprise us so much? We come across the double-yolked egg, do we not? And the twin banana? Why not the double soul—or in this case the quadruple soul—in the single body?"

" The double soul?" protested the Canon.

Dr. Campbell Clark turned his piercing blue eyes on him.

" What else can we call it? That is to say—if the personality is the soul?"

" It is a good thing such a state of affairs is only in the nature of a ' freak,' " remarked Sir George. " If the case were common, it would give rise to pretty complications."

" The condition is, of course, quite abnormal," agreed the doctor. " It was a great pity that a longer study could not have been made, but all that was put an end to by Felicie's unexpected death."

" There was something queer about that, if I remember rightly," said the lawyer slowly.

Dr. Campbell Clark nodded.

" A most unaccountable business. The girl was found one morning dead in bed. She had clearly been strangled. But to everyone's stupefaction it was presently proved beyond doubt that she had actually strangled herself. The marks on her neck were those of her own fingers. A method of suicide which, though not physically impossible, must have necessitated terrific muscular strength and almost superhuman will power. What had driven the girl to such straits has never been found out. Of course her mental balance must always have been precarious. Still, there it is. The curtain has been rung down for ever on the mystery of Felicie Bault."

It was then that the man in the far corner laughed.

The other three men jumped as though shot. They had totally forgotten the existence of the fourth amongst them. As they stared towards the place where he sat, still huddled in his overcoat, he laughed again.

" You must excuse me, gentlemen," he said, in perfect English that had, nevertheless, a foreign flavour.

He sat up, displaying a pale face with a small jet-black moustache.

" Yes, you must excuse me," he said, with a mock bow. " But really! in science, is the last word ever said?"

" You know something of the case we have been discussing?" asked the doctor courteously.

" Of the case? No. But I knew her."

" Felicie Bault?"

" Yes. And Annette Ravel also. You have not heard of Annette Ravel, I see? And yet the story of the one is the story of the other. Believe me, you know nothing of Felicie Bault if you do not also know the history of Annette Ravel."

He drew out a watch and looked at it.

" Just half an hour before the next stop. I have time to tell you the story—that is, if you care to hear it?"

" Please tell it to us," said the doctor quietly.

" Delighted," said the Canon. " Delighted."

Sir George Durand merely composed himself in an attitude of keen attention.

" My name, gentlemen," began their strange travelling companion, " is Raoul Letardeau. You have spoken just now of an English lady, Miss Slater, who interested herself in works of charity. I was born in that Brittany fishing village and when my parents were both killed in a railway accident it was Miss Slater who came to the rescue and saved me from the equivalent of your English workhouse. There were some twenty children under her care, girls and boys. Amongst these children were Felicie Bault and Annette Ravel. If I cannot make you understand the personality of Annette, gentlemen, you will understand nothing. She was the child of what you call a ' fille de joie ' who had died of consumption abandoned by her lover. The mother had been a dancer, and Annette, too, had the desire to dance. When I saw her first she was eleven years old, a little shrimp of a thing with eyes that alternately mocked and promised—a little creature all fire and life. And at once —yes, at once—she made me her slave. It was ' Raoul, do this for me.' ' Raoul, do that for me.' And me, I obeyed. Already I worshipped her, and she knew it.

" We would go down to the shore together, we three —for Felicie would come with us. And there Annette would pull off her shoes and stockings and dance on the sand. And then when she sank down breathless, she would tell us of what she meant to do and to be.

" ' See you, I shall be famous. Yes, exceedingly famous. I will have hundreds and thousands of silk stockings—the finest silk. And I shall live in an exquisite apartment. All my lovers shall be young and handsome as well as being rich. And when I dance all Paris shall come to see me. They will yell and call and shout and go mad over my dancing. And in the winters I shall not dance. I shall go south to the sunlight. There are villas there with orange trees. I shall have one of them. I shall lie in the sun on silk cushions, eating oranges. As for you, Raoul, I will never forget you, however great and rich and famous I shall be, I will protect you and advance your career. Felicie here shall be my maid—no, her hands are too clumsy. Look at them, how large and coarse they are.'

" Felicie would grow angry at that. And then Annette would go on teasing her.

" ' She is so ladylike, Felicie—so elegant, so refined. She is a princess in disguise—ha, ha.'

" ' My father and mother were married, which is more than yours were,' Felicie would growl out spitefully.

" ' Yes, and your father killed your mother. A pretty thing, to be a murderer's daughter.'

" ' Your father left your mother to rot,' Felicie would rejoin.

" ' Ah! yes.' Annette became thoughtful. ' *Pauvre Maman*. One must keep strong and well. It is everything to keep strong and well.'

" ' I am as strong as a horse,' Felicie boasted.

" And indeed she was. She had twice the strength of any other girl in the Home. And she was never ill.

" But she was stupid, you comprehend, stupid like a brute beast. I often wondered why she followed Annette round as she did. It was, with her, a kind of fascination. Sometimes, I think, she actually hated Annette, and indeed Annette was not kind to her. She jeered at her slowness and stupidity, and baited her in front of the others. I have seen Felicie grow quite white with rage. Sometimes I have thought that she would fasten her fingers round Annette's neck and choke the life out of her. She was not nimble-witted enough to reply to Annette's taunts, but she did learn in time to make one retort which never failed. That was a reference to her own health and strength. She had learned (what I had

always known) that Annette envied her her strong
physique, and she struck instinctively at the weak spot
in her enemy's armour.

" One day Annette came to me in great glee.

" ' Raoul,' she said. ' We shall have fun to-day with
that stupid Felicie. We shall die of laughing.'

" ' What are you going to do?'

" ' Come behind the little shed, and I will tell you.'

" It seemed that Annette had got hold of some book.
Part of it she did not understand, and indeed the whole
thing was much over her head. It was an early work on
hypnotism.

" ' A bright object, they say. The brass knob of my
bed, it twirls round. I made Felicie look at it last
night. " Look at it steadily," I said. " Do not take your
eyes off it." And then I twirled it. Raoul, I was
frightened. Her eyes looked so queer—so queer.
" Felicie, you will do what I say always," I said. " I
will do what you say always, Annette," she answered.
And then—and then—I said: " To-morrow you will
bring a tallow candle out into the playground at twelve
o'clock and start to eat it. And if anyone asks you, you
will say that it is the best *galette* you ever tasted." Oh!
Raoul, think of it!'

" ' But she'll never do such a thing,' I objected.

" ' The book says so. Not that I can quite believe it
—but, oh! Raoul, if the book is all true, how we shall
amuse ourselves!'

" I, too, thought the idea very funny. We passed
word round to the comrades and at twelve o'clock we
were all in the playground. Punctual to the minute,
out came Felicie with a stump of candle in her hand.
Will you believe me, Messieurs, she began solemnly
to nibble at it? We were all in hysterics! Every now
and then one or other of the children would go up to
her and say solemnly: ' It is good, what you eat there,

eh, Felicie?' And she would answer. ' But, yes, it is
the best *galette* I ever tasted.' And then we would shriek
with laughter. We laughed at last so loud that the
noise seemed to wake up Felicie to a realisation of what
she was doing. She blinked her eyes in a puzzled way,
looked at the candle, then at us. She passed her hand
over her forehead.

" ' But what is it that I do here?' she muttered.

" ' You are eating a candle,' we screamed.

" ' *I* made you do it. *I* made you do it,' cried
Annette, dancing about.

" Felicie stared for a moment. Then she went slowly
up to Annette.

" ' So it is you—it is you who have made me ridiculous? I seem to remember. Ah! I will kill you for
this.'

" She spoke in a very quiet tone, but Annette rushed
suddenly away and hid behind me.

" ' Save me, Raoul! I am afraid of Felicie. It was
only a joke, Felicie. Only a joke.'

" ' I do not like these jokes,' said Felicie. ' You
understand? I hate you. I hate you all.'

" She suddenly burst out crying and rushed away.

" Annette was, I think, scared by the result of her
experiment, and did not try to repeat it. But from that
day on, her ascendency over Felicie seemed to grow
stronger.

" Felicie, I now believe, always hated her, but nevertheless she could not keep away from her. She used
to follow Annette around like a dog.

" Soon after that, Messieurs, employment was found
for me, and I only came to the Home for occasional
holidays. Annette's desire to become a dancer was not
taken seriously, but she developed a very pretty singing voice as she grew older and Miss Slater consented
to her being trained as a singer.

" She was not lazy, Annette. She worked feverishly, without rest. Miss Slater was obliged to prevent her doing too much. She spoke to me once about her.

" ' You have always been fond of Annette,' she said. ' Persuade her not to work too hard. She has a little cough lately that I do not like.'

" My work took me far afield soon afterwards. I received one or two letters from Annette at first, but then came silence. For five years after that I was abroad.

" Quite by chance, when I returned to Paris, my attention was caught by a poster advertising Annette Ravelli with a picture of the lady. I recognised her at once. That night I went to the theatre in question. Annette sang in French and Italian. On the stage she was wonderful. Afterwards I went to her dressing-room. She received me at once.

" ' Why, Raoul,' she cried, stretching out her whitened hands to me. ' This is splendid. Where have you been all these years?'

" I would have told her, but she did not really want to listen.

" ' You see, I have very nearly arrived!'

" She waved a triumphant hand round the room filled with bouquets.

" ' The good Miss Slater must be proud of your success.'

" ' That old one? No, indeed. She designed me, you know, for the Conservatoire. Decorous concert singing. But me, I am an artist. It is here, on the variety stage, that I can express myself.'

" Just then a handsome middle-aged man came in. He was very distinguished. By his manner I soon saw that he was Annette's protector. He looked sideways at me, and Annette explained.

" ' A friend of my infancy. He passes through Paris, sees my picture on a poster *et voilà!*'

" The man was then very affable and courteous. In my presence he produced a ruby and diamond bracelet and clasped it on Annette's wrist. As I rose to go, she threw me a glance of triumph and a whisper.

" ' I arrive, do I not? You see? All the world is before me.'

" But as I left the room, I heard her cough, a sharp dry cough. I knew what it meant, that cough. It was the legacy of her consumptive mother.

" I saw her next two years later. She had gone for refuge to Miss Slater. Her career had broken down. She was in a state of advanced consumption for which the doctors said nothing could be done.

" Ah! I shall never forget her as I saw her then! She was lying in a kind of shelter in the garden. She was kept outdoors night and day. Her cheeks were hollow and flushed, her eyes bright and feverish and she coughed repeatedly.

" She greeted me with a kind of desperation that startled me.

" ' It is good to see you, Raoul. You know what they say—that I may not get well? They say it behind my back, you understand. To me they are soothing and consolatory. But it is not true, Raoul, it is not true! I shall not permit myself to die. Die? With beautiful life stretching in front of me? It is the will to live that matters. All the great doctors say that nowadays. I am not one of the feeble ones who let go. Already I feel myself infinitely better—infinitely better, do you hear?'

" She raised herself on her elbow to drive her words home, then fell back, attacked by a fit of coughing that racked her thin body.

" ' The cough—it is nothing,' she gasped. ' And hæmorrhages do not frighten me. I shall surprise the

doctors. It is the will that counts. Remember, Raoul,
I am going to live.'

" It was pitiful, you understand, pitiful.

" Just then, Felicie Bault came out with a tray. A
glass of hot milk. She gave it to Annette and watched
her drink it with an expression that I could not fathom.
There was a kind of smug satisfaction in it.

" Annette too caught the look. She flung the glass
down angrily, so that it smashed to bits.

" ' You see her? That is how she always looks at
me. She is glad I am going to die! Yes, she gloats over
it. She who is well and strong. Look at her, never
a day's illness, that one! And all for nothing. What
good is that great carcass of hers to her? What can
she make of it?'

" Felicie stooped and picked up the broken fragments
of glass.

" ' I do not mind what she says,' she observed in a
sing-song voice. ' What does it matter? I am a respectable girl, I am. As for her. She will be knowing
the fires of Purgatory before very long. I am a Christian.
I say nothing.'

" ' You hate me,' cried Annette. ' You have always
hated me. Ah! but I can charm you, all the same. I
can make you do what I want. See now, if I asked you
to, you would go down on your knees before me now
on the grass.'

" ' You are absurd,' said Felicie uneasily.

" ' But, yes, you will do it. You will. To please me.
Down on your knees. I ask it of you, I, Annette.
Down on your knees, Felicie.'

" Whether it was the wonderful pleading in the voice,
or some deeper motive, Felicie obeyed. She sank
slowly on to her knees, her arms spread wide, her face
vacant and stupid.

" Annette flung back her head and laughed—peal upon peal of laughter.

" ' Look at her, with her stupid face! How ridiculous she looks. You can get up now, Felicie, thank you! It is of no use to scowl at me. I am your mistress. You have to do what I say.'

" She lay back on her pillows exhausted. Felicie picked up the tray and moved slowly away. Once she looked back over her shoulder, and the smouldering resentment in her eyes startled me.

" I was not there when Annette died. But it was terrible, it seems. She clung to life. She fought against death like a madwoman. Again and again she gasped out: ' I will not die—do you hear me? I will not die. I will live—live——'

" Miss Slater told me all this when I came to see her six months later.

" ' My poor Raoul,' she said kindly. ' You loved her, did you not?'

" ' Always—always. But of what use could I be to her? Let us not talk of it. She is dead—she so brilliant, so full of burning life. . . .'

" Miss Slater was a sympathetic woman. She went on to talk of other things. She was very worried about Felicie, so she told me. The girl had had a queer sort of nervous breakdown, and ever since she had been very strange in manner.

" ' You know,' said Miss Slater, after a momentary hesitation, ' that she is learning the piano?'

" I did not know it, and was very much surprised to hear it. Felicie—learning the piano! I would have declared the girl would not know one note for another.

" ' She has talent, they say,' continued Miss Slater. ' I can't understand it. I have always put her down as—well, Raoul, you know yourself, she was always a stupid girl.'

" I nodded.

" ' She is so strange in her manner sometimes—I really don't know what to make of it.'

" A few minutes later I entered the Salle de Lecture. Felicie was playing the piano. She was playing the air that I had heard Annette sing in Paris. You understand, Messieurs, it gave me quite a turn. And then, hearing me, she broke off suddenly and looked round at me, her eyes full of mockery and intelligence. For a moment I thought—— Well, I will not tell you what I thought.

" ' Tiens!' she said. ' So it is you—*Monsieur* Raoul.'

" I cannot describe the way she said it. To Annette I had never ceased to be Raoul. But Felicie, since we had met as grown-ups, always addressed me as *Monsieur* Raoul. But the way she said it now was different— as though the *Monsieur*, slightly stressed, was somehow very amusing.

" ' Why, Felicie,' I stammered.   ' You look quite different to-day?'

" ' Do I?' she said reflectively.   ' It is odd, that. But do not be so solemn, Raoul—decidedly I shall call you Raoul—did we not play together as children?— Life was made for laughter. Let us talk of the poor Annette—she who is dead and buried. Is she in Purgatory, I wonder, or where?'

" And she hummed a snatch of song—untunefully enough, but the words caught my attention.

" ' Felicie,' I cried. ' You speak Italian?'

" ' Why not, Raoul? I am not as stupid as I pretend to be, perhaps.' She laughed at my mystification.

" ' I don't understand——' I began.

" ' But I will tell you. I am a very fine actress, though no one suspects it. I can play many parts—and play them very well.'

" She laughed again and ran quickly out of the room before I could stop her.

" I saw her again before I left. She was asleep in an arm-chair. She was snoring heavily. I stood and watched her, fascinated, yet repelled. Suddenly she woke with a start. Her eyes, dull and lifeless, met mine.

" ' Monsieur Raoul,' she muttered mechanically.

" ' Yes, Felicie. I am going now. Will you play to me again before I go?'

" ' I? Play? You are laughing at me, Monsieur Raoul.'

" ' Don't you remember playing to me this morning?'

" She shook her head.

" ' I play? How can a poor girl like me play.'

" She paused for a minute as though in thought, then beckoned me nearer.

" ' Monsieur Raoul, there are strange things going on in this house! They play tricks upon you. They alter the clocks. Yes, yes, I know what I am saying. And it is all her doing.'

" ' Whose doing?' I asked, startled.

" ' That Annette's. That wicked one's. When she was alive she always tormented me. Now that she is dead, she comes back from the dead to torment me.'

" I stared at Felicie. I could see now that she was in an extremity of terror, her eyes starting from her head.

" ' She is bad, that one. She is bad, I tell you. She would take the bread from your mouth, the clothes from your back, *the soul from your body*. . . .'

" She clutched me suddenly.

" ' I am afraid, I tell you—afraid. I hear her voice —not in my ear—no, not in my ear. Here, in my head——' She tapped her forehead. ' She will drive

me away—drive me away altogther, and then what shall
I do, what will become of me?'

" Her voice rose almost to a shriek. She had in her
eyes the look of the terrified brute beast at bay. . . .

" Suddenly she smiled, a pleasant smile, full of cunning, with something in it that made me shiver.

" ' If it should come to it, Monsieur Raoul, I am
very strong with my hands—very strong with my hands.'

" I had never noticed her hands particularly before.
I looked at them now and shuddered in spite of myself.
Squat brutal fingers, and as Felicie had said, terribly
strong. . . . I cannot explain to you the nausea that
swept over me. With hands such as these her father
must have strangled her mother. . . .

" That was the last time I ever saw Felicie Bault.
Immediately afterwards I went abroad—to South
America. I returned from there two years after her
death. Something I had read in the newspapers of her
life and sudden death. I have heard fuller details to-
night—from you—gentlemen! Felicie 3 and Felicie 4
—I wonder? She was a good actress, you know!"

The train suddenly slackened speed. The man in the
corner sat erect and buttoned his overcoat more closely.

" What is your theory?" asked the lawyer, leaning
forward.

" I can hardly believe——" began Canon Parfitt, and
stopped.

The doctor said nothing. He was gazing steadily at
Raoul Lepardeau.

" *The clothes from your back, the soul from your
body,*" quoted the Frenchman lightly. He stood up.
" I say to you, Messieurs, that the history of Felicie
Bault is the history of Annette Ravel. You did not know
her, gentlemen. I did. *She was very fond of life. . . .*"

His hand on the door, ready to spring out, he turned

suddenly and bending down tapped Canon Parfitt on the chest.

" M. le docteur over there, he said just now, that all *this* "—his hand smote the Canon's stomach, and the Canon winced—" was only a residence. Tell me, if you find a burglar in your house what do you do? Shoot him, do you not?"

" No," cried the Canon. " No, indeed—I mean—not in this country."

But he spoke the last words to empty air. The carriage door banged.

The clergyman, the lawyer and the doctor were alone. The fourth corner was vacant.

THE GIPSY

MACFARLANE had often noticed that his friend, Dickie Carpenter, had a strange aversion to gipsies. He had never known the reason for it. But when Dickie's engagement to Esther Lawes was broken off, there was a momentary tearing down of reserves between the two men.

Macfarlane had been engaged to the younger sister, Rachel, for about a year. He had known both the Lawes girls since they were children. Slow and cautious in all things, he had been unwilling to admit to himself the growing attraction that Rachel's childlike face and honest brown eyes had for him. Not a beauty like Esther, no! But unutterably truer and sweeter. With Dickie's engagement to the elder sister, the bond between the two men seemed to be drawn closer.

And now, after a few brief weeks, that engagement was off again, and Dickie, simple Dickie, hard hit. So far in his young life all had gone so smoothly. His career in the navy had been well chosen. His craving for the sea was inborn. There was something of the Viking about him, primitive and direct, a nature on which subtleties of thought were wasted. He belonged to that inarticulate order of young Englishmen who dislike any form of emotion, and who find it peculiarly hard to explain their mental processes in words. . . .

Macfarlane, that dour Scot, with a Celtic imagination hidden away somewhere, listened and smoked while his friend floundered along in a sea of words. He had known an unburdening was coming. But he had expected the subject matter to be different. To begin with, anyway, there was no mention of Esther Lawes. Only, it seemed, the story of a childish terror.

" It all started with a dream I had when I was a kid. Not a nightmare exactly. She—the gipsy, you know—would just come into any old dream—even a good dream (or a kid's idea of what's good—a party and crackers and things). I'd be enjoying myself no end, and then I'd feel, I'd *know*, that if I looked up, *she'd* be there, standing as she always stood, watching me. . . . With sad eyes, you know, as though she understood something that I didn't. . . . Can't explain why it rattled me so—but it did! Every time! I used to wake up howling with terror, and my old nurse used to say: ' There! Master Dickie's had one of his gipsy dreams again!' "

" Ever been frightened by real gipsies?"

" Never saw one till later. That was queer, too. I was chasing a pup of mine. He'd run away. I got out through the garden door, and along one of the forest paths. We lived in the New Forest then, you know. I came to a sort of clearing at the end, with a wooden bridge over a stream. And just beside it a gipsy was standing—with a red handkerchief over her head—just the same as in my dream. And at once I was frightened! She looked at me, you know. . . . Just the same look —as though she knew something I didn't, and was sorry about it. . . . And then she said quite quietly, nodding her head at me: ' *I shouldn't go that way, if I were you.*' I can't tell you why, but it frightened me to death. I dashed past her on to the bridge. I suppose it was rotten. Anyway, it gave way, and I was chucked into the stream. It was running pretty fast, and I was nearly drowned. Beastly to be nearly drowned. I've never forgotten it. And I felt it had all to do with the gipsy. . . ."

" Actually, though, she warned you against it?"

" I suppose you could put it like that," Dickie
paused, then went on: " I've told you about this dream
of mine, not because it has anything to do with what
happened after (at least, I suppose it hasn't), but because it's the jumping off point, as it were. You'll
understand now what I mean by the ' gipsy feeling.'
So I'll go on to that first night at the Lawes'. I'd just
come back from the west coast then. It was awfully
rum to be in England again. The Lawses were old
friends of my people's. I hadn't seen the girls since
I was about seven, but young Arthur was a great pal
of mine, and after he died, Esther used to write to
me, and send me out papers. Awfully jolly letters, she
wrote! Cheered me up no end. I always wished I
was a better hand at writing back. I was awfully keen
to see her. It seemed odd to know a girl quite well
from her letters, and not otherwise. Well, I went down
to the Lawes' place first thing. Esther was away when I
arrived, but was expected back that evening. I sat
next to Rachel at dinner, and as I looked up and down
the long table a queer feeling came over me. I felt
someone was watching me, and it made me uncomfortable. Then I saw her——"

" Saw who?"

" Mrs. Haworth—what I'm telling you about."

It was on the tip of Macfarlane's tongue to say: " I
thought you were telling me about Esther Lawes." But
he remained silent, and Dickie went on.

" There was something about her quite different from
all the rest. She was sitting next to old Lawes—listening to him very gravely with her head bent down. She
had some of that red tulle stuff round her neck. It had
got torn, I think, anyway it stood up behind her head
like little tongues of flame. . . . I said to Rachel:
' Who's that woman over there. Dark—with a red
scarf!' "

" Do you mean Alistair Haworth? She's got a red scarf. But she's fair. *Very* fair."

" So she was, you know. Her hair was a lovely pale shining yellow. Yet I could have sworn positively she was dark. Queer what tricks one's eyes play on one. . . . After dinner, Rachel introduced us, and we walked up and down in the garden. We talked about reincarnation. . . ."

" Rather out of your line, Dickie!"

" I suppose it is. I remember saying that it seemed to be a jolly sensible way of accounting for how one seems to know some people right off—as if you'd met them before. She said: ' You mean lovers . . .' There was something queer about the way she said it —something soft and eager. It reminded me of something—but I couldn't remember what. We went on jawing a bit, and then old Lawes called us from the terrace—said Esther had come, and wanted to see me. Mrs. Haworth put her hand on my arm and said: ' You're going in?' ' Yes,' I said. ' I suppose we'd better,' and then—then——"

" Well?"

" It sounds such rot. Mrs. Haworth said: ' *I shouldn't go in if I were you. . . .*' He paused. " It frightened me, you know. It frightened me badly. That's why I told you about the dream. . . . Because, you see, she said it just the same way—quietly, as though she knew something I didn't. It wasn't just a pretty woman who wanted to keep me out in the garden with her. Her voice was just kind—and very sorry. Almost as though she knew what was to come. . . . I suppose it was rude, but I turned and left her—almost ran to the house. It seemed like safety. I knew then that I'd been afraid of her from the first. It was a relief to see old Lawes. Esther was there beside him. . . ." He hesitated a minute, and then muttered rather ob-

scurely: " There was no question—the moment I saw
her. I knew I'd got it in the neck."

Macfarlane's mind flew swiftly to Esther Lawes. He
had once heard her summed up as " Six foot one of
Jewish perfection." A shrewd portrait, he thought, as
he remembered her unusual height and the long slenderness of her, the marble whiteness of her face with its
delicate down-drooping nose, and the black splendour
of hair and eyes. Yes, he did not wonder that the
boyish simplicity of Dickie had capitulated. Esther
could never have made his own pulses beat one jot
faster, but he admitted her magnificence.

" And then," continued Dickie, " we got engaged."

" At once?"

" Well, after about a week. It took her about a fortnight after that to find out that she didn't care after
all. . . ." He gave a short bitter laugh.

" It was the last evening before I went back to the
old ship. I was coming back from the village through
the woods—and then I saw *her*—Mrs. Haworth. I mean.
She had on a red tam-o'-shanter, and—just for a
minute, you know—it made me jump! I've told you
about my dream, so you'll understand. . . . Then we
walked along a bit. Not that there was a word Esther
couldn't have heard, you know. . . ."

" No?" Macfarlane looked at his friend curiously.
Strange how people told you things of which they themselves were unconscious!

" And then, when I was turning to go back to the
house, she stopped me. She said: ' You'll be home
soon enough. *I shouldn't go back too soon if I were
you.* . . .' And then I *knew*—that there was something beastly waiting for me . . . and . . . as soon as
I got back Esther met me, and told me—that she'd found
out she didn't really care. . . ."

Macfarlane grunted sympathetically. "And Mrs. Haworth?" he asked.

"I never saw her again—until to-night."

"To-night?"

"Yes. At that doctor Johnny's nursing home. They had a look at my leg, the one that got messed up in that torpedo business. It's worried me a bit lately. The old chap advised an operation—it'll be quite a simple thing. Then as I left the place, I ran into a girl in a red jumper over her nurse's things, and she said: '*I wouldn't have that operation, if I were you.* . . .' Then I saw it was Mrs. Haworth. She passed on so quickly I couldn't stop her. I met another nurse, and asked about her. But she said there wasn't anyone of that name in the home. . . . Queer. . . ."

"Sure it was her?"

"Oh! yes, you see—she's very beautiful. . . ." He paused, and then added: "I shall have the old op, of course—but—but in case my number *should* be up——"

"Rot!"

"Of course it's rot. But all the same I'm glad I told you about this gipsy business. . . . You know, there's more of it if only I could remember. . . ."

2

Macfarlane walked up the steep moorland road. He
turned in at the gate of a house near the crest of the
hill. Setting his jaw squarely, he pulled the bell.

" Is Mrs. Haworth in?"

" Yes, sir. I'll tell her." The maid left him in a low
long room, with windows that gave on the wildness of
the moorland. He frowned a little. Was he making
a colossal ass of himself?

Then he started. A low voice was singing overhead:

> " *The gipsy woman*
> *Lives on the moor*———"

The voice broke off. Macfarlane's heart beat a shade
faster. The door opened.

The bewildering, almost Scandinavian fairness of her
came as a shock. In spite of Dickie's description, he
had imagined her gipsy dark. . . . And he suddenly
remembered Dickie's words, and the peculiar tone of
them. " *You see, she's very beautiful. . . .*" Perfect unquestionable beauty is rare, and perfect unquestionable beauty was what Alistair Haworth
possessed.

He caught himself up, and advanced towards her.
" I'm afraid you don't know me from Adam. I got your
address from the Lawes. But—I'm a friend of Dickie
Carpenter's."

She looked at him closely for a minute or two. Then
she said: " I was going out. Up on the moor. Will
you come too?"

She pushed open the window, and stepped out on the

hillside. He followed her. A heavy, rather foolish-looking man was sitting in a basket-chair smoking.

" My husband! We're going out on the moor, Maurice. And then Mr. Macfarlane will come back to lunch with us. You will, won't you?"

" Thanks very much." He followed her easy stride up the hill, and thought to himself: " Why? Why, on God's earth, marry *that*?"

Alistair made her way to some rocks. " We'll sit here. And you shall tell me—what you came to tell me."

" You knew?"

" I always know when bad things are coming. It is bad, isn't it? About Dickie?"

" He underwent a slight operation—quite successfully. But his heart must have been weak. He died under the anæsthetic.",

What he expected to see on her face, he scarcely knew—hardly that look of utter eternal weariness. . . . He heard her murmur: " Again—to wait—so long—so long. . . ." She looked up: " Yes, what were you going to say?"

" Only this. Someone warned him against this operation. A nurse. He thought it was you. Was it?"

She shook her head. " No, it wasn't me. But I've got a cousin who is a nurse. She's rather like me in a dim light. I dare say that was it." She looked up at him again. " It doesn't matter, does it?" And then suddenly her eyes widened. She drew in her breath. " Oh!" she said. " Oh! How funny! You don't understand. . . ."

Macfarlane was puzzled. She was still staring at him.

" I thought you did. . . . You *should* do. You look as though you'd got it, too. . . ."

" Got what?"

" The gift—curse—call it what you like. I believe

you have. Look hard at that hollow in the rocks.
Don't think of anything, just look. . . . Ah!'' she
marked his slight start. '' Well—you saw something?''

'' It must have been imagination. Just for a second
I saw it full of—blood!''

She nodded. '' I knew you had it. That's the place
where the old sun-worshippers sacrificed victims. I
knew that before anyone told me. And there are times
when I know just how they felt about it—almost as
though I'd been there myself. . . . And there's something about the moor that makes me feel as though I
were coming back home. . . . Of course it's natural
that I should have the gift. I'm a Ferguesson. There's
second sight in the family. And my mother was a
medium until my father married her. Cristine was her
name. She was rather celebrated.''

'' Do you mean by ' the gift ' the power of being
able to see things before they happen?''

'' Yes, forwards or backwards—it's all the same. For
instance, I saw you wondering why I married Maurice
—oh! yes, you did!—It's simply because I've always
known that there's something dreadful hanging over
him. . . . I wanted to save him from it. . . .Women
are like that. With my gift, I ought to be able to prevent it happening . . . if one ever can. . . . I couldn't
help Dickie. And Dickie wouldn't understand. . . .
He was afraid. He was very young.''

'' Twenty-two.''

'' And I'm thirty. But I didn't mean that. There
are so many ways of being divided, length and height
and breadth . . . but to be divided by time is the
worst way of all. . . .'' She fell into a long brooding
silence.

The low peal of a gong from the house below roused
them.

At lunch, Macfarlane watched Maurice Haworth. He

was undoubtedly madly in love with his wife. There was the unquestioning happy fondness of a dog in his eyes. Macfarlane marked also the tenderness of her response, with its hint of maternity. After lunch he took his leave.

" I'm staying down at the inn for a day or so. May I come and see you again? To-morrow, perhaps?"

" Of course. But——"

" But what——"

She brushed her hand quickly across her eyes. " I don't know. I—I fancied that we shouldn't meet again —that's all. . . . Good-bye."

He went down the road slowly. In spite of himself, a cold hand seemed tightening round his heart. Nothing in her words, of course, but——

A motor swept round the corner. He flattened himself against the hedge . . . only just in time. A curious greyish pallor crept across his face. . . .

3

" Good Lord, my nerves are in a rotten state,"
muttered Macfarlane, as he awoke the following morning. He reviewed the events of the afternoon before
dispassionately. The motor, the short-cut to the inn
and the sudden mist that had made him lose his way
with the knowledge that a dangerous bog was no distance
off. Then the chimney pot that had fallen off the
inn, and the smell of burning in the night which he had
traced to a cinder on his hearthrug. Nothing in it all!
Nothing at all—but for her words, and that deep un-
acknowledged certainty in his heart that she *knew*. . . .

He flung off the bedclothes with sudden energy. He
must go up and see her first thing. That would break
the spell. That is, *if he got there safely*. . . . Lord,
what a fool he was!

He could eat little breakfast. Ten o'clock saw him
starting up the road. At ten-thirty his hand was on
the bell. Then, and not till then, he permitted himself
to draw a long breath of relief.

" Is Mrs. Haworth in?"

It was the same elderly woman who had opened the
door before. But her face was different—ravaged with
grief.

" Oh! sir, oh! sir, you haven't heard then?"

" Heard what?"

" Miss Alistair, the pretty lamb. It was her tonic.
She took it every night. The poor captain is beside
himself, he's nearly mad. He took the wrong bottle
off the shelf in the dark. . . . They sent for the doctor,
but he was too late——"

And swiftly there recurred to Macfarlane the words:
" *I've always known there was something dreadful*

hanging over him. I ought to be able to prevent it happening—if one ever can——'' Ah! but one couldn't cheat Fate. . . . Strange fatality of vision that had destroyed where it sought to save. . . .

The old servant went on: '' My pretty lamb! So sweet and gentle she was, and so sorry for anything in trouble. Couldn't bear anyone to be hurt.'' She hesitated, then added: '' Would you like to go up and see her, sir? I think, from what she said, that you must have known her long ago. A *very* long time ago, she said. . . .''

Macfarlane followed the old woman up the stairs, into the room over the drawing-room where he had heard the voice singing the day before. There was stained glass at the top of the windows. It threw a red light on the head of the bed. . . . *A gipsy with a red handkerchief over her head.* . . . Nonsense, his nerves were playing tricks again. He took a long last look at Alistair Haworth.

4

" There's a lady to see you, sir."

" Eh?" Macfarlane looked at the landlady abstractedly. " Oh! I beg your pardon, Mrs. Rowse, I've been seeing ghosts."

" Not really, sir? There's queer things to be seen on the moor after nightfall, I know. There's the white lady, and the Devil's blacksmith, and the sailor and the gipsy——"

" What's that? A sailor and a gipsy?"

" So they say, sir. It was quite a tale in my young days. Crossed in love they were, a while back. . . . But they've not walked for many a long day now."

" No? I wonder if—perhaps—they will again now. . . ."

" Lor! sir, what things you do say! About that young lady——"

" What young lady?"

" The one that's waiting to see you. She's in the parlour. Miss Lawes, she said her name was."

" Oh!"

Rachel! He felt a curious feeling of contraction, a shifting of perspective. He had been peeping through at another world. He had forgotten Rachel, for Rachel belonged to this life only. . . . Again that curious shifting of perspective, that slipping back to a world of three dimensions only.

He opened the parlour door. Rachel—with her honest brown eyes. And suddenly, like a man awakening from a dream, a warm rush of glad reality swept over him. He was alive—alive! He thought: " There's only one life one can be *sure* about! This one!"

" Rachel!" he said, and, lifting her chin, he kissed her lips.

THE LAMP

I

IT was undoubtedly an old house. The whole square was old, with that disapproving dignified old age often met with in a cathedral town. But No. 19 gave the impression of an elder among elders; it had a veritable patriarchal solemnity; it towered greyest of the grey, haughtiest of the haughty, chillest of the chill. Austere, forbidding, and stamped with that particular desolation attaching to all houses that have been long untenanted, it reigned above the other dwellings.

In any other town it would have been freely labelled " haunted," but Weyminster was averse from ghosts and considered them hardly respectable except as the appanage of a " county family." So No. 19 was never alluded to as a haunted house; but nevertheless it remained, year after year, " To be Let or Sold."

Mrs. Lancaster looked at the house with approval as she drove up with the talkative house agent, who was in an unusually hilarious mood at the idea of getting No. 19 off his books. He inserted the key in the door without ceasing his appreciative comments.

" How long has the house been empty?" inquired Mrs. Lancaster, cutting short his flow of language rather brusquely.

Mr. Raddish (of Raddish and Foplow) became slightly confused.

" Er—er—some time," he remarked blandly.

" So I should think," said Mrs. Lancaster drily.

The dimly lighted hall was chill with a sinister chill. A more imaginative woman might have shivered, but

87

this woman happened to be eminently practical. She was tall with much dark brown hair just tinged with grey and rather cold blue eyes.

She went over the house from attic to cellar, asking a pertinent question from time to time. The inspection over, she came back into one of the front rooms looking out on the square and faced the agent with a resolute mien.

" What is the matter with the house?"

Mr. Raddish was taken by surprise.

" Of course, an unfurnished house is always a little gloomy," he parried feebly.

" Nonsense," said Mrs. Lancaster.   " The rent is ridiculously low for such a house—purely nominal. There must be some reason for it. I suppose the house is haunted?"

Mr. Raddish gave a nervous little start but said nothing.

Mrs. Lancaster eyed him keenly. After a few moments she spoke again.

" Of course that is all nonsense, I don't believe in ghosts or anything of that sort, and personally it is no deterrent to my taking the house; but servants, unfortunately, are very credulous and easily frightened. It would be kind of you to tell me exactly what—what thing *is* supposed to haunt this place."

" I—er—really don't know," stammered the house agent.

" I am sure you must," said the lady quietly.   " I cannot take the house without knowing. What was it? A murder?"

" Oh! no," cried Mr. Raddish, shocked by the idea of anything so alien to the respectability of the square. " It's—it's—only a child."

" A child?"

" Yes."

" I don't know the story exactly," he continued reluctantly. " Of course, there are all kinds of different
versions, but I believe that about thirty years ago a
man going by the name of Williams took No. 19.
Nothing was known of him; he kept no servants; he had
no friends; he seldom went out in the day time. He
had one child, a little boy. After he had been there
about two months, he went up to London, and had
barely set foot in the metropolis before he was recognised as being a man ' wanted ' by the police on some
charge—exactly what, I do not know. But it must
have been a grave one, because, sooner than give himself up, he shot himself. Meanwhile, the child lived on
here, alone in the house. He had food for a little time,
and he waited day after day for his father's return. Unfortunately, it had been impressed upon him that he
was never under any circumstances to go out of the
house or to speak to anyone. He was a weak, ailing,
little creature, and did not dream of disobeying this
command. In the night, the neighbours, not knowing
that his father had gone away, often heard him sobbing
in the awful loneliness and desolation of the empty
house."

Mr. Raddish paused.

" And—er—the child starved to death," he concluded, in the same tones as he might have announced
that it had just begun to rain.

" And it is the child's ghost that is supposed to haunt
the place?" asked Mrs. Lancaster.

" It is nothing of consequence really," Mr. Raddish
hastened to assure her. " There's nothing *seen*, not
seen, only people say, ridiculous, of course, but they
do say they hear—the child—crying, you know."

Mrs. Lancaster moved towards the front door.

" I like the house very much," she said. " I shall

get nothing as good for the price. I will think it over and let you know.''

" It really looks very cheerful, doesn't it, Papa?''

Mrs. Lancaster surveyed her new domain with approval. Gay rugs, well-polished furniture, and many knick-knacks, had quite transformed the gloomy aspect of No. 19.

She spoke to a thin, bent old man with stooping shoulders and a delicate mystical face. Mr. Winburn did not resemble his daughter; indeed no greater contrast could be imagined than that presented by her resolute practicalness and his dreamy abstraction.

" Yes,'' he answered with a smile, " no one would dream the house was haunted.''

" Papa, don't talk nonsense! On our first day too.''

Mr. Winburn smiled.

" Very well, my dear, we will agree that there are no such things as ghosts.''

" And please,'' continued Mrs. Lancaster, " don't say a word before Geoff. He's so imaginative.''

Geoff was Mrs. Lancaster's little boy. The family consisted of Mr. Winburn, his widowed daughter, and Geoffrey.

Rain had begun to beat again the window—pitter-patter, pitter-patter.

" Listen,'' said Mr. Winburn. " Is it not like little footsteps?''

" It's more like rain,'' said Mrs. Lancaster, with a smile.

" But *that, that* is a footstep,'' cried her father, bending forward to listen.

Mrs. Lancaster laughed outright.

" That's Geoff coming downstairs.''

Mr. Winburn was obliged to laugh too. They were having tea in the hall, and he had been sitting with his back to the staircase. He now turned his chair round to face it.

Little Geoffrey was coming down, rather slowly and sedately, with a child's awe of a strange place. The stairs were of polished oak, uncarpeted. He came across and stood by his mother. Mr. Winburn gave a slight start. As the child was crossing the floor, he distinctly heard another pair of footsteps on the stairs, as of some-one following Geoffrey. Dragging footsteps, curiously painful they were. Then he shrugged his shoulders in-credulously. "The rain, no doubt," he thought.

"I'm looking at the spongecakes," remarked Geoff with the admirably detached air of one who points out an interesting fact.

His mother hastened to comply with the hint.

"Well, Sonny, how do you like your new home?" she asked.

"Lots," replied Geoffrey with his mouth generously filled. "Pounds and pounds and pounds." After this last assertion, which was evidently expressive of the deepest contentment, he relapsed into silence, only anxious to remove the spongecake from the sight of man in the least time possible.

Having bolted the last mouthful, he burst forth into speech.

"Oh! Mummy, there's attics here, Jane says; and can I go at once and *eggz*plore them? And there might be a secret door, Jane says there isn't, but I think there must be, and, anyhow, I know there'll be *pipes, water pipes* (with a face full of ecstasy) and can I play with them, and, oh! can I go and see the Boi-i-ler?" He spun out the last word with such evident rapture that his grandfather left ashamed to reflect that this peerless delight of childhood only conjured up to his imagina-tion the picture of hot water that wasn't hot, and heavy and numerous plumber's bills.

" We'll see about the attics to-morrow, darling,"
said Mrs. Lancaster. " Suppose you fetch your bricks
and build a nice house, or an engine."

" Don't want to build an 'ouse."

" *H*ouse."

" House, or h'engine h'either."

" Build a boiler," suggested his grandfather.

Geoffrey brightened.

" With pipes?"

" Yes, lots of pipes."

Geoffrey ran away happily to fetch his bricks.

The rain was still falling. Mr. Winburn listened. Yes,
it must have been the rain he had heard; but it did
sound like footsteps.

He had a queer dream that night.

He dreamt that he was walking through a town, a
great city it seemed to him. But it was a children's
city; there were no grown-up people there, nothing but
children, crowds of them. In his dream they all rushed
to the stranger crying: " Have you brought him?" It
seemed that he understood what they meant and shook
his head sadly.   When they saw this, the children
turned away and began to cry, sobbing bitterly.

The city and the children faded away and he awoke
to find himself in bed, but the sobbing was still in his
ears.   Though wide awake, he heard it distinctly; and
he remembered that Geoffrey slept on the floor below,
while this sound of a child's sorrow descended from
above. He sat up and struck a match. Instantly the
sobbing ceased.

Mr. Winburn did not tell his daughter of the dream or
its sequel.   That it was no trick of his imagination, he
was convinced; indeed soon afterwards he heard it again
in the day time.   The wind was howling in the chimney

but *this* was a separate sound—distinct, unmistakable: pitiful little heartbroken sobs.

He found out too, that he was not the only one to hear them. He overheard the housemaid saying to the parlourmaid that she " didn't think as that there nurse was kind to Master Geoffrey, she'd 'eard 'im crying 'is little 'eart out only that very morning." Geoffrey had come down to breakfast and lunch beaming with health and happiness; and Mr. Winburn knew that it was not Geoff who had been crying, but that other child whose dragging footsteps had startled him more than once.

Mrs. Lancaster alone never heard anything. Her ears were not perhaps attuned to catch sounds from another world.

Yet one day she also received a shock.

" Mummy," said Geoff plaintively. " I wish you'd let me play with that little boy."

Mrs. Lancaster looked up from her writing-table with a smile.

" What little boy, dear?"

" I don't know his name. He was in a attic, sitting on the floor crying, but he ran away when he saw me. I suppose he was *shy* (with slight contempt), not like a *big* boy, and then, when I was in the nursery building, I saw him standing in the door watching me build, and he looked so awful lonely and as though he wanted to play wiv me. I said: ' Come and build a h'engine,' but he didn't say nothing, just looked as— as though he saw a lot of chocolates, and his Mummy had told him not to touch them." Geoff sighed, sad personal reminiscences evidently recurring to him. " But when I asked Jane who he was and told her I wanted to play wiv him, he said there wasn't no little boy in the 'ouse and not to tell naughty stories. I don't love Jane at all."

H.D.   G

Mrs. Lancaster got up.

" Jane was right. There was no little boy."

" But I saw him. Oh! Mummy, do let me play wiv him, he did look so awful lonely and unhappy. I *do* want to do something to ' make him better.' "

Mrs. Lancaster was about to speak again, but her father shook his head.

" Geoff," he said very gently, " that poor little boy *is* lonely, and perhaps you may do something to comfort him; but you must find out how by yourself—like a puzzle—do you see?"

" Is it because I am getting *big* I must do it all my lone?"

" Yes, because you are getting big."

As the boy left the room, Mrs. Lancaster turned to her father impatiently.

" Papa, this is absurd. To encourage the boy to believe the servants' idle tales!"

" No servant has told the child anything," said the old man gently. " He's seen—what I *hear*, what I could see perhaps if I were his age."

" But it's such nonsense! Why don't I see it or hear it?"

Mr. Winburn smiled, a curiously tired smile, but did not reply.

" Why?" repeated his daughter. " And why did you tell him he could help the—the—thing. It's—it's all so impossible."

The old man looked at her with his thoughtful glance.

" Why not?" he said. " Do you remember these words:

" *What Lamp has Destiny to guide*
Her little Children stumbling in the Dark?
' A Blind Understanding,' Heaven replied.

" Geoffrey has that—a blind understanding. All children possess it. It is only as we grow older that we lose it, that we cast it away from us. Sometimes, when we are quite old, a faint gleam comes back to us, but the Lamp burns brightest in childhood. That is why I think Geoffrey may help."

" I don't understand," murmured Mrs. Lancaster feebly.

" No more do I. That—that child is in trouble and wants—to be set free. But how? I do not know, but —it's awful to think of it—sobbing its heart out—a *child*."

A month after this conversation Geoffrey fell very ill. The east wind had been severe, and he was not a strong child. The doctor shook his head and said that it was a grave case. To Mr. Winburn he divulged more and confessed that the case was quite hopeless. " The child would never have lived to grow up, under any circumstances," he added. " There has been serious lung trouble for a long time."

It was when nursing Geoff that Mrs. Lancaster became aware of that—other child. At first the sobs were an indistinguishable part of the wind, but gradually they became more distinct, more unmistakable. Finally she heard them in moments of dead calm: a child's sobs— dull, hopeless, heartbroken.

Geoff grew steadily worse and in his delirium he spoke of the " little boy " again and again. " I do want to help him get away, I do!" he cried.

Succeeding the delirium there came a state of lethargy. Geoffrey lay very still, hardly breathing, sunk in oblivion. There was nothing to do but wait and watch. Then there came a still night, clear and calm, without one breath of wind.

Suddenly the child stirred. His eyes opened. He looked past his mother towards the open door. He tried to speak and she bent down to catch the half-breathed words.

" All right, I'm comin'," he whispered; then he sank back.

The mother felt suddenly terrified, she crossed the room to her father. Somewhere near them the other child was laughing. Joyful, contented, triumphant, the silvery laughter echoed through the room.

" I'm frightened; I'm frightened," she moaned.

He put his arm round her protectingly. A sudden gust of wind made them both start, but it passed swiftly and left the air quiet as before.

The laughter had ceased and there crept to them a faint sound, so faint as hardly to be heard, but growing louder till they could distinguish it. Footsteps—light footsteps, swiftly departing.

Pitter-patter, pitter-patter, they ran—those well-known halting little feet. Yet—surely—now *other* footsteps suddenly mingled with them, moving with a quicker and a lighter tread.

With one accord they hastened to the door.

Down, down, down, past the door, close to them, pitter-patter, pitter-patter, went the unseen feet of the little children *together*.

Mrs. Lancaster looked up wildly.

" There are *two* of them—*two*!"

Grey with sudden fear, she turned towards the cot in the corner, but her father restrained her gently, and pointed away.

" There," he said simply.

Pitter-patter, pitter-patter—fainter and fainter.

And then—silence.

WIRELESS

"ABOVE all, avoid worry and excitement," said Dr. Meynell, in the comfortable fashion affected by doctors.

Mrs. Harter, as is often the case with people hearing these soothing but meaningless words, seemed more doubtful than relieved.

"There is a certain cardiac weakness," continued the doctor fluently, "but nothing to be alarmed about. I can assure you of that."

"All the same," he added, "it might be as well to have a lift installed. Eh? What about it?"

Mrs. Harter looked worried.

Dr. Meynell, on the contrary, looked pleased with himself. The reason he liked attending rich patients rather than poor ones was that he could exercise his active imagination in prescribing for their ailments.

"Yes, a lift," said Dr. Meynell, trying to think of something else even more dashing—and failing. "Then we shall avoid all undue exertion. Daily exercise on the level on a fine day, but avoid walking up hills. And above all," he added happily, "plenty of distraction for the mind. Don't dwell on your health."

To the old lady's nephew, Charles Ridgeway, the doctor was slightly more explicit.

"Do not misunderstand me," he said. "Your aunt may live for years, probably will. At the same time, shock or over-exertion might carry her off like that!" He snapped his fingers. "She must lead a very quiet life. No exertion. No fatigue. But, of course, she must not be allowed to brood. She must be kept cheerful and the mind well distracted."

" Distracted," said Charles Ridgeway thoughtfully.

Charles was a thoughtful young man. He was also a young man who believed in furthering his own inclinations whenever possible.

That evening he suggested the installation of a wireless set.

Mrs. Harter, already seriously upset at the thought of the lift, was disturbed and unwilling. Charles was fluent and persuasive.

" I do not know that I care for these new-fangled things," said Mrs. Harter piteously. " The waves, you know—the electric waves. They might affect me."

Charles in a superior and kindly fashion pointed out the futility of this idea.

Mrs. Harter, whose knowledge of the subject was of the vaguest, but who was tenacious of her own opinion, remained unconvinced.

" All that electricity," she murmured timorously. " You may say what you like, Charles, but some people *are* affected by electricity. I always have a terrible headache before a thunderstorm. I know that."

She nodded her head triumphantly.

Charles was a patient young man. He was also persistent.

" My dear Aunt Mary," he said, " let me make the thing clear to you."

He was something of an authority on the subject. He delivered now quite a lecture on the theme; warming to his task, he spoke of bright-emitter valves, of dull-emitter valves, of high frequency and low frequency, of amplification and of condensers.

Mrs. Harter, submerged in a sea of words that she did not understand, surrendered.

" Of course, Charles," she murmured, " if you really think——"

" My dear Aunt Mary," said Charles enthusiastically. " It is the very thing for you, to keep you from moping and all that."

The lift prescribed by Dr. Meynell was installed shortly afterwards and was very nearly the death of Mrs. Harter since, like many other old ladies, she had a rooted objection to strange men in the house. She suspected them one and all of having designs on her old silver.

After the lift the wireless set arrived. Mrs. Harter was left to contemplate the, to her, repellant object—a large ungainly-looking box, studded with knobs.

It took all Charles' enthusiasm to reconcile her to it.

Charles was in his element, he turned knobs, discoursing eloquently the while.

Mrs. Harter sat in her high-backed chair, patient and polite, with a rooted conviction in her own mind that these new-fangled notions were neither more nor less than unmitigated nuisances.

" Listen, Aunt Mary, we are on to Berlin, isn't that splendid? Can you hear the fellow?"

" I can't hear anything except a good deal of buzzing and clicking," said Mrs. Harter.

Charles continued to twirl knobs. " Brussels," he announced with enthusiasm.

" It is really?" said Mrs. Harter with no more than a trace of interest.

Charles again turned knobs and an unearthly howl echoed forth into the room.

" Now we seem to be on to the Dogs' Home," said Mrs. Harter, who was an old lady with a certain amount of spirit.

" Ha, ha!" said Charles, " you will have your joke, won't you, Aunt Mary? Very good that!"

Mrs. Harter could not help smiling at him. She was very fond of Charles. For some years a niece, Miriam Harter, had lived with her. She had intended to make the girl her heiress, but Miriam had not been a success. She was impatient and obviously bored by her aunt's society. She was always out, " gadding about " as Mrs. Harter called it. In the end, she had entangled herself with a young man of whom her aunt thoroughly disapproved. Miriam had been returned to her mother with a curt note much as if she had been goods on approval. She had married the young man in question and Mrs. Harter usually sent her a handkerchief case or a table-centre at Christmas.

Having found nieces disappointing, Mrs. Harter turned her attention to nephews. Charles, from the first, had been an unqualified success. He was always pleasantly deferential to his aunt, and listened with an appearance of intense interest to the reminiscences of her youth. In this he was a great contrast to Miriam, who had been frankly bored and showed it. Charles was never bored, he was always good-tempered, always gay. He told his aunt many times a day that she was a perfectly marvellous old lady.

Highly satisfied with her new acquisition, Mrs. Harter had written to her lawyer with instructions as to the making of a new will. This was sent to her, duly approved by her and signed.

And now even in the matter of the wireless, Charles was soon proved to have won fresh laurels.

Mrs. Harter, at first antagonistic, became tolerant and finally fascinated. She enjoyed it very much better when Charles was out. The trouble with Charles was that he could not leave the thing alone. Mrs. Harter would be seated in her chair comfortably listening to a symphony concert or a lecture on Lucrezia Borgia or Pond Life, quite happy and at peace with the world. Not so Charles. The harmony would be shattered by discordant shrieks while he enthusiastically attempted to get foreign stations. But on those evenings when Charles was dining out with friends Mrs. Harter enjoyed the wireless very much indeed. She would turn on two switches, sit in her high-backed chair and enjoy the programme of the evening.

It was about three months after the wireless had been installed that the first eerie happening occurred. Charles was absent at a bridge party.

The programme for that evening was a ballad concert. A well-known soprano was singing " Annie Laurie," and in the middle of " Annie Laurie " a strange thing happened. There was a sudden break, the music ceased for a moment, the buzzing, clicking noise continued and then that too died away. There was dead silence, and then very faintly a low buzzing sound was heard.

Mrs. Harter got the impression, why she did not know, that the machine was tuned in to somewhere very far away, and then clearly and distinctly a voice spoke, a man's voice with a faint Irish accent.

" *Mary—can you hear me, Mary? It is Patrick speaking. . . . I am coming for you soon. You will be ready, won't you, Mary?*"

Then, almost immediately, the strains of " Annie Laurie " once more filled the room.

Mrs. Harter sat rigid in her chair, her hands clenched on each arm of it. Had she been dreaming? Patrick! Patrick's voice! Patrick's voice in this very room, speaking to her. No, it must be a dream, a hallucination perhaps. She must just have dropped off to sleep for a minute or two. A curious thing to have dreamed—that her dead husband's voice should speak to her over the ether. It frightened her just a little. What were the words he had said?

" I am coming for you soon, Mary. You will be ready, won't you?"

Was it, could it be a premonition? Cardiac weakness. Her heart. After all, she was getting on in years.

" It's a warning—that's what it is," said Mrs. Harter, rising slowly and painfully from her chair, and added characteristically:

" All that money wasted on putting in a lift!"

She said nothing of her experience to anyone, but for the next day or two she was thoughtful and a little preoccupied.

And then came the second occasion. Again she was alone in the room. The wireless, which had been playing an orchestral selection, died away with the same suddenness as before. Again there was silence, the sense of distance, and finally Patrick's voice, not as it had been in life—but a voice rarefied, far away, with a strange unearthly quality.

" Patrick speaking to you, Mary. I will be coming for you very soon now. . . ."

Then click, buzz, and the orchestral selection was in full swing again.

Mrs. Harter glanced at the clock. No, she had not been asleep this time. Awake and in full possession of her faculties, she had heard Patrick's voice speaking. It was no hallucination, she was sure of that. In a confused way she tried to think over all that Charles had explained to her of the theory of ether waves.

Could it be that Patrick had *really* spoken to her? That his actual voice had been wafted through space? There were missing wave lengths or something of that kind. She remembered Charles speaking of " gaps in the scale." Perhaps the missing waves explained all the so-called psychological phenomena? No, there was nothing inherently impossible in the idea. Patrick had spoken to her. He had availed himself of modern science to prepare her for what must soon be coming.

Mrs. Harter rang the bell for her maid, Elizabeth.

Elizabeth was a tall gaunt woman of sixty. Beneath an unbending exterior she concealed a wealth of affection and tenderness for her mistress.

" Elizabeth," said Mrs. Harter when her faithful retainer had appeared, " you remember what I told you? The top left-hand drawer of my bureau. It is locked, the long key with the white label. Everything is there ready."

" Ready, ma'am?"

" For my burial," snorted Mrs. Harter. " You know perfectly well what I mean, Elizabeth. You helped me to put the things there yourself."

Elizabeth's face began to work strangely.

" Oh, ma'am," she wailed, " don't dwell on such things. I thought you was a sight better."

" We have all got to go sometime or another," said Mrs. Harter practically. " I am over my three score years and ten, Elizabeth. There, there, don't make a fool of yourself. If you must cry, go and cry somewhere else."

Elizabeth retired, still sniffing.

Mrs. Harter looked after her with a good deal of affection.

" Silly old fool, but faithful," she said, " very faithful. Let me see, was it a hundred pounds, or only fifty I left her? It ought to be a hundred. She has been with me a long time."

The point worried the old lady and the next day she sat down and wrote to her lawyer asking if he would send her her will so that she might look over it. It was that same day that Charles startled her by something he said at lunch.

" By the way, Aunt Mary," he said, " who is that funny old josser up in the spare room? The picture over the mantelpiece, I mean. The old johnny with the beaver and side whiskers?"

Mrs. Harter looked at him austerely.

" That is your Uncle Patrick as a young man," she said.

" Oh, I say, Aunt Mary, I am awfully sorry. I didn't mean to be rude."

Mrs. Harter accepted the apology with a dignified bend of the head.

Charles went on rather uncertainly:

" I just wondered. You see——"

He stopped undecidedly and Mrs. Harter said sharply:

" Well? What were you going to say?"

" Nothing," said Charles hastily. " Nothing that makes sense, I mean."

For the moment the old lady said nothing more, but later that day, when they were alone together, she returned to the subject.

" I wish you would tell me, Charles, what it was made you ask me about that picture of your uncle."

Charles looked embarrassed.

" I told you, Aunt Mary. It was nothing but a silly fancy of mine—quite absurd."

" Charles," said Mrs. Harter in her most autocratic voice, " I insist upon knowing."

" Well, my dear aunt, if you will have it, I fancied I saw him—the man in the picture, I mean—looking out of the end window when I was coming up the drive last night. Some effect of the light, I suppose. I wondered who on earth he could be, the face was so—early Victorian, if you know what I mean. And then Elizabeth said there was no one, no visitor or stranger in the house, and later in the evening I happened to drift into the spare room, and there was the picture over the mantel-piece. My man to the life! It is quite easily explained, really, I expect. Sub-conscious and all that. Must have noticed the picture before without realising that I had noticed it, and then just fancied the face at the window."

" The end window?" said Mrs. Harter sharply.

" Yes, why?"

" Nothing," said Mrs. Harter.

But she was startled all the same. That room had been her husband's dressing-room.

That same evening, Charles again being absent, Mrs. Harter sat listening to the wireless with feverish im-patience. If for the third time she heard the mysterious voice, it would prove to her finally and without a shadow of doubt that she was really in communication with some other world.

Although her heart beat faster, she was not surprised when the same break occurred, and after the usual interval of deathly silence the faint far-away Irish voice spoke once more.

" *Mary—you are prepared now. . . . On Friday I shall come for you. . . . Friday at half-past nine. . . . Do not be afraid—there will be no pain. . . . Be ready. . . .*"

Then, almost cutting short the last word, the music of the orchestra broke out again, clamorous and discordant.

Mrs. Harter sat very still for a minute or two. Her face had gone white and she looked blue and pinched round the lips.

Presently she got up and sat down at her writing-desk. In a somewhat shaky hand she wrote the following lines:

" *To-night, at 9.15, I have distinctly heard the voice of my dead husband. He told me that he would come for*

*me on Friday night at 9.30. If I should die on that day
and at that hour I should like the facts made known so
as to prove beyond question the possibility of communicating with the spirit world.*—MARY HARTER."

Mrs. Harter read over what she had written, enclosed
it in an envelope and addressed the envelope. Then
she rang the bell which was promptly answered by Elizabeth. Mrs. Harter got up from her desk and gave the
note she had just written to the old woman.

" Elizabeth," she said, " if I should die on Friday
night I should like that note given to Dr. Meynell. No "
—as Elizabeth appeared to be about to protest—" do not
argue with me. You have often told me you believe in
premonitions. I have a premonition now. There is one
thing more. I have left you in my will £50. I should
like you to have £100. If I am not able to go to the
bank myself before I die Mr. Charles will see to it."

As before, Mrs. Harter cut short Elizabeth's tearful
protests. In pursuance of her determination, the old
lady spoke to her nephew on the subject the following
morning.

" Remember, Charles, that if anything should happen
to me, Elizabeth is to have an extra £50."

" You are very gloomy these days, Aunt Mary," said
Charles cheerfully. " What is going to happen to you?
According to Dr. Meynell, we shall be celebrating your
hundredth birthday in twenty years or so!"

Mrs. Harter smiled affectionately at him but did not
answer. After a minute or two she said:

" What are you doing on Friday evening, Charles?"

Charles looked a trifle surprised.

" As a matter of fact, the Ewings asked me to go in
and play bridge, but if you would rather I stayed at
home——"

" No," said Mrs. Harter with determination. " Certainly not. I mean it, Charles. On that night of all nights I should much rather be alone."

Charles looked at her curiously, but Mrs. Harter vouchsafed no further information. She was an old lady of courage and determination. She felt that she must go through with her strange experience single-handed.

Friday evening found the house very silent. Mrs. Harter sat as usual in her straight-backed chair drawn up to the fireplace. All her preparations were made. That morning she had been to the bank, had drawn out £50 in notes and had handed them over to Elizabeth despite the latter's tearful protests. She had sorted and arranged all her personal belongings and had labelled one or two pieces of jewellery with the names of friends or relations. She had also written out a list of instructions for Charles. The Worcester tea service was to go to Cousin Emma. The Sevres jars to young William, and so on.

Now she looked at the long envelope she held in her hand and drew from it a folded document. This was her will sent to her by Mr. Hopkinson in accordance with her instructions. She had already read it carefully, but now she looked over it once more to refresh her memory. It was a short, concise document. A bequest of £50 to Elizabeth Marshall in consideration of faithful service; two bequests of £500 to a sister and a first cousin, and the remainder to her beloved nephew Charles Ridgeway.

Mrs. Harter nodded her head several times. Charles would be a very rich man when she was dead. Well, he had been a dear good boy to her. Always kind, always affectionate, and with a merry tongue which never failed to please her.

She looked at the clock. Three minutes to the half-hour. Well, she was ready. And she was calm—quite calm. Although she repeated these last words to herself several times, her heart beat strangely and unevenly. She hardly realised it herself, but she was strung up to a fine point of overwrought nerves.

Half-past nine. The wireless was switched on. What would she hear? A familiar voice announcing the weather forecast or that far-away voice belonging to a man who had died twenty-five years before?

But she heard neither. Instead there came a familiar sound, a sound she knew well but which to-night made her feel as though an icy hand were laid on her heart. A fumbling at the front door. . . .

It came again. And then a cold blast seemed to sweep through the room. Mrs. Harter had now no doubt what her sensations were. She was afraid. . . . She was more than afraid—she was terrified. . . .

And suddenly there came to her the thought: *" Twenty-five years is a long time. Patrick is a stranger to me now."*

Terror! That was what was invading her.

A soft step outside the door—a soft halting footstep. Then the door swung silently open. . . .

Mrs. Harter staggered to her feet, swaying slightly from side to side, her eyes fixed on the open doorway, something slipped from her fingers into the grate.

She gave a strangled cry which died in her throat. In the dim light of the doorway stood a familiar figure with chestnut beard and whiskers and an old-fashioned Victorian coat.

Patrick had come for her!

Her heart gave one terrified leap and stood still. She slipped to the ground in a huddled heap.

There Elizabeth found her, an hour later.

Dr. Meynell was called at once and Charles Ridgeway

was hastily recalled from his bridge party. But nothing could be done. Mrs. Harter had gone beyond human aid.

It was not until two days later that Elizabeth remembered the note given to her by her mistress. Dr. Meynell read it with great interest and showed it to Charles Ridgeway.

"A very curious coincidence," he said. "It seems clear that your aunt had been having hallucinations about her dead husband's voice. She must have strung herself up to such a point that the excitement was fatal and when the time actually came she died of the shock."

"Auto-suggestion?" said Charles.

"Something of the sort. I will let you know the result of the autopsy as soon as possible, though I have no doubt of it myself. In the circumstances, an autopsy was desirable, though purely as a matter of form.

Charles nodded comprehendingly.

On the preceding night, when the household was in bed, he had removed a certain wire which ran from the back of the wireless cabinet to his bedroom on the floor above. Also, since the evening had been a chilly one, he had asked Elizabeth to light a fire in his room, and in that fire he had burned a chestnut beard and whiskers. Some Victorian clothing belonging to his late uncle he replaced in the camphor-scented chest in the attic.

As far as he could see, he was perfectly safe. His plan, the shadowy outline of which had first formed in his brain when Doctor Meynell had told him that his aunt might with due care live for many years, had succeeded admirably. A sudden shock, Dr. Meynell had said. Charles, that affectionate young man, beloved of old ladies, smiled to himself.

When the doctor had departed, Charles went about his

duties mechanically. Certain funeral arrangements had to be finally settled. Relatives coming from a distance had to have trains looked out for them. In one or two cases they would have to stay the night. Charles went about it all efficiently and methodically, to the accompaniment of an undercurrent of his own thoughts.

A very good stroke of business! That was the burden of them. Nobody, least of all his dead aunt, had known in what perilous straits Charles stood. His activities, carefully concealed from the world, had landed him where the shadow of a prison loomed ahead.

Exposure and ruin had stared him in the face unless he could in a few short months raise a considerable sum of money. Well—that was all right now. Charles smiled to himself. Thanks to—yes, call it a practical joke—nothing criminal about *that*—he was saved. He was now a very rich man. He had no anxieties on the subject, for Mrs. Harter had never made any secret of her intentions.

Chiming in very appositely with these thoughts, Elizabeth put her head round the door and informed him that Mr. Hopkinson was here and would like to see him.

About time, too, Charles thought. Repressing a tendency to whistle, he composed his face to one of suitable gravity and repaired to the library. There he greeted the precise old gentleman who had been for over a quarter of a century the late Mrs. Harter's legal adviser.

The lawyer seated himself at Charles' invitation and with a dry little cough entered upon business matters.

" I did not quite understand your letter to me, Mr. Ridgeway. You seemed to be under the impression that the late Mrs. Harter's will was in our keeping? "

Charles stared at him.

" But surely—I've heard my aunt say as much."

" Oh! quite so, quite so. It *was* in our keeping."

" *Was?*"

" That is what I said. Mrs. Harter wrote to us, asking that it might be forwarded to her on Tuesday last."

An uneasy feeling crept over Charles. He felt a far-off
premonition of unpleasantness.

" Doubtless it will come to light amongst her papers,"
continued the lawyer smoothly.

Charles said nothing. He was afraid to trust his
tongue. He had already been through Mrs. Harter's
papers pretty thoroughly, well enough to be quite certain
that no will was amongst them. In a minute or two,
when he had regained control of himself, he said so.
His voice sounded unreal to himself, and he had a
sensation as of cold water trickling down his back.

" Has anyone been through her personal effects?"
asked the lawyer.

Charles replied that her own maid, Elizabeth, had
done so. At Mr. Hopkinson's suggestion, Elizabeth was
sent for. She came promptly, grim and upright, and
answered the questions put to her.

She had been through all her mistress's clothes and
personal belongings. She was quite sure that there had
been no legal document such as a will amongst them.
She knew what the will looked like—her poor mistress
had had it in her hand only the morning of her death.

" You are sure of that?" asked the lawyer sharply.

" Yes, sir. She told me so. And she made me take
fifty pounds in notes. The will was in a long blue
envelope."

" Quite right," said Mr. Hopkinson.

" Now I come to think of it," continued Elizabeth,
" that same blue envelope was lying on this table the
morning after—but empty. I laid it on the desk."

" I remember seeing it there," said Charles.

He got up and went over to the desk. In a minute or
two he turned round with an envelope in his hand which

he handed to Mr. Hopkinson. The latter examined it and nodded his head.

"That is the envelope in which I despatched the will on Tuesday last."

Both men looked hard at Elizabeth.

"Is there anything more, sir?" she inquired respectfully.

"Not at present, thank you."

Elizabeth went towards the door.

"One minute," said the lawyer. "Was there a fire in the grate that evening?"

"Yes, sir, there was always a fire."

"Thank you, that will do."

Elizabeth went out. Charles leaned forward, resting a shaking hand on the table.

"What do you think? What are you driving at?"

Mr. Hopkinson shook his head.

"We must still hope the will may turn up. If it does not——"

"Well, if it does not?"

"I am afraid there is only one conclusion possible. Your aunt sent for that will in order to destroy it. Not wishing Elizabeth to lose by that, she gave her the amount of her legacy in cash."

"But why?" cried Charles wildly. "Why?"

Mr. Hopkinson coughed. A dry cough.

"You have had no—er—disagreement with your aunt, Mr. Ridgeway?" he murmured.

Charles gasped.

"No, indeed," he cried warmly. "We were on the kindliest, most affectionate terms, right up to the end."

"Ah!" said Mr. Hopkinson, not looking at him.

It came to Charles with a shock that the lawyer did not believe him. Who knew what this dry old stick might not have heard? Rumours of Charles' doings might have come round to him. What more natural than that he should suppose that these same rumours had come to Mrs. Harter, and that aunt and nephew should have had an altercation on the subject?

But it wasn't so! Charles knew one of the bitterest moments of his career. His lies had been believed. Now that he spoke the truth, belief was withheld. The irony of it!

Of course his aunt had never burnt the will! Of course——

His thoughts came to a sudden check. What was that picture rising before his eyes? An old lady with one hand clasped to her heart . . . something slipping . . . a paper . . . falling on the red-hot embers. . . .

Charles' face grew livid. He heard a hoarse voice— his own—asking:

" If that will's never found——?"

" There is a former will of Mrs. Harter's still extant. Dated September, 1920. By it Mrs. Harter leaves everything to her niece, Miriam Harter, now Miriam Robinson."

What was the old fool saying? Miriam? Miriam with her nondescript husband, and her four whining brats. All his cleverness—for Miriam!

The telephone rang sharply at his elbow. He took up the receiver. It was the doctor's voice, hearty and kindly.

" That you, Ridgeway? Thought you'd like to know. The autopsy's just concluded. Cause of death as I surmised. But as a matter of fact the cardiac trouble was much more serious than I suspected when she was alive. With the utmost care, she couldn't have lived longer than two months at the outside. Thought you'd like to know. Might console you more or less."

" Excuse me," said Charles, " would you mind saying that again?"

" She couldn't have lived longer than two months,"

said the doctor in a slightly louder tone. "All things work out for the best, you know, my dear fellow——"

But Charles had slammed back the receiver on its hook. He was conscious of the lawyer's voice speaking from a long way off.

"Dear me, Mr. Ridgeway, are you ill?"

Damn them all! The smug-faced lawyer. That poisonous old ass Meynell. No hope in front of him—only the shadow of the prison wall. . . .

He felt that Somebody had been playing with him—playing with him like a cat with a mouse. Somebody must be laughing. . . .

THE WITNESS FOR THE PROSECUTION

MR. MAYHERNE adjusted his pince-nez and cleared his throat with a little dry as dust cough that was wholly typical of him. Then he looked again at the man opposite him, the man charged with wilful murder.

Mr. Mayherne was a small man, precise in manner, neatly, not to say foppishly dressed, with a pair of very shrewd and piercing grey eyes. By no means a fool. Indeed, as a solicitor, Mr. Mayherne's reputation stood very high. His voice, when he spoke to his client, was dry but not unsympathetic.

" I must impress upon you again that you are in very grave danger, and that the utmost frankness is necessary."

Leonard Vole, who had been staring in a dazed fashion at the blank wall in front of him, transferred his glance to the solicitor.

" I know," he said hopelessly. " You keep telling me so. But I can't seem to realise yet that I'm charged with murder—*murder*. And such a dastardly crime too."

Mr. Mayherne was practical, not emotional. He coughed again, took off his pince-nez, polished them carefully, and replaced them on his nose. Then he said:

" Yes, yes, yes. Now, my dear Mr. Vole, we're going to make a determined effort to get you off—and we shall succeed—we shall succeed. But I must have all the facts. I must know just how damaging the case against you is likely to be. Then we can fix upon the best line of defence."

Still the young man looked at him in the same dazed, hopeless fashion. To Mr. Mayherne the case had seemed black enough, and the guilt of the prisoner assured. Now, for the first time, he felt a doubt.

" You think I'm guilty," said Leonard Vole, in a low voice. " But, by God, I swear I'm not! It looks pretty black against me, I know that. I'm like a man caught in a net—the meshes of it all round me, entangling me whichever way I turn. But I didn't do it, Mr. Mayherne, I didn't do it!"

In such a position a man was bound to protest his innocence. Mr. Mayherne knew that. Yet, in spite of himself, he was impressed. It might be, after all, that Leonard Vole was innocent.

" You are right, Mr. Vole," he said gravely. " The case does look very black against you. Nevertheless, I accept your assurance. Now, let us get to facts. I want you to tell me in your own words exactly how you came to make the acquaintance of Miss Emily French."

" It was one day in Oxford Street. I saw an elderly lady crossing the road. She was carrying a lot of parcels. In the middle of the street she dropped them, tried to recover them, found a 'bus was almost on top of her and just managed to reach the curb safely, dazed and bewildered by people having shouted at her. I recovered her parcels, wiped the mud off them as best I could, retied the string of one, and returned them to her."

" There was no question of your having saved her life?"

" Oh! dear me, no. All I did was to perform a common act of courtesy. She was extremely grateful, thanked me warmly, and said something about my manners not being those of most of the younger generation—I can't remember the exact words. Then I lifted my hat and went on. I never expected to see her again. But life is full of coincidences. That very evening I came across her at a party at a friend's house. She recognised me at once and asked that I should be introduced to her. I then found out that she was a Miss Emily French and that she lived at Cricklewood. I talked to her for some time. She was, I imagine, an old lady who took sudden and violent fancies to people. She took one to me on the strength of a perfectly simple action which anyone might have performed. On leaving, she shook me warmly by the hand, and asked me to come and see her. I replied, of course, that I should be very pleased to do so, and she then urged me to name a day. I did not want particularly to go, but it would have seemed churlish to refuse, so I fixed on the following Saturday. After she had gone, I learned something about her from my friends. That she was rich, eccentric, lived alone with one maid and owned no less than eight cats.''

'' I see,'' said Mr. Mayherne. '' The question of her being well off came up as early as that?''

'' If you mean that I inquired——'' began Leonard Vole hotly, but Mr. Mayherne stilled him with a gesture.

'' I have to look at the case as it will be presented by the other side. An ordinary observer would not have supposed Miss French to be a lady of means. She lived poorly, almost humbly. Unless you had been told the contrary, you would in all probability have considered her to be in poor circumstances—at any rate to begin with. Who was it exactly who told you that she was well off?''

'' My friend, George Harvey, at whose house the party took place.''

'' Is he likely to remember having done so?''

'' I really don't know. Of course it is some time ago now.''

'' Quite so, Mr. Vole. You see, the first aim of the prosecution will be to establish that you were in low water financially—that is true, is it not?''

Leonard Vole flushed.

" Yes," he said, in a low voice. " I'd been having a run of infernal bad luck just then."

" Quite so," said Mr. Mayherne again. " That being, as I say, in low water financially, you met this rich old lady and cultivated her acquaintance assiduously. Now if we are in a position to say that you had no idea she was well off, and that you visited her out of pure kindness of heart——"

" Which is the case."

" I dare say. I am not disputing the point. I am looking at it from the outside point of view. A great deal depends on the memory of Mr. Harvey. Is he likely to remember that conversation or is he not? Could he be confused by counsel into believing that it took place later?"

Leonard Vole reflected for some minutes. Then he said steadily enough, but with a rather paler face:

" I do not think that that line would be successful, Mr. Mayherne. Several of those present heard his remark, and one or two of them chaffed me about my conquest of a rich old lady."

The solicitor endeavoured to hide his disappointment with a wave of the hand.

" Unfortunate," he said. " But I congratulate you upon your plain speaking, Mr. Vole. It is to you I look to guide me. Your judgment is quite right. To persist in the line I spoke of would have been disastrous. We must leave that point. You made the acquaintance of Miss French, you called upon her, the acquaintanceship progressed. We want a clear reason for all this. Why did you, a young man of thirty-three, good-looking, fond of sport, popular with your friends, devote so much of your time to an elderly woman with whom you could hardly have anything in common?"

Leonard Vole flung out his hands in a nervous gesture.

" I can't tell you—I really can't tell you. After the first visit, she pressed me to come again, spoke of being lonely and unhappy. She made it difficult for me to refuse. She showed so plainly her fondness and affection for me that I was placed in an awkward position. You see, Mr. Mayherne, I've got a weak nature—I drift—I'm one of those people who can't say ' No.' And believe me or not, as you like, after the third or fourth visit I paid her I found myself getting genuinely fond of the old thing. My mother died when I was young, an aunt brought me up, and she too died before I was fifteen. If I told you that I genuinely enjoyed being mothered and pampered, I dare say you'd only laugh."

Mr. Mayherne did not laugh. Instead he took off his pince-nez again and polished them, always a sign with him that he was thinking deeply.

" I accept your explanation, Mr. Vole," he said at last. " I believe it to be psychologically probable. Whether a jury would take that view of it is another matter. Please continue your narrative. When was it that Miss French first asked you to look into her business affairs?"

" After my third or fourth visit to her. She understood very little of money matters, and was worried about some investments."

Mr. Mayherne looked up sharply.

" Be careful, Mr. Vole. The maid, Janet Mackenzie, declares that her mistress was a good woman of business and transacted all her own affairs, and this is borne out by the testimony of her bankers."

" I can't help that," said Vole earnestly. " That's what she said to me."

Mr. Mayherne looked at him for a moment or two in silence. Though he had no intention of saying so, his belief in Leonard Vole's innocence was at that moment strengthened. He knew something of the mentality of elderly ladies. He saw Miss French, infatuated with the good-looking young man, hunting about for pretexts that should bring him to the house. What more likely than that she should plead ignorance of business, and beg him to help her with her money affairs? She was enough of a woman of the world to realise that any man is slightly flattered by such an admission of his superiority. Leonard Vole had been flattered. Perhaps, too, she had not been averse to letting this young man know that she was wealthy. Emily French had been a strong-willed old woman, willing to pay her price for what she wanted. All this passed rapidly through Mr. Mayherne's mind, but he gave no indication of it, and asked instead a further question.

" And you did handle her affairs for her at her request?"

" I did."

" Mr. Vole," said the solicitor, " I am going to ask you a very serious question, and one to which it is vital I should have a truthful answer. You were in low water financially. You had the handling of an old lady's affairs —an old lady who, according to her own statement, knew little or nothing of business. Did you at any time, or in any manner, convert to your own use the securities which you handled? Did you engage in any transaction for your own pecuniary advantage which will not bear the light of day?" He quelled the other's response. " Wait a minute before you answer. There are two courses open to us. Either we can make a feature of your probity and honesty in conducting her affairs whilst pointing out how unlikely it is that you would commit murder to obtain money which you might have obtained by such infinitely easier means. If, on the other hand, there is anything in your dealings which the prosecution will get hold of—if, to put it baldly, it it can be proved that you swindled the old lady in any way, we must take the line that you had no motive for the murder, since she was already a profitable source of income to you. You perceive the distinction. Now, I beg of you, take your time before you reply.''

But Leonard Vole took no time at all.

'' My dealings with Miss French's affairs are all perfectly fair and above board. I acted for her interests to the very best of my ability, as anyone will find who looks into the matter.''

'' Thank you,'' said Mr. Mayherne. '' You relieve my mind very much. I pay you the compliment of believing that you are far too clever to lie to me over such an important matter.''

'' Surely,'' said Vole eagerly, '' the strongest point in my favour is the lack of motive. Granted that I cultivated the acquaintanceship of a rich old lady in the hopes of getting money out of her—that, I gather, is the substance of what you have been saying—surely her death frustrates all my hopes?''

The solicitor looked at him steadily. Then, very deliberately, he repeated his unconscious trick with his pince-nez. It was not until they were firmly replaced on his nose that he spoke.

'' Are you not aware, Mr. Vole, that Miss French left a will under which you are the principal beneficiary?''

'' What?'' The prisoner sprang to his feet. His dismay was obvious and unforced. '' My God! What are you saying? She left her money to me?''

Mr. Mayherne nodded slowly. Vole sank down aagin, his head in his hands.

'' You pretend you know nothing of this will?''

'' Pretend? There's no pretence about it. I knew nothing about it.''

'' What would you say if I told you that the maid, Janet Mackenzie, swears that you *did* know? That her

mistress told her distinctly that she had consulted you
in the matter, and told you of her intentions?''

'' Say? That she's lying! No, I go too fast. Janet
is an elderly woman. She was a faithful watchdog to her
mistress, and she didn't like me. She was jealous and
suspicious. I should say that Miss French confided her
intentions to Janet, and that Janet either mistook something she said, or else was convinced in her own mind
that I had persuaded the old lady into doing it. I dare
say that she believes herself now that Miss French
actually told her so.''

'' You don't think she dislikes you enough to lie
deliberately about the matter?''

Leonard Vole looked shocked and startled.

'' No, indeed! Why should she?''

'' I don't know,'' said Mr. Mayherne thoughtfully.
'' But she's very bitter against you.''

The wretched young man groaned again.

'' I'm beginning to see,'' he muttered. '' It's frightful.
I made up to her, that's what they'll say, I got her to
make a will leaving her money to me, and then I go there
that night, and there's nobody in the house—they find
her the next day—oh! my God, it's awful!''

'' You are wrong about there being nobody in the
house,'' said Mr. Mayherne. '' Janet, as you remember,
was to go out for the evening. She went, but about half-
past nine she returned to fetch the pattern of a blouse
sleeve which she had promised to a friend. She let herself in by the back door, went upstairs and fetched it.
and went out again. She heard voices in the sitting-room,
though she could not distinguish what they said, but she
will swear that one of them was Miss French's and one
was a man's.''

'' At half-past nine,'' said Leonard Vole. '' At half-
past nine. . . .'' He sprang to his feet. '' But then I'm
saved—saved——''

" What do you mean, saved?" cried Mr. Mayherne, astonished.

" *By half-past nine I was at home again!* My wife can prove that. I left Miss French about five minutes to nine. I arrived home about twenty-past nine. My wife was there waiting for me. Oh! thank God—thank God! And bless Janet Mackenzie's sleeve pattern."

In his exuberance, he hardly noticed that the grave expression of the solicitor's face had not altered. But the latter's words brought him down to earth with a bump.

" Who, then, in your opinion, murdered Miss French?"

" Why, a burglar, of course, as was thought at first. The window was forced, you remember. She was killed with a heavy blow from a crowbar, and the crowbar was found lying on the floor beside the body. And several articles were missing. But for Janet's absurd suspicions and dislike of me, the police would never have swerved from the right track."

" That will hardly do, Mr. Vole," said the solicitor. " The things that were missing were mere trifles of no value, taken as a blind. And the marks on the window were not at all conclusive. Besides, think for yourself. You say you were no longer in the house by half-past nine. Who, then, was the man Janet heard talking to Miss French in the sitting-room? She would hardly be having an amicable conversation with a burglar?"

" No," said Vole. " No——" He looked puzzled and discouraged. " But anyway," he added with reviving spirit, " it lets me out. I've got an *alibi*. You must see Romaine—my wife—at once."

" Certainly," acquiesced the lawyer. " I should already have seen Mrs. Vole but for her being absent when you were arrested. I wired to Scotland at once, and I understand that she arrives back to-night. I am going to call upon her immediately I leave here.''

Vole nodded, a great expression of satisfaction settling down over his face.

'' Yes, Romaine will tell you. My God! it's a lucky chance that.''

'' Excuse me, Mr. Vole, but you are very fond of your wife?''

'' Of course.''

'' And she of you?''

'' Romaine is devoted to me. She'd do anything in the world for me.''

He spoke enthusiastically, but the solicitor's heart sank a little lower. The testimony of a devoted wife—would it gain credence?

'' Was there anyone else who saw you return at nine-twenty. A maid, for instance?''

'' We have no maid.''

'' Did you meet anyone in the street on the way back?''

'' Nobody I knew. I rode part of the way in a 'bus. The conductor might remember.''

Mr. Mayherne shook his head doubtfully.

'' There is no one, then, who can confirm your wife's testimony?''

'' No. But it isn't necessary, surely?''

'' I dare say not. I dare say not,'' said Mr. Mayherne hastily. '' Now there's just one thing more. Did Miss French know that you were a married man?''

'' Oh, yes.''

'' Yet you never took your wife to see her. Why was that?''

For the first time, Leonard Vole's answer came halting and uncertain.

'' Well—I don't know.''

'' Are you aware that Janet Mackenzie says her

mistress believed you to be single, and contemplated marrying you in the future?''

Vole laughed.

'' Absurd! There was forty years difference in age between us.''

'' It has been done,'' said the solicitor drily. '' The fact remains. Your wife never met Miss French?''

'' No——'' Again the constraint.

'' You will permit me to say,'' said the lawyer, '' that I hardly understand your attitude in the matter.''

Vole flushed, hesitated, and then spoke.

'' I'll make a clean breast of it. I was hard up, as you know. I hoped that Miss French might lend me some money. She was fond of me, but she wasn't at all interested in the struggles of a young couple. Early on, I found that she had taken it for granted that my wife and I didn't get on—were living apart. Mr. May-herne—I wanted the money—for Romaine's sake. I said nothing, and allowed the old lady to think what she chose. She spoke of my being an adopted son to her. There was never any question of marriage—that must be just Janet's imagination.''

'' And that is all?''

'' Yes—that is all.''

Was there just a shade of hesitation in the words? The lawyer fancied so. He rose and held out his hand.

'' Good-bye, Mr. Vole.'' He looked into the haggard young face and spoke with an unusual impulse. '' I believe in your innocence in spite of the multitude of facts arrayed against you. I hope to prove it and vindicate you completely.''

Vole smiled back at him.

'' You'll find the alibi is all right,'' he said cheerfully. Again he hardly noticed that the other did not respond.

'' The whole thing hinges a good deal on the testimony

H.D.   I

of Janet Mackenzie," said Mr. Mayherne. " She hates
you. That much is clear."

" She can hardly hate me," protested the young man.
The solicitor shook his head as he went out.

" Now for Mrs. Vole," he said to himself.

He was seriously disturbed by the way the thing was
shaping.

The Voles lived in a small shabby house near Paddington Green. It was to this house that Mr. Mayherne went.

In answer to his ring, a big slatternly woman,
obviously a charwoman, answered the door.

" Mrs. Vole? Has she returned yet?"

" Got back an hour ago. But I dunno if you can see
her."

" If you will take my card to her," said Mr. Mayherne
quietly, " I am quite sure that she will do so."

The woman looked at him doubtfully, wiped her hand
on her apron and took the card. Then she closed the
door in his face and left him on the step outside.

In a few minutes, however, she returned with a slightly
altered manner.

" Come inside, please."

She ushered him into a tiny drawing-room. Mr. Mayherne, examining a drawing on the wall, started up
suddenly to face a tall pale woman who had entered so
quietly that he had not heard her.

" Mr. Mayherne? You are my husband's solicitor,
are you not? You have come from him? Will you please
sit down?"

Until she spoke he had not realised that she was not
English. Now, observing her more closely, he noticed
the high cheekbones, the dense blue-black of the hair,
and an occasional very slight movement of the hands
that was distinctly foreign. A strange woman, very
quiet. So quiet as to make one uneasy. From the very

first Mr. Mayherne was conscious that he was up against
something that he did not understand.

"Now, my dear Mrs. Vole," he began, "you must
not give way——"

He stopped. It was so very obvious that Romaine
Vole had not the slightest intention of giving way. She
was perfectly calm and composed.

"Will you please tell me all about it?" she said. "I
must know everything. Do not think to spare me. I
want to know the worst." She hesitated, then repeated
in a lower tone, with a curious emphasis which the lawyer
did not understand: "I want to know the worst."

Mr. Mayherne went over his interview with Leonard
Vole. She listened attentively, nodding her head now
and then.

"I see," she said, when he had finished. "He wants
me to say that he came in at twenty minutes past nine
that night?"

"He did come in at that time?" said Mr. Mayherne
sharply.

"That is not the point," she said coldly. "Will my
saying so acquit him? Will they believe me?"

Mr. Mayherne was taken aback. She had gone so
quickly to the core of the matter.

"That is what I want to know," she said. "Will it
be enough? Is there anyone else who can support my
evidence?"

There was a suppressed eagerness in her manner that
made him vaguely uneasy.

"So far there is no one else," he said reluctantly.

"I see," said Romaine Vole.

She sat for a minute or two perfectly still. A little
smile played over her lips.

The lawyer's feeling of alarm grew stronger and
stronger.

" Mrs. Vole——" he began. " I know what you must feel——"

" Do you?" she said. " I wonder."

" In the circumstances——"

" In the circumstances—I intend to play a lone hand."

He looked at her in dismay.

" But, my dear Mrs. Vole—you are overwrought. Being so devoted to your husband——"

" I beg your pardon?"

The sharpness of her voice made him start. He repeated in a hesitating manner:

" Being so devoted to your husband——"

Romaine Vole nodded slowly, the same strange smile on her lips.

" Did he tell you that I was devoted to him?" she asked softly. " Ah! yes, I can see he did. How stupid men are! Stupid—stupid—stupid——"

She rose suddenly to her feet. All the intense emotion that the lawyer had been conscious of in the atmosphere was now concentrated in her tone.

" I hate him, I tell you! I hate him. I hate him. I hate him! I would like to see him hanged by the neck till he is dead."

The lawyer recoiled before her and the smouldering passion in her eyes.

She advanced a step nearer, and continued vehemently:

" Perhaps I *shall* see it. Supposing I tell you that he did not come in that night at twenty past nine, but at twenty past *ten*? You say that he tells you he knew nothing about the money coming to him. Supposing I tell you he knew all about it, and counted on it, and committed murder to get it? Supposing I tell you that he admitted to me that night when he came in what he had done? That there was blood on his coat? What then? Supposing that I stand up in court and say all these things?"

Her eyes seemed to challenge him. With an effort, he concealed his growing dismay, and endeavoured to speak in a rational tone.

" You cannot be asked to give evidence against your husband——"

" He is not my husband!"

The words came out so quickly that he fancied he had misunderstood her.

" I beg your pardon? I——"

" He is not my husband."

The silence was so intense that you could have heard a pin drop.

" I was an actress in Vienna. My husband is alive but in a madhouse. So we could not marry. I am glad now."

She nodded defiantly.

" I should like you to tell me one thing," said Mr. Mayherne. He contrived to appear as cool and unemotional as ever. " Why are you so bitter against Leonard Vole?"

She shook her head, smiling a little.

" Yes, you would like to know. But I shall not tell you. I will keep my secret. . . ."

Mr. Mayherne gave his dry little cough and rose.

" There seems no point in prolonging this interview," he remarked. " You will hear from me again after I have communicated with my client."

She came closer to him, looking into his eyes with her own wonderful dark ones.

" Tell me," she said, " did you believe—honestly—that he was innocent when you came here to-day?"

" I did," said Mr. Mayherne.

" You poor little man," she laughed.

" And I believe so still," finished the lawyer. " Good-evening, madam."

He went out of the room, taking with him the memory of her startled face.

" This is going to be the devil of a business," said Mr. Mayherne to himself as he strode along the street.

Extraordinary, the whole thing. An extraordinary woman. A very dangerous woman. Women were the devil when they got their knife into you.

What was to be done? That wretched young man hadn't a leg to stand upon. Of course, possibly he did commit the crime. . . .

" No," said Mr. Mayherne to himself. " No—there's almost too much evidence against him. I don't believe this woman. She was trumping up the whole story. But she'll never bring it into court."

He wished he felt more conviction on the point.

The police court proceedings were brief and dramatic. The principal witnesses for the prosecution were Janet Mackenzie, maid to the dead woman, and Romaine Heilger, Austrian subject, the mistress of the prisoner.

Mr. Mayherne sat in court and listened to the damning story that the latter told. It was on the lines she had indicated to him in their interview.

The prisoner reserved his defence and was committed for trial.

Mr. Mayherne was at his wits' end. The case against Leonard Vole was black beyond words. Even the famous K.C. who was engaged for the defence held out little hope.

" If we can shake that Austrian woman's testimony, we might do something," he said dubiously. " But it's a bad business."

Mr. Mayherne had concentrated his energies on one single point. Assuming Leonard Vole to be speaking

the truth, and to have left the murdered woman's house
at nine o'clock, who was the man whom Janet heard
talking to Miss French at half-past nine?

The only ray of light was in the shape of a scapegrace
nephew who had in bygone days cajoled and threatened
his aunt out of various sums of money. Janet Mackenzie,
the solicitor learned, had always been attached to this
young man, and had never ceased urging his claims
upon her mistress. It certainly seemed possible that it
was this nephew who had been with Miss French after
Leonard Vole left, especially as he was not to be found
in any of his old haunts.

In all other directions, the lawyer's researches had
been negative in their result. No one had seen Leonard
Vole entering his own house, or leaving that of Miss
French. No one had seen any other man enter or leave
the house in Cricklewood. All inquiries drew blank.

It was the eve of the trial when Mr. Mayherne received
the letter which was to lead his thoughts in an entirely
new direction.

It came by the six o'clock post. An illiterate scrawl,
written on common paper and enclosed in a dirty
envelope with the stamp stuck on crooked.

Mr. Mayherne read it through once or twice before he
grasped its meaning.

" DEAR MISTER:

" Youre the lawyer chap wot acks for the young feller.
If you want that painted foreign hussy showd up for
wot she is an her pack of lies you come to 16 Shaw's
Rents Stepney to-night It ull cawst you 2 hundred
quid Arsk for Missis Mogson."

The solicitor read and re-read this strange epistle. It
might, of course, be a hoax, but when he thought it
over, he became increasingly convinced that it was

genuine, and also convinced that it was the one hope for the prisoner. The evidence of Romaine Heilger damned him completely, and the line the defence meant to pursue, the line that the evidence of a woman who had admittedly lived an immoral life was not to be trusted, was at best a weak one.

Mr. Mayherne's mind was made up. It was his duty to save his client at all costs. He must go to Shaw's Rents.

He had some difficulty in finding the place, a ramshackle building in an evil-smelling slum, but at last he did so, and on inquiry for Mrs. Mogson was sent up to a room on the third floor. On this door he knocked, and getting no answer, knocked again.

At this second knock, he heard a shuffling sound inside, and presently the door was opened cautiously half an inch and a bent figure peered out.

Suddenly the woman, for it was a woman, gave a chuckle and opened the door wider.

" So it's you, dearie," she said, in a wheezy voice. " Nobody with you, is there? No playing tricks? That's right. You can come in—you can come in."

With some reluctance the lawyer stepped across the threshold into the small dirty room, with its flickering gas jet. There was an untidy unmade bed in a corner, a plain deal table and two rickety chairs. For the first time Mr. Mayherne had a full view of the tenant of this unsavoury apartment. She was a woman of middle age, bent in figure, with a mass of untidy grey hair and a scarf wound tightly round her face. She saw him looking at this and laughed again, the same curious toneless chuckle.

" Wondering why I hide my beauty, dear? He, he, he. Afraid it may tempt you, eh? But you shall see— you shall see."

She drew aside the scarf and the lawyer recoiled in-

voluntarily before the almost formless blur of scarlet.
She replaced the scarf again.

"So you're not wanting to kiss me, dearie? He, he,
I don't wonder. And yet I was a pretty girl once—not
so long ago as you'd think, either.   Vitriol, dearie,
vitriol—that's what did that. Ah! but I'll be even with
'em——"

She burst into a hideous torrent of profanity which
Mr. Mayherne tried vainly to quell. She fell silent at
last, her hands clenching and unclenching themselves
nervously.

"Enough of that," said the lawyer sternly. "I've
come here because I have reason to believe you can give
me information which will clear my client, Leonard Vole.
Is that the case?"

Her eyes leered at him cunningly.

"What about the money, dearie?" she wheezed.
"Two hundred quid, you remember."

"It is your duty to give evidence, and you can be
called upon to do so."

"That won't do, dearie. I'm an old woman, and I
know nothing. But you give me two hundred quid,
and perhaps I can give you a hint or two. See?"

"What kind of hint?"

"What should you say to a letter? A letter from
her. Never mind how I got hold of it. That's my business. It'll do the trick. But I want my two hundred
quid."

Mr. Mayherne looked at her coldly, and made up his
mind.

"I'll give you ten pounds, nothing more. And only
that if this letter is what you say it is."

"Ten pounds?" She screamed and raved at him.

"Twenty," said Mr. Mayherne, "and that's my last
word."

He rose as if to go. Then, watching her closely, he

drew out a pocket-book, and counted out twenty one-pound notes.

" You see," he said. " That is all I have with me. You can take it or leave it."

But already he knew that the sight of the money was too much for her. She cursed and raved impotently, but at last she gave in. Going over to the bed, she drew something out from beneath the tattered mattress.

" Here you are, damn you!" she snarled. " It's the top one you want."

It was a bundle of letters that she threw to him, and Mr. Mayherne untied them and scanned them in his usual cool, methodical manner. The woman, watching him eagerly, could gain no clue from his impassive face.

He read each letter through, then returned again to the top one and read it a second time. Then he tied the whole bundle up again carefully.

They were love letters, written by Romaine Heilger, and the man they were written to was not Leonard Vole. The top letter was dated the day of the latter's arrest.

" I spoke true, dearie, didn't I?" whined the woman. " It'll do for her, that letter?"

Mr. Mayherne put the letters in his pocket, then he asked a question.

" How did you get hold of this correspondence?"

" That's telling," she said with a leer. " But I know something more. I heard in court what that hussy said. Find out where *she* was at twenty past ten, the time she says she was at home. Ask at the Lion Road Cinema. They'll remember—a fine upstanding girl like that—curse her!"

" Who is the man?" asked Mr. Mayherne. " There's only a Christian name here."

The other's voice grew thick and hoarse, her hands clenched and unclenched. Finally she lifted one to her face.

" He's the man that did this to me. Many years ago now. She took him away from me—a chit of a girl she was then. And when I went after him—and went for him too—he threw the cursed stuff at me! And she laughed—damn her! I've had it in for her for years. Followed her, I have, spied upon her. And now I've got her! She'll suffer for this, won't she, Mr. Lawyer? She'll suffer?"

" She will probably be sentenced to a term of imprisonment for perjury," said Mr. Mayherne quietly.

" Shut away—that's what I want. You're going, are you? Where's my money? Where's that good money?"

Without a word, Mr. Mayherne put down the notes on the table. Then, drawing a deep breath, he turned and left the squalid room. Looking back, he saw the old woman crooning over the money.

He wasted no time. He found the cinema in Lion Road easily enough, and, shown a photograph of Romaine Heilger, the commissionaire recognised her at once. She had arrived at the cinema with a man some time after ten o'clock on the evening in question. He had not noticed her escort particularly, but he remembered the lady who had spoken to him about the picture that was showing. They stayed until the end, about an hour later.

Mr. Mayherne was satisfied. Romaine Heilger's evidence was a tissue of lies from beginning to end. She had evolved it out of her passionate hatred. The lawyer wondered whether he would ever know what lay behind that hatred. What had Leonard Vole done to her? He had seemed dumbfounded when the solicitor had reported her attitude to him. He had declared earnestly that such a thing was incredible—yet it had seemed to Mr. Mayherne that after the first astonishment his protests had lacked sincerity.

He *did* know. Mr. Mayherne was convinced of it. He

knew, but he had no intention of revealing the fact. The secret between those two remained a secret. Mr. Mayherne wondered if some day he should come to learn what it was.

The solicitor glanced at his watch. It was late, but time was everything. He hailed a taxi and gave an address.

" Sir Charles must know of this at once," he murmured to himself as he got in.

The trial of Leonard Vole for the murder of Emily French aroused widespread interest. In the first place the prisoner was young and good-looking, then he was accused of a particularly dastardly crime, and there was the further interest of Romaine Heilger, the principal witness for the prosecution. There had been pictures of her in many papers, and several fictitious stories as to her origin and history.

The proceedings opened quietly enough. Various technical evidence came first. Then Janet Mackenzie was called. She told substantially the same story as before. In cross-examination counsel for the defence succeeded in getting her to contradict herself once or twice over her account of Vole's association with Miss French, he emphasised the fact that though she had heard a man's voice in the sitting-room that night, there was nothing to show that it was Vole who was there, and he managed to drive home a feeling that jealousy and dislike of the prisoner were at the bottom of a good deal of her evidence.

Then the next witness was called.

" Your name is Romaine Heilger?"

" Yes."

" You are an Austrian subject?"

" Yes."

" For the last three years you have lived with the prisoner and passed yourself off as his wife?"

Just for a moment Romaine Heilger's eyes met those of the man in the dock. Her expression held something curious and unfathomable.

" Yes."

The questions went on. Word by word the damning facts came out. On the night in question the prisoner had taken out a crowbar with him. He had returned at twenty minutes past ten, and had confessed to having killed the old lady. His cuffs had been stained with blood, and he had burned them in the kitchen stove. He had terrorised her into silence by means of threats.

As the story proceeded, the feeling of the court which had, to begin with, been slightly favourable to the prisoner, now set dead against him. He himself sat with downcast head and moody air, as though he knew he were doomed.

Yet it might have been noted that her own counsel sought to restrain Romaine's animosity. He would have preferred her to be a more unbiased witness.

Formidable and ponderous, counsel for the defence arose.

He put it to her that her story was a malicious fabrication from start to finish, that she had not even been in her own house at the time in question, that she was in love with another man and was deliberately seeking to send Vole to his death for a crime he did not commit.

Romaine denied these allegations with superb insolence.

Then came the surprising denouement, the production of the letter. It was read aloud in court in the midst of a breathless stillness.

" *Max, beloved, the Fates have delivered him into our*

hands! He has been arrested for murder—but, yes, the murder of an old lady! Leonard who would not hurt a fly! At last I shall have my revenge. The poor chicken! I shall say that he came in that night with blood upon him—that he confessed to me. I shall hang him, Max—and when he hangs he will know and realise that it was Romaine who sent him to his death. And then—happiness, Beloved! Happiness at last!"

There were experts present ready to swear that the handwriting was that of Romaine Heilger, but they were not needed. Confronted with the letter, Romaine broke down utterly and confessed everything. Leonard Vole had returned to the house at the time he said, twenty past nine. She had invented the whole story to ruin him.

With the collapse of Romaine Heilger, the case for the Crown collapsed also. Sir Charles called his few witnesses, the prisoner himself went into the box and told his story in a manly straightforward manner, unshaken by cross-examination.

The prosecution endeavoured to rally, but without great success. The judge's summing up was not wholly favourable to the prisoner, but a reaction had set in and the jury needed little time to consider their verdict.

" We find the prisoner not guilty."

Leonard Vole was free!

Little Mr. Mayherne hurried from his seat. He must congratulate his client.

He found himself polishing his pince-nez vigorously, and checked himself. His wife had told him only the night before that he was getting a habit of it. Curious things, habits. People themselves never knew they had them.

An interesting case—a very interesting case. That woman, now, Romaine Heilger.

The case was dominated for him still by the exotic figure of Romaine Heilger. She had seemed a pale quiet woman in the house at Paddington, but in court she had flamed out against the sober background. She had flaunted herself like a tropical flower.

If he closed his eyes he could see her now, tall and vehement, her exquisite body bent forward a little, her right hand clenching and unclenching itself unconsciously all the time.

Curious things, habits. That gesture of hers with the hand was her habit, he supposed. Yet he had seen some-one else do it quite lately. Who was it now? Quite lately——

He drew in his breath with a gasp as it came back to him. *The woman in Shaw's Rents.* . . .

He stood still, his head whirling. It was impossible —impossible—— Yet, Romaine Heilger was an actress.

The K.C. came up behind him and clapped him on the shoulder.

" Congratulated our man yet? He's had a narrow shave, you know. Come along and see him."

But the little lawyer shook off the other's hand.

He wanted one thing only—to see Romaine Heilger face to face.

He did not see her until some time later, and the place of their meeting is not relevant.

" So you guessed," she said, when he had told her all that was in his mind. " The face? Oh! that was easy enough, and the light of that gas jet was too bad for you to see the make-up."

" But why—why——"

" Why did I play a lone hand?" She smiled a little, remembering the last time she had used the words.

" Such an elaborate comedy!"

" My friend—I had to save him. The evidence of a woman devoted to him would not have been enough—

you hinted as much yourself. But I know something of the psychology of crowds. Let my evidence be wrung from me, as an admission, damning me in the eyes of the law, and a reaction in favour of the prisoner would immediately set in."

" And the bundle of letters?"

" One alone, the vital one, might have seemed like a—what do you call it?—put-up job."

" Then the man called Max?"

" Never existed, my friend."

" I still think," said little Mr. Mayherne, in an aggrieved manner, " that we could have got him off by the—er—normal procedure."

" I dared not risk it. You see, you *thought* he was innocent——"

" And you *knew* it? I see," said little Mr. Mayherne.

" My dear Mr. Mayherne," said Romaine, " you do not see at all. I knew—he was guilty!"

THE MYSTERY OF THE
BLUE JAR

JACK HARTINGTON surveyed his topped drive
ruefully. Standing by the ball, he looked back to
the tee, measuring the distance. His face was elo-
quent of the disgusted contempt which he felt. With a
sigh he drew out his iron, executed two vicious swings
with it, annihilating in turn a dandelion and a tuft of
grass, and then addressed himself firmly to the ball.

It is hard when you are twenty-four years of age, and
your one ambition in life is to reduce your handicap at
golf, to be forced to give time and attention to the
problem of earning your living. Five and a half days
out of the seven saw Jack imprisoned in a kind of
mahogany tomb in the city. Saturday afternoon and
Sunday were religiously devoted to the real business
of life, and in an excess of zeal he had taken rooms at
the small hotel near Stourton Heath links, and rose daily
at the hour of six a.m. to get in an hour's practice before catching the 8.46 to town.

The only disadvantage to the plan was that he seemed
constitutionally unable to hit anything at that hour
in the morning. A foozled iron succeeded a muffed drive.
His mashie shots ran merrily along the ground, and four
putts seemed to be the minimum on any green.

Jack sighed, grasped his iron firmly and repeated to
himself the magic words, " Left arm right through, and
don't look up."

He swung back—and then stopped, petrified, as a
shrill cry rent the silence of the summer's morning.

" Murder," it called. " Help! Murder!"

It was a woman's voice, and it died away at the end into a sort of gurgling sigh.

Jack flung down his club and ran in the direction of the sound. It had come from somewhere quite near at hand. This particular part of the course was quite wild country, and there were few houses about. In fact, there was only one near at hand, a small picturesque cottage, which Jack had often noticed for its air of old world daintiness. It was towards this cottage that he ran. It was hidden from him by a heather-covered slope, but he rounded this and in less than a minute was standing with his hand on the small latched gate.

There was a girl standing in the garden, and for a moment Jack jumped to the natural conclusion that it was she who had uttered the cry for help. But he quickly changed his mind.

She had a little basket in her hand, half-full of weeds, and had evidently just straightened herself up from weeding a wide border of pansies. Her eyes, Jack noticed, were just like pansies themselves, velvety and soft and dark, and more violet than blue. She was like a pansy altogether, in her straight purple linen gown.

The girl was looking at Jack with an expression midway between annoyance and surprise.

"I beg your pardon," said the young man. "But did you cry out just now?"

"I? No, indeed."

Her surprise was so genuine that Jack felt confused. Her voice was very soft and pretty with a slight foreign inflection.

"But you must have heard it," he exclaimed. "It came from somewhere just near here."

She stared at him.

"I heard nothing at all."

Jack in his turn stared at her. It was perfectly incredible that she should not have heard that agonised appeal for help. And yet her calmness was so evident that he could not believe she was lying to him.

" It came from somewhere close at hand," he insisted.

She was looking at him suspiciously now.

" What did it say?" she asked.

" Murder—help! Murder!"

" Murder—help, murder," repeated the girl. " Somebody has played a trick on you, Monsieur. Who could be murdered here?"

Jack looked about him with a confused idea of discovering a dead body upon a garden path. Yet he was still perfectly sure that the cry he had heard was real and not a product of his imagination. He looked up at the cottage windows. Everything seemed perfectly still and peaceful.

" Do you want to search our house?" asked the girl drily.

She was so clearly sceptical that Jack's confusion grew deeper than ever. He turned away.

" I'm sorry," he said. " It must have come from higher up in the woods."

He raised his cap and retreated. Glancing back over his shoulder, he saw that the girl had calmly resumed her weeding.

For some time he hunted through the woods, but could find no sign of anything unusual having occurred. Yet he was as positive as ever that he had really heard the cry. In the end, he gave up the search and hurried home to bolt his breakfast and catch the 8.46 by the usual narrow margin of a second or so. His conscience pricked him a little as he sat in the train. Ought he not to have immediately reported what he had heard to the police? That he had not done so was solely owing to the pansy girl's incredulity. She had clearly suspected him of romancing—possibly the police might do the same. *Was* he absolutely certain that he had heard the cry?

By now he was not nearly so positive as he had been —the natural result of trying to recapture a lost sensation. Was it some bird's cry in the distance that he had twisted into the semblance of a woman's voice?

But he rejected the suggestion angrily. It was a woman's voice, and he had heard it. He remembered looking at his watch just before the cry had come. As nearly as possible it must have been five and twenty minutes past seven when he had heard the call. That might be a fact useful to the police if—if anything should be discovered.

Going home that evening, he scanned the evening papers anxiously to see if there were any mention of a crime having been committed. But there was nothing, and he hardly knew whether to be relieved or disappointed.

The following morning was wet—so wet that even the most ardent golfer might have his enthusiasm damped. Jack rose at the last possible moment, gulped his breakfast, ran for the train and again eagerly scanned the papers. Still no mention of any gruesome discovery having been made. The evening papers told the same tale.

" Queer," said Jack to himself, " but there it is. Probably some blinking little boys having a game together up in the woods."

He was out early the following morning. As he passed the cottage, he noted out of the tail of his eye that the girl was out in the garden again weeding. Evidently a habit of hers. He did a particularly good approach shot, and hoped that she had noticed it. As he teed up on the next tee, he glanced at his watch.

" Just five and twenty past seven," he murmured. " I wonder——"

The words were frozen on his lips. From behind him came the same cry which had so startled him before. A woman's voice, in dire distress.

" *Murder—help, murder!*"

Jack raced back. The pansy girl was standing by the gate. She looked startled, and Jack ran up to her triumphantly, crying out:

" You heard it this time, anyway."

Her eyes were wide with some emotion he could not fathom but he noticed that she shrank back from him as he approached, and even glanced back at the house, as though she meditated running to it for shelter.

She shook her head, staring at him.

" I heard nothing at all," she said wonderingly.

It was as though she had struck him a blow between the eyes. Her sincerity was so evident that he could not disbelieve her. Yet he couldn't have imagined it—he couldn't—he couldn't——

He heard her voice speaking gently—almost with sympathy.

" You have had the shell-shock, yes?"

In a flash he understood her look of fear, her glance back at the house. She thought that he suffered from delusions. . . .

And then, like a douche of cold water, came the horrible thought, was she right? *Did* he suffer from delusions? Obsessed by the horror of the thought, he turned and stumbled away without vouchsafing a word. The girl watched him go, sighed, shook her head, and bent down to her weeding again.

Jack endeavoured to reason matters out with himself. " If I hear the damned thing again at twenty-five minutes past seven," he said to himself, " it's clear that I've got hold of a hallucination of some sort. But I won't hear it."

He was nervous all that day, and went to bed early

determined to put the matter to the proof the following morning.

As was perhaps natural in such a case, he remained awake half the night, and finally overslept himself. It was twenty past seven by the time he was clear of the hotel and running towards the links. He realised that he would not be able to get to the fatal spot by twenty-five past, but surely, if the voice was a hallucination pure and simple, he would hear it anywhere. He ran on, his eyes fixed on the hands of his watch.

Twenty-five past. From far off came the echo of a woman's voice, calling. The words could not be distinguished, but he was convinced that it was the same cry he had heard before, and that it came from the same spot, somewhere in the neighbourhood of the cottage.

Strangely enough, that fact reassured him. It might, after all, be a hoax. Unlikely as it seemed, the girl herself might be playing a trick on him. He set his shoulders resolutely, and took out a club from his golf bag. He would play the few holes up to the cottage.

The girl was in the garden as usual. She looked up this morning, and when he raised his cap to her, said good-morning rather shyly. . . . She looked, he thought, lovelier than ever.

" Nice day, isn't it?" Jack called out cheerily, cursing the unavoidable banality of the observation.

" Yes, indeed, it is lovely."

" Good for the garden, I expect?"

The girl smiled a little, disclosing a fascinating dimple.

" Alas, no! For my flowers the rain is needed. See, they are all dried up."

Jack accepted the invitation of her gesture, and came up to the low hedge dividing the garden from the course, looking over it into the garden.

" They seem all right," he remarked awkwardly, conscious as he spoke of the girl's slightly pitying glance running over him.

" The sun is good, is it not?" she said. " For the flowers one can always water them. But the sun gives strength and repairs the health. Monsieur is much better to-day, I can see."

Her encouraging tone annoyed Jack intensely.

" Curse it all," he said to himself. " I believe she's trying to cure me by suggestion."

" I'm perfectly well," he said irritably.

" That is good then," returned the girl quickly and soothingly.

Jack had the irritating feeling that she didn't believe him.

He played a few more holes and hurried back to breakfast. As he ate it, he was conscious, not for the first time, of the close scrutiny of a man who sat at the table next to him. He was a man of middle-age, with a powerful forceful face. He had a small dark beard and very piercing grey eyes, and an ease and assurance of manner which placed him among the higher ranks of the professional classes. His name, Jack knew, was Lavington, and he had heard vague rumours as to his being a well-known medical specialist, but as Jack was not a frequenter of Harley Street, the name had conveyed little or nothing to him.

But this morning he was very conscious of the quiet observation under which he was being kept, and it frightened him a little. Was his secret written plainly in his face for all to see? Did this man, by reason of his professional calling, know that there was something amiss in the hidden grey matter.

Jack shivered at the thought. Was it true? Was he really going mad? Was the whole thing a hallucination, or was it a gigantic hoax?

And suddenly a very simple way of testing the solution occurred to him. He had hitherto been alone on his round. Supposing someone else was with him? Then one out of the three things might happen. The voice might be silent. They might both hear it. Or—he only might hear it.

That evening he proceeded to carry his plan into effect. Lavington was the man he wanted with him. They fell into conversation easily enough—the older man might have been waiting for such an opening. It was clear that for some reason or other Jack interested him. The latter was able to come quite easily and naturally to the suggestion that they might play a few holes together before breakfast. The arrangement was made for the following morning.

They started out a little before seven. It was a perfect day, still and cloudless, but not too warm. The doctor was playing well, Jack wretchedly. His whole mind was intent on the forthcoming crisis. He kept glancing surreptitiously at his watch. They reached the seventh tee, between which and the hole the cottage was situated, about twenty past seven.

The girl, as usual, was in the garden as they passed. She did not look up as they passed.

The two balls lay on the green, Jack's near the hole, the doctor's some little distance away.

" I've got this for it," said Lavington. " I must go for it, I suppose."

He bent down, judging the line he should take. Jack stood rigid, his eyes glued on his watch. It was exactly twenty-five minutes past seven.

The ball ran swiftly along the grass, stopped on the edge of the hole, hesitated and dropped in.

" Good putt," said Jack. His voice sounded hoarse and unlike himself. . . . He shoved his wrist watch farther up his arm with a sigh of overwhelming relief. Nothing had happened. The spell was broken.

" If you don't mind waiting a minute," he said, " I think I'll have a pipe."

They paused a while on the eighth tee. Jack filled and lit the pipe with fingers that trembled a little in spite of himself. An enormous weight seemed to have lifted from his mind.

" Lord, what a good day it is," he remarked, staring at the prospect ahead of him with great contentment. " Go on, Lavington, your swipe."

And then it came. Just at the very instant the doctor was hitting. A woman's voice, high and agonised.

" Murder—Help! Murder!"

The pipe fell from Jack's nerveless hand, as he spun round in the direction of the sound, and then, remembering, gazed breathlessly at his companion.

Lavington was looking down the course, shading his eyes.

" A bit short—just cleared the bunker, though, I think."

He had heard nothing.

The world seemed to spin round with Jack. He took a step or two, lurching heavily. When he recovered himself, he was lying on the short turf, and Lavington was bending over him.

" There, take it easy now, take it easy."

" What did I do?"

" You fainted, young man—or gave a very good try at it."

" My God!" said Jack, and groaned.

" What's the trouble? Something on your mind?"

" I'll tell you in one minute, but I'd like to ask you something first."

The doctor lit his own pipe and settled himself on the bank.

"Ask anything you like," he said comfortably.

"You've been watching me for the last day or two. Why?"

Lavington's eyes twinkled a little.

"That's rather an awkward question. A cat can look at a king, you know."

"Don't put me off. I'm in earnest. Why was it? I've a vital reason for asking."

Lavington's face grew serious.

"I'll answer you quite honestly. I recognised in you all the signs of a man labouring under a sense of acute strain, and it intrigued me what that strain could be."

"I can tell you that easily enough," said Jack bitterly. "I'm going mad."

He stopped dramatically, but his statement not seeming to arouse the interest and consternation he expected, he repeated it.

"I tell you I'm going mad."

"Very curious," murmured Lavington. "Very curious indeed."

Jack felt indignant.

"I suppose that's all it does seem to you. Doctors are so damned callous."

"Come, come, my young friend, you're talking at random. To begin with, although I have taken my degree, I do not practise medicine. Strictly speaking, I am not a doctor—not a doctor of the body, that is."

Jack looked at him keenly.

"Of the mind?"

"Yes, in a sense, but more truly I call myself a doctor of the soul."

"Oh!"

"I perceive the disparagement in your tone, and yet we must use some word to denote the active principle which can be separated and exist independently of its fleshy home, the body. You've got to come to terms with the soul, you know, young man, it isn't just a religious term invented by clergymen. But we'll call it the mind, or the subconscious self, or any term that suits you better. You took offence at my tone just now, but I can assure you that it really did strike me as very curious that such a well-balanced and perfectly normal young man as yourself should suffer from the delusion that he was going out of his mind."

" I'm out of my mind all right. Absolutely balmy."

" You will forgive me for saying so, but I don't believe it."

" I suffer from delusions."

" After dinner?"

" No, in the morning."

" Can't be done," said the doctor, relighting his pipe which had gone out.

" I tell you I hear things that no one else hears."

" One man in a thousand can see the moons of Jupiter. Because the other nine hundred and ninety nine can't see them there's no reason to doubt that the moons of Jupiter exist, and certainly no reason for calling the thousandth man a lunatic."

" The moons of Jupiter are a proved scientific fact."

" It's quite possible that the delusions of to-day may be the proved scientific facts of to-morrow."

In spite of himself, Lavington's matter-of-fact manner was having its effect upon Jack. He felt immeasurably soothed and cheered. The doctor looked at him attentively for a minute or two and then nodded.

" That's better," he said. " The trouble with you young fellows is that you're so cocksure nothing can exist outside your own philosophy that you get the wind up when something occurs to jolt you out of that opinion. Let's hear your grounds for believing that you're going mad, and we'll decide whether or not to lock you up afterwards."

As faithfully as he could, Jack narrated the whole series of occurrences.

" But what I can't understand," he ended, " is why this morning it should come at half-past seven—five minutes late."

Lavington thought for a minute or two. Then——

" What's the time now by your watch?" he asked.

" Quarter to eight," replied Jack, consulting it.

" That's simple enough, then. Mine says twenty to eight. Your watch is five minutes fast. That's a very interesting and important point—to me. In fact, it's invaluable."

" In what way?"

Jack was beginning to get interested.

" Well, the obvious explanation is that on the first morning you *did* hear some such cry—may have been a joke, may not. On the following mornings, you suggestioned yourself to hear it at exactly the same time."

" I'm sure I didn't."

" Not consciously, of course, but the subconscious plays us some funny tricks, you know. But anyway, that explanation won't wash. If it was a case of suggestion, you would have heard the cry at twenty-five minutes past seven by your watch, and you could never have heard it when the time, as you thought, was past."

" Well, then?"

" Well—it's obvious, isn't it? This cry for help occupies a perfectly definite place and time in space. The place is the vicinity of that cottage and the time is twenty-five minutes past seven."

" Yes, but why should *I* be the one to hear it? I don't believe in ghosts and all that spook stuff—spirits rapping and all the rest of it. Why should I hear the damned thing?"

" Ah! that we can't tell at present. It's a curious

thing that many of the best mediums are made out of confirmed sceptics. It isn't the people who are interested in occult phenomena who get the manifestations. Some people see and hear things that other people don't—we don't know why, and nine times out of ten they don't want to see or hear them, and are convinced that they are suffering from delusions—just as you were. It's like electricity. Some substances are good conductors, others are non-conductors, and for a long time we didn't know why, and had to be content just to accept the fact. Nowadays we do know why. Some day, no doubt, we shall know why you hear this thing and I and the girl don't. Everything's governed by natural law, you know —there's no such thing really as the supernatural. Finding out the laws that govern so called psychic phenomena is going to be a tough job—but every little helps."

" But what am I going to *do*?" asked Jack.

Lavington chuckled.

" Practical, I see. Well, my young friend, you are going to have a good breakfast and get off to the city without worrying your head further about things you don't understand. I, on the other hand, am going to poke about, and see what I can find out about that cottage back there. That's where the mystery centres, I dare swear."

Jack rose to his feet.

" Right, sir. I'm on, but, I say——"

" Yes?"

Jack flushed awkwardly.

" I'm sure the girl's all right," he muttered.

Lavington looked amused.

" You didn't tell me she was a pretty girl! Well, cheer up, I think the mystery started before her time."

Jack arrived home that evening in a perfect fever of curiosity. He was by now pinning his faith blindly to Lavington. The doctor had accepted the matter so naturally, had been so matter-of-fact and unperturbed by it, that Jack was impressed.

He found his new friend waiting for him in the hall when he came down for dinner, and the doctor suggested that they should dine together at the same table.

"Any news, sir?" asked Jack anxiously.

"I've collected the life history of Heather Cottage all right. It was tenanted first by an old gardener and his wife. The old man died, and the old woman went to her daughter. Then a builder got hold of it, and modernised it with great success, selling it to a city gentleman who used it for week-ends. About a year ago, he sold it to some people called Turner—Mr. and Mrs. Turner. They seem to have been rather a curious couple from all I can make out. He was an Englishman, his wife was popularly supposed to be partly Russian, and was a very handsome exotic-looking woman. They lived very quietly, seeing no one, and hardly ever going outside the cottage garden. The local rumour goes that they were afraid of something—but I don't think we ought to rely on that.

"And then suddenly one day they departed, cleared out one morning early, and never came back. The agents here got a letter from Mr. Turner, written from London, instructing him to sell up the place as quickly as possible. The furniture was sold off, and the house itself was sold to a Mr. Mauleverer. He only actually lived in it a fortnight—then he advertised it to be let furnished. The people who have it now are a consumptive French professor and his daughter. They have been there just ten days."

Jack digested this in silence.

"I don't see that that gets us any forrader," he said at last. "Do you?"

"I rather want to know more about the Turners," said Lavington quietly. "They left very early in the morning, you remember. As far as I can make out, nobody actually saw them go. Mr. Turner has been seen since—but I can't find anybody who has seen Mrs. Turner."

Jack paled.

" It can't be—you don't mean——"

" Don't excite yourself, young man. The influence of anyone at the point of death—and especially of violent death—upon their surroundings is very strong. Those surroundings might conceivably absorb that influence, transmitting it in turn to a suitably tuned receiver—in this case yourself."

" But why me?" murmured Jack rebelliously. " Why not someone who could do some good?"

" You are regarding the force as intelligent and purposeful, instead of blind and mechanical. I do not believe myself in earth-bound spirits, haunting a spot for one particular purpose. But the thing I have seen, again and again, until I can hardly believe it to be pure coincidence, is a kind of blind groping towards justice —a subterranean moving of blind forces, always working obscurely towards that end. . . ."

He shook himself—as though casting off some obsession that preoccupied him, and turned to Jack with a ready smile.

" Let us banish the subject—for to-night at all events," he suggested.

Jack agreed readily enough, but did not find it so easy to banish the subject from his own mind.

During the week-end, he made vigorous inquiries of his own, but succeeded in eliciting little more than the doctor had done. He had definitely given up playing golf before breakfast.

The next link in the chain came from an unexpected quarter. On getting back one day, Jack was informed that a young lady was waiting to see him. To his in-

tense surprise it proved to be the girl of the garden—
the pansy girl, as he always called her in his own mind.
She was very nervous and confused.

" You will forgive me, Monsieur, for coming to seek
you like this? But there is something I want to tell
you—I——"

She looked round uncertainly.

" Come in here," said Jack promptly, leading the
way into the now deserted " Ladies' Drawing-room " of
the hotel, a dreary apartment, with a good deal of red
plush about it. " Now, sit down, Miss, Miss——"

" Marchaud, Monsieur. Felise Marchaud."

" Sit down, Mademoiselle Marchaud, and tell me all
about it."

Felise sat down obediently. She was dressed in dark
green to-day, and the beauty and charm of the proud
little face was more evident than ever. Jack's heart beat
faster as he sat down beside her.

" It is like this," explained Felise. " We have been
here but a short time, and from the beginning we hear
the house—our so sweet little house—is haunted. No
servant will stay in it. That does not matter so much
—me, I can do the *ménage* and cook easily enough."

" Angel," thought the infatuated young man. " She's
wonderful."

But he maintained an outward semblance of businesslike attention.

" This talk of ghosts, I think it is all folly—that is
until four days ago. Monsieur, four nights running, I
have had the same dream. A lady stands there—she is
beautiful, tall and very fair. In her hands she holds a
blue china jar. She is distressed—very distressed, and
continually she holds out the jar to me, as though imploring me to do something with it—but alas! she cannot speak, and I—I do not know what she asks. That
was the dream for the first two nights—but the night be-

fore last, there was more of it. She and the blue jar
faded away, and suddenly I heard her voice crying
out—I know it is her voice, you comprehend—and, oh!
Monsieur, the words she says are those you spoke to me
that morning. ' Murder—Help! Murder!' I awoke in
terror. I say to myself—it is a nightmare, the words
you heard are an accident. But last night the dream
came again. Monsieur, what is it? You too have
heard. What shall we do?"

Felise's face was terrified. Her small hands clasped
themselves together, and she gazed appealingly at Jack.
The latter affected an unconcern he did not feel.

" That's all right, Mademoiselle Marchaud.   You
mustn't worry. I tell you what I'd like you to do, if
you don't mind, repeat the whole story to a friend of
mine who is staying here, a Dr. Lavington."

Felise signified her willingness to adopt this course,
and Jack went off in search of Lavington. He returned with him a few minutes later.

Lavington gave the girl a keen scrutiny as he acknowledged Jack's hurried introductions. With a few reassuring words, he soon put the girl at her ease, and
he, in his turn, listened attentively to her story.

" Very curious," he said, when she had finished.
" You have told your father of this?"

Felise shook her head.

" I have not liked to worry him. He is very ill
still "—her eyes filled with tears—" I keep from him
anything that might excite or agitate him."

" I understand," said Lavington kindly. " And I
am glad you came to us, Mademoiselle Marchaud. Hartington here, as you know, had an experience something
similar to yours. I think I may say that we are well
on the track now. There is nothing else that you can
think of?"

Felise gave a quick movement.

"Of course! How stupid I am. It is the point of the whole story. Look, Monsieur, at what I found at the back of one of the cupboards where it had slipped behind the shelf."

She held out to them a dirty piece of drawing-paper on which was executed roughly in water colours a sketch of a woman. It was a mere daub, but the likeness was probably good enough. It represented a tall fair woman, with something subtly un-English in her face. She was standing by a table on which was standing a blue china jar.

"I only found it this morning," explained Felise. "Monsieur le docteur, that is the face of the woman I saw in my dream, and that is the identical blue jar."

"Extraordinary," commented Lavington. "The key to the mystery is evidently the blue jar. It looks like a Chinese jar to me, probably an old one. It seems to have a curious raised pattern over it."

"It is Chinese," declared Jack. "I have seen an exactly similar one in my uncle's collection—he is a great collector of Chinese porcelain, you know, and I remember noticing a jar just like this a short time ago."

"The Chinese jar," mused Lavington. He remained a minute or two lost in thought, then raised his head suddenly, a curious light shining in his eyes. "Hartington, how long has your uncle had that jar?"

"How long? I really don't know."

"Think. Did he buy it lately?"

"I don't know—yes, I believe he did, now I come to think of it. I'm not very interested in porcelain myself, but I remember his showing me his 'recent acquisitions,' and this was one of them."

"Less than two months ago? The Turners left Heather Cottage just two months ago."

"Yes, I believe it was."

"Your uncle attends country sales sometimes?"

" He's always tooling round to sales."

" Then there is no inherent improbability in our assuming that he bought this particular piece of porcelain at the sale of the Turners' things. A curious coincidence—or perhaps what I call the groping of blind justice. Hartington, you must find out from your uncle at once where he bought this jar."

Jack's face fell.

" I'm afraid that's impossible. Uncle George is away on the Continent. I don't even know where to write to him."

" How long will he be away?"

" Three weeks to a month at least."

There was a silence. Felise sat looking anxiously from one man to the other.

" Is there nothing that we can do?" she asked timidly.

" Yes, there is one thing," said Lavington, in a tone of suppressed excitement. " It is unusual, perhaps, but I believe that it will succeed. Hartington, you must get hold of that jar. Bring it down here, and, if Mademoiselle permits, we will spend a night in Heather Cottage, taking the blue jar with us."

Jack felt his skin creep uncomfortably.

" What do you think will happen?" he asked uneasily.

" I have not the slightest idea—but I honestly believe that the mystery will be solved and the ghost laid. Quite possibly there may be a false bottom to the jar and something is concealed inside it. It no phenomena occurs, we must use our own ingenuity."

Felise clasped her hands.

" It is a wonderful idea," she exclaimed.

Her eyes were alight with enthusiasm. Jack did not feel nearly so enthusiastic—in fact, he was inwardly funking it badly, but nothing would have induced him to admit the fact before Felise. The doctor acted as though his suggestion were the most natural one in the world.

"When can you get the jar?" asked Felise, turning to Jack.

"To-morrow," said the latter, unwillingly.

He had to go through with it now, but the memory of that frenzied cry for help that had haunted him each morning was something to be ruthlessly thrust down and not thought about more than could be helped.

He went to his uncle's house the following evening, and took away the jar in question. He was more than ever convinced when he saw it again that it was the identical one pictured in the water colour sketch, but carefully as he looked it over he could see no sign that it contained a secret receptacle of any kind.

It was eleven o'clock when he and Lavington arrived at Heather Cottage. Felise was on the look-out for them, and opened the door softly before they had time to knock.

"Come in," she whispered. "My father is asleep upstairs, and we must not wake him. I have made coffee for you in here."

She led the way into a small cosy sitting-room. A spirit lamp stood in the grate, and bending over it, she brewed them both some fragrant coffee.

Then Jack unfastened the Chinese jar from its many wrappings. Felise gasped as her eyes fell on it.

"But yes, but yes," she cried eagerly. "That is it— I would know it anywhere."

Meanwhile Lavington was making his own preparations. He removed all the ornaments from a small table and set it in the middle of the room. Round it he placed three chairs. Then, taking the blue jar from Jack, he placed it in the centre of the table.

" Now," he said, " we are ready. Turn off the lights, and let us sit round the table in the darkness."

The others obeyed him. Lavington's voice spoke again out of the darkness.

" Think of nothing—or of everything. Do not force the mind. It is possible that one of us has mediumistic powers. If so, that person will go into a trance. Remember, there is nothing to fear. Cast out fear from your hearts, and drift—drift——"

His voice died away and there was silence. Minute by minute, the silence seemed to grow more pregnant with possibilities. It was all very well for Lavington to say " Cast out fear." It was not fear that Jack felt—it was panic. And he was almost certain that Felise felt the same way. Suddenly he heard her voice, low and terrified.

" Something terrible is going to happen. I feel it."

" Cast out fear," said Lavington. " Do not fight against the influence."

The darkness seemed to get darker and the silence more acute. And nearer and nearer came that indefinable sense of menace.

Jack felt himself choking—stifling—the evil thing was very near. . . .

And then the moment of conflict passed. He was drifting—drifting down stream—his lids closed—peace—darkness. . . .

Jack stirred slightly. His head was heavy—heavy as lead. Where was he?

Sunshine . . . birds. . . . He lay staring up at the sky.

Then it all came back to him. The sitting. The little room. Felise and the doctor. What had happened?

He sat up, his head throbbing unpleasantly, and looked round him. He was lying in a little copse not far from the cottage. No one else was near him. He took out his watch. To his amazement it registered half-past twelve.

Jack struggled to his feet, and ran as fast as he could in the direction of the cottage. They must have been alarmed by his failure to come out of the trance, and carried him out into the open air.

Arrived at the cottage, he knocked loudly on the door. But there was no answer, and no signs of life about it. They must have gone off to get help. Or else—Jack felt an indefinable fear invade him. What had happened last night?

He made his way back to the hotel as quickly as possible. He was about to make some inquiries at the office, when he was diverted by a colossal punch in the ribs which nearly knocked him off his feet. Turning in some indignation, he beheld a white-haired old gentleman wheezing with mirth.

" Didn't expect me, my boy. Didn't expect me, hey?" said this individual.

" Why, Uncle George, I thought you were miles away—in Italy somewhere."

" Ah! but I wasn't. Landed at Dover last night. Thought I'd motor up to town and stop here to see you on the way. And what did I find. Out all night, hey? Nice goings on——"

" Uncle George," Jack checked him firmly. " I've got the most extraordinary story to tell you. I dare say you won't believe it."

" I dare say I shan't," laughed the old man. " But do your best, my boy."

" But I must have something to eat," continued Jack. " I'm famished."

He led the way to the dining-room, and over a substantial repast, he narrated the whole story.

" And God knows what's become of them," he ended. His uncle seemed on the verge of apoplexy.

" The jar," he managed to ejaculate at last. " THE BLUE JAR! What's become of that?"

Jack stared at him in non-comprehension, but submerged in the torrent of words that followed he began to understand.

It came with a rush: " Ming—unique—gem of my collection—worth ten thousand pounds at least—offer from Hoggenheimer, the American millionaire—only one of its kind in the world.—Confound it, sir, what have you done with my BLUE JAR?"

Jack rushed from the room. He must find Lavington. The young lady at the office eyed him coldly.

" Dr. Lavington left late last night—by motor. He left a note for you."

Jack tore it open. It was short and to the point.

" MY DEAR YOUNG FRIEND,

" Is the day of the supernatural over? Not quite—especially when tricked out in new scientific language. Kindest regards from Felise, invalid father, and myself. We have twelve hours start, which ought to be ample.

" Yours ever,

" AMBROSE LAVINGTON,

" *Doctor of the Soul.*"

THE STRANGE CASE OF
SIR ANDREW CARMICHAEL

(Taken from the notes of the late Dr. Edward Carstairs, M.D., the eminent psychologist.)

I AM perfectly aware that there are two distinct ways of looking at the strange and tragic events which I have set down here. My own opinion has never wavered. I have been persuaded to write the story out in full, and indeed I believe it to be due to science that such strange and inexplicable facts should not be buried in oblivion.

It was a wire from my friend, Dr. Settle, that first introduced me to the matter. Beyond mentioning the name Carmichael, the wire was not explicit, but in obedience to it I took the 12.20 train from Paddington to Wolden, in Herefordshire.

The name of Carmichael was not unfamiliar to me. I had been slightly acquainted with the late Sir William Carmichael of Wolden, though I had seen nothing of him for the last eleven years. He had, I knew, one son, the present baronet, who must now be a young man of about twenty-three. I remembered vaguely having heard some rumours about Sir William's second marriage, but could recall nothing definite unless it were a vague impression detrimental to the second Lady Carmichael.

Settle met me at the station.

" Good of you to come," he said as he wrung my hand.

" Not at all. I understand this is something in my line?"

" Very much so."

" A mental case, then?" I hazarded. " Possessing some unusual features?"

We had collected my luggage by this time and were seated in a dog-cart driving away from the station in the direction of Wolden, which lay about three miles away. Settle did not answer for a minute or two. Then he burst out suddenly.

" The whole thing's incomprehensible! Here is a young man, twenty-three years of age, thoroughly normal in every respect. A pleasant amiable boy, with no more than his fair share of conceit, not brilliant intellectually perhaps, but an excellent type of the ordinary upper-class young Englishman. Goes to bed in his usual health one evening, and is found the next morning wandering about the village in a semi-idiotic condition, incapable of recognising his nearest and dearest."

" Ah!" I said, stimulated. This case promised to be interesting. " Complete loss of memory? And this occurred——?"

" Yesterday morning. The 9th of August."

" And there has been nothing—no shock that you know of—to account for this state?"

" Nothing."

I had a sudden suspicion.

" Are you keeping anything back?"

" N—no."

His hesitation confirmed my suspicion.

" I must know everything."

" It's nothing to do with Arthur. It's to do with— with the house."

" With the house," I repeated, astonished.

" You've had a great deal to do with that sort of

thing, haven't you, Carstairs? You've ' tested ' so-called haunted houses. What's your opinion of the whole thing?"

" In nine cases out of ten, fraud," I replied. " But the tenth—well, I have come across phenomena that is absolutely unexplainable from the ordinary materialistic standpoint. I am a believer in the occult."

Settle nodded. We were just turning in at the Park gates. He pointed with his whip at a low-lying white mansion on the side of a hill.

" That's the house," he said. " And—there's *something* in that house, something uncanny—horrible. We all feel it. . . . And I'm not a superstitious man. . . ."

" What form does it take?" I asked.

He looked straight in front of him. " I'd rather you knew nothing. You see, if you—coming here unbiased —knowing nothing about it—see it too—well——"

" Yes," I said, " it's better so. But I should be glad if you will tell me a little more about the family."

" Sir William," said Settle, " was twice married. Arthur is the child of his first wife. Nine years ago he married again, and the present Lady Carmichael is something of a mystery. She is only half English, and, I suspect, has Asiatic blood in her veins."

He paused.

" Settle," I said, " you don't like Lady Carmichael."

He admitted it frankly. " No, I don't. There has always seemed to me to be something sinister about her. Well, to continue, by his second wife Sir William had another child, also a boy, who is now eight years old. Sir William died three years ago, and Arthur came into the title and place. His stepmother and half-brother continued to live with him at Wolden. The estate, I must tell you, is very much impoverished. Nearly the whole of Sir Arthur's income goes to keeping it up. A few hundreds a year was all Sir William could leave his wife, but fortunately Arthur has always got on splendidly with his stepmother, and has been only too delighted to have her live with him. Now——''

'' Yes?''

'' Two months ago Arthur became engaged to a charming girl, a Miss Phyllis Patterson.'' He added, lowering his voice with a touch of emotion: '' They were to have been married next month. She is staying here now. You can imagine her distress——''

I bowed my head silently.

We were driving up close to the house now. On our right the green lawn sloped gently away. And suddenly I saw a most charming picture. A young girl was coming slowly across the lawn to the house. She wore no hat, and the sunlight enhanced the gleam of her glorious golden hair. She carried a great basket of roses, and a beautiful grey Persian cat twined itself lovingly round her feet as she walked.

I looked at Settle interrogatively.

'' That is Miss Patterson,'' he said.

'' Poor girl,'' I said, '' poor girl. What a picture she makes with her roses and her grey cat.''

I heard a faint sound and looked quickly round at my friend. The reins had slipped out of his fingers, and his face was quite white.

'' What's the matter?'' I exclaimed.

He recovered himself with an effort.

'' Nothing,'' he said, '' nothing.''

In a few moments more we had arrived, and I was following him into the green drawing-room, where tea was laid out.

A middle-aged but still beautiful woman rose as we entered and came forward with an outstretched hand.

'' This is my friend, Dr. Carstairs, Lady Carmichael.''

I cannot explain the instinctive wave of repulsion that

swept over me as I took the proffered hand of this charming and stately woman who moved with the dark and languorous grace that recalled Settle's surmise of Oriental blood.

" It is very good of you to come, Dr. Carstairs," she said in a low musical voice, " and to try and help us in our great trouble."

I made some trivial reply and she handed me my tea.

In a few minutes the girl I had seen on the lawn outside entered the room. The cat was no longer with her, but she still carried the basket of roses in her hand. Settle introduced me and she came forward impulsively.

" Oh! Dr. Carstairs, Dr. Settle has told us so much about you. I have a feeling that you will be able to do something for poor Arthur."

Miss Patterson was certainly a very lovely girl, though her cheeks were pale, and her frank eyes were outlined with dark circles.

" My dear young lady," I said reassuringly, " indeed you must not despair. These cases of lost memory, or secondary personality, are often of very short duration. At any minute the patient may return to his full powers."

She shook her head. " I can't believe in this being a second personality," she said. " *This* isn't Arthur at all. It is *no* personality of his. It isn't *him*. I——"

" Phyllis, dear," said Lady Carmichael's soft voice, " here is your tea."

And something in the expression of her eyes as they rested on the girl told me that Lady Carmichael had little love for her prospective daughter-in-law.

Miss Patterson declined the tea, and I said, to ease the conversation: " Isn't the pussy cat going to have a saucer of milk?"

She looked at me rather strangely.

" The—pussy cat?"

" Yes, your companion of a few moments ago in the garden——"

I was interrupted by a crash. Lady Carmichael had upset the tea kettle, and the hot water was pouring all over the floor. I remedied the matter, and Phyllis Patterson looked questioningly at Settle. He rose.

" Would you like to see your patient now, Carstairs?"

I followed him at once. Miss Patterson came with us. We went upstairs and Settle took a key from his pocket.

" He sometimes has a fit of wandering," he explained. " So I usually lock the door when I'm away from the house."

He turned the key in the lock and we went in.

A young man was sitting on the window seat where the last rays of the westerly sun struck broad and yellow. He sat curiously still, rather hunched together, with every muscle relaxed. I thought at first that he was quite unaware of our presence until I suddenly saw that, under immovable lids, he was watching us closely. His eyes dropped as they met mine, and he blinked. But he did not move.

" Come, Arthur," said Settle cheerfully. " Miss Patterson and a friend of mine have come to see you."

But the young fellow on the window seat only blinked. Yet a moment or two later I saw him watching us again —furtively and secretly.

" Want your tea?" asked Settle, still loudly and cheerfully, as though talking to a child.

He set on the table a cup full of milk. I lifted my eyebrows in surprise, and Settle smiled.

" Funny thing," he said, " the only drink he'll touch is milk."

In a moment or two, without undue haste, Sir Arthur uncoiled himself, limb by limb, from his huddled position, and walked slowly over to the table. I recognised suddenly that his movements were absolutely silent, his feet made no sound as they trod. Just as he reached the table he gave a tremendous stretch, poised on one leg forward, the other stretching out behind him. He prolonged this exercise to its utmost extent, and then yawned. Never have I seen such a yawn! It seemed to swallow up his entire face.

He now turned his attention to the milk, bending down to the table until his lips touched the fluid.

Settle answered my inquiring look.

" Won't make use of his hands at all. Seems to have returned to a primitive state. Odd, isn't it?"

I felt Phyllis Patterson shrink against me a little, and I laid my hand soothingly on her arm.

The milk was finished at last, and Arthur Carmichael stretched himself once more, and then with the same quiet noiseless footsteps he regained the window seat, where he sat, huddled up as before, blinking at us.

Miss Patterson drew us out into the corridor. She was trembling all over.

" Oh! Dr. Carstairs," she cried. " It *isn't* him—that thing in there isn't Arthur! I should feel—I should know——"

I shook my head sadly.

" The brain can play strange tricks, Miss Patterson."

I confess that I was puzzled by the case. It presented unusual features. Though I had never seen young Carmichael before there was something about his peculiar manner of walking, and the way he blinked, that reminded me of someone or something that I could not quite place.

Our dinner that night was a quiet affair, the burden of conversation being sustained by Lady Carmichael and myself. When the ladies had withdrawn Settle asked me my impression of my hostess.

"I must confess," I said, "that for no cause or reason I dislike her intensely. You were quite right, she has Eastern blood, and, I should say, possesses marked occult powers. She is a woman of extraordinary magnetic force."

Settle seemed on the point of saying something, but checked himself and merely remarked after a minute or two: "She is absolutely devoted to her little son."

We sat in the green drawing-room again after dinner. We had just finished coffee and were conversing rather stiffly on the topics of the day when the cat began to miaw piteously for admission outside the door. No one took any notice, and, as I am fond of animals, after a moment or two I rose.

"May I let the poor thing in?" I asked Lady Carmichael.

Her face seemed very white, I thought, but she made a faint gesture of the head which I took as assent and, going to the door, I opened it. But the corridor outside was quite empty.

"Strange," I said, "I could have sworn I heard a cat."

As I came back to my chair I noticed they were all watching me intently. It somehow made me feel a little uncomfortable.

We retired to bed early. Settle accompanied me to my room.

"Got everything you want?" he asked, looking round.

"Yes, thanks."

He still lingered rather awkwardly as though there was something he wanted to say but could not quite get out.

"By the way," I remarked. "you said there was something uncanny about this house? As yet it seems most normal."

" You call it a cheerful house?"

" Hardly that, under the circumstances. It is obviously under the shadow of a great sorrow. But as regards any abnormal influence, I should give it a clean bill of health."

" Good-night," said Settle abruptly. " And pleasant dreams."

Dream I certainly did. Miss Patterson's grey cat seemed to have impressed itself upon my brain. All night long, it seemed to me, I dreamt of the wretched animal.

Awaking with a start, I suddenly realised what had brought the cat so forcibly into my thoughts. The creature was miawing persistently outside my door. Impossible to sleep with that racket going on. I lit my candle and went to the door. But the passage outside my room was empty, though the miawing still continued. A new idea struck me. The unfortunate animal was shut up somewhere, unable to get out. To the left was the end of the passage, where Lady Carmichael's room was situated. I turned therefore to the right, but had taken but a few paces when the noise broke out again from behind me. I turned sharply and the sound came again, this time distinctly on the *right* of me.

Something, probably a draught in the corridor, made me shiver, and I went sharply back to my room. Everything was silent now, and I was soon asleep once more —to wake to another glorious summer's day.

As I was dressing I saw from my window the disturber of my night's rest. The grey cat was creeping slowly and stealthily across the lawn. I judged its object of attack to be a small flock of birds who were busy chirruping and preening themselves not far away.

And then a very curious thing happened. The cat came straight on and passed through the midst of the

birds, its fur almost brushing against them—and the
birds did not fly away. I could not understand it—the
thing seemed incomprehensible.

So vividly did it impress me that I could not refrain
from mentioning it at breakfast.

" Do you know?" I said to Lady Carmichael, " that
you have a very unusual cat?"

I heard the quick rattle of a cup on a saucer, and I
saw Phyllis Patterson, her lips parted and her breath
coming quickly, gazing earnestly at me.

There was a moment's silence, and then Lady Carmichael said in a distinctly disagreeable manner: " I
think you must have made a mistake. There is no cat
here. I have never had a cat."

It was evident that I had managed to put my foot in
it badly, so I hastily changed the subject.

But the matter puzzled me. Why had Lady Carmichael declared there was no cat in the house? Was it
perhaps Miss Patterson's, and its presence concealed
from the mistress of the house? Lady Carmichael might
have one of those strange antipathies to cats which are
so often met with nowadays. It hardly seemed a
plausible explanation, but I was forced to rest content
with it for the moment.

Our patient was still in the same condition. This
time I made a thorough examination and was able to
study him more closely than the night before. At my
suggestion it was arranged that he should spend as
much time with the family as possible. I hoped not only
to have a better opportunity of observing him when he
was off his guard, but that the ordinary every-day
routine might awaken some gleam of intelligence. His
demeanour, however, remained unchanged. He was
quiet and docile, seemed vacant, but was, in point of
fact, intensely and rather slyly watchful. One thing

H.D.   M

certainly came as a surprise to me, the intense affection
he displayed towards his stepmother. Miss Patterson
he ignored completely, but he always managed to sit as
near Lady Carmichael as possible, and once I saw him
rub his head against her shoulder in a dumb expression
of love.

I was worried about the case. I could not but feel
that there was some clue to the whole matter which had
so far escaped me.

" This is a very strange case," I said to Settle.

" Yes," said he, " it's very—suggestive."

He looked at me—rather furtively, I thought.

" Tell me," he said. " He doesn't—remind you of
anything?"

The words struck me disagreeably, reminding me of
my impression of the day before.

" Remind me of what?" I asked.

He shook his head.

" Perhaps it's my fancy," he muttered. " Just my
fancy."

And he would say no more on the matter.

Altogether there was mystery shrouding the affair. I
was still obsessed with that baffling feeling of having
missed the clue that should elucidate it to me. And
concerning a lesser matter there was also mystery. I
mean that trifling affair of the grey cat. For some reason
or other the thing was getting on my nerves. I dreamed
of cats—I continually fancied I heard them. Now and
then in the distance I caught a glimpse of the beautiful
animal. And the fact that there was some mystery
connected with it fretted me unbearably. On a sudden
impulse I applied one afternoon to the footman for
information.

" Can you tell me anything," I said, " about the
cat I see?"

" The cat, sir?" He appeared politely surprised.

" Wasn't there—isn't there—a cat?"

" Her ladyship *had* a cat, sir. A great pet. Had to be put away though. A great pity, as it was a beautiful animal."

" A grey cat?" I asked slowly.

" Yes, sir. A Persian."

" And you say it was destroyed?"

" Yes, sir."

" You're quite sure it was destroyed?"

" Oh! quite sure, sir. Her ladyship wouldn't have him sent to the vet—but did it herself. A little less than a week ago now. He's buried out there under the copper beech, sir." And he went out of the room, leaving me to my meditations.

Why had Lady Carmichael affirmed so positively that she had never had a cat?

I felt an intuition that this trifling affair of the cat was in some way significant. I found Settle and took him aside.

" Settle," I said. " I want to ask you a question. Have you, or have you not, both seen and heard a cat in this house?"

He did not seem surprised at the question. Rather did he seem to have been expecting it.

" I've heard it," he said. " I've not seen it."

" But that first day," I cried. " On the lawn with Miss Patterson!"

He looked at me very steadily.

" I saw Miss Patterson walking across the lawn. Nothing else."

I began to understand. " Then," I said, " the cat——?"

He nodded.

" I wanted to see if you—unprejudiced—would hear what we all hear . . .?"

" You all hear it then?"

He nodded again.

" It's strange," I murmured thoughtfully. " I never heard of a cat haunting a place before."

I told him what I had learnt from the footman, and he expressed surprise.

" That's news to me. I didn't know that."

" But what does it mean?" I asked helplessly.

He shook his head. " Heaven only knows! But I'll tell you, Carstairs—I'm afraid. The—thing's voice sounds—menacing."

" Menacing?" I said sharply. " To whom?"

He spread out his hands. " I can't say."

It was not till that evening after dinner that I realised the meaning of his words. We were sitting in the green drawing-room, as on the night of my arrival, when it came—the loud insistent miawing of a cat outside the door. But this time it was unmistakably angry in its tone—a fierce cat yowl, long-drawn and menacing. And then as it ceased the brass hook outside the door was rattled violently as by a cat's paw.

Settle started up.

" I swear that's real," he cried.

He rushed to the door and flung it open.

There was nothing there.

He came back mopping his brow. Phyllis was pale and trembling, Lady Carmichael deathly white. Only Arthur, squatting contentedly like a child, his head against his stepmother's knee, was calm and undisturbed.

Miss Patterson laid her hand on my arm as we went upstairs.

" Oh! Dr. Carstairs," she cried. " What is it? What does it all mean?"

" We don't know yet, my dear young lady," I said.

" But I mean to find out. But you mustn't be afraid. I am convinced there is no danger to you personally."

She looked at me doubtfully. " You think that?"

" I am sure of it," I answered firmly. I remembered the loving way the grey cat had twined itself round her feet, and I had no misgivings. The menace was not for her.

I was some time dropping off to sleep, but at length I fell into an uneasy slumber from which I awoke with a sense of shock. I heard a scratching sputtering noise as of something being violently ripped or torn. I sprang out of bed and rushed out into the passage. At the same moment Settle burst out of his room opposite. The sound came from our left.

" You hear it, Carstairs?" he cried. " You hear it?"

We came swiftly up to Lady Carmichael's door. Nothing had passed us, but the noise had ceased. Our candles glittered blankly on the shiny panels of Lady Carmichael's door. We stared at one another.

" You know what it was?" he half whispered.

I nodded. " A cat's claws ripping and tearing something." I shivered a little. Suddenly I gave an exclamation and lowered the candle I held.

" Look here, Settle."

" Here " was a chair that rested against the wall— and the seat of it was ripped and torn in long strips. . . .

We examined it closely. He looked at me and I nodded.

" Cat's claws," he said, drawing in his breath sharply. " Unmistakable." His eyes went from the chair to the closed door. " That's the person who is menaced. Lady Carmichael!"

I slept no more that night. Things had come to a pass where something must be done. As far as I knew there was only one person who had the key to the situation.

I suspected Lady Carmichael of knowing more than she chose to tell.

She was deathly pale when she came down the next morning, and only toyed with the food on her plate. I was sure that only an iron determination kept her from breaking down. After breakfast I requested a few words with her. I went straight to the point.

" Lady Carmichael," I said. " I have reason to believe that you are in very grave danger."

" Indeed?" She braved it out with wonderful unconcern.

" There is in this house," I continued, " a Thing— a Presence—that is obviously hostile to you."

" What nonsense," she murmured scornfully. " As if I believed in any rubbish of that kind."

" The chair outside your door," I remarked dryly, " was ripped to ribbons last night."

" Indeed?" With raised eyebrows she pretended surprise, but I saw that I had told her nothing she did not know. " Some stupid practical joke, I suppose."

" It was not that," I replied with some feeling. " And I want you to tell me—for your own sake——" I paused.

" Tell you what?" she queried.

" Anything that can throw light on the matter," I said gravely.

She laughed.

" I know nothing," she said. " Absolutely nothing."

And no warnings of danger could induce her to relax the statement. Yet I was convinced that she *did* know a great deal more than any of us, and held some clue to the affair of which we were absolutely ignorant. But I saw that it was quite impossible to make her speak.

I determined, however, to take every precaution that I could, convinced as I was that she was menaced by a very real and immediate danger. Before she went to her room the following night Settle and I made a thorough examination of it. We had agreed that we would take it in turns to watch in the passage.

I took the first watch, which passed without incident, and at three o'clock Settle relieved me. I was tired after my sleepless night the day before, and dropped off at once. And I had a very curious dream.

I dreamed that the grey cat was sitting at the foot of my bed and that its eyes were fixed on mine with a curious pleading. Then, with the ease of dreams, I knew that the creature wanted me to follow it. I did so, and it led me down the great staircase and right to the opposite wing of the house to a room which was obviously the library. It paused there at one side of the room and raised its front paws till they rested on one of the lower shelves of books, while it gazed at me once more with that same moving look of appeal.

Then—cat and library faded, and I awoke to find that morning had come.

Settle's watch had passed without incident, but he was keenly interested to hear of my dream. At my request he took me to the library, which coincided in every particular with my vision of it. I could even point out the exact spot where the animal had given me that last sad look.

We both stood there in silent perplexity. Suddenly an idea occurred to me, and I stooped to read the titles of the books in that exact place. I noticed that there was a gap in the line.

" Some book had been taken out of here," I said to Settle.

He stooped also to the shelf.

" Hallo," he said. " There's a nail at the back here that has torn off a fragment of the missing volume."

He detached the little scrap of paper with care. It

was not more than an inch square—but on it were printed two significant words: " The cat. . . ."

We looked at each other.

" This thing gives me the creeps," said Settle. " It's simply horribly uncanny."

" I'd give anything to know," I said, " what book it is that is missing from here. Do you think there is any way of finding out?"

" May be a catalogue somewhere. Perhaps Lady Carmichael——"

I shook my head.

" Lady Carmichael will tell you nothing."

" You think so?"

" I am sure of it. While we are guessing and feeling about in the dark Lady Carmichael *knows*. And for reasons of her own she will say nothing. She prefers to run a most horrible risk sooner than break silence."

The day passed with an uneventfulness that reminded me of the calm before a storm. And I had a strange feeling that the problem was near solution. I was groping about in the dark, but soon I should see. The facts were all there, ready, waiting for the little flash of illumination that should weld them together and show out their significance.

And come it did! In the strangest way!

It was when we were all sitting together in the green drawing-room as usual after dinner. We had been very silent. So noiseless indeed was the room that a little mouse ran across the floor—and in an instant the thing happened.

With one long spring Arthur Carmichael leapt from his chair. His quivering body was swift as an arrow on the mouse's track. It had disappeared behind the wainscoting, and there he crouched—watchful—his body still trembling with eagerness.

It was horrible! I have never known such a paralysing moment. I was no longer puzzled as to that something that Arthur Carmichael reminded me of with his stealthy feet and watching eyes. And in a flash an explanation, wild, incredible, unbelievable, swept into my mind. I rejected it as impossible—unthinkable! But I could not dismiss it from my thoughts.

I hardly remember what happened next. The whole thing seemed blurred and unreal. I know that somehow we got upstairs and said our good-nights briefly, almost with a dread of meeting each other's eyes, lest we should see there some confirmation of our own fears.

Settle established himself outside Lady Carmichael's door to take the first watch, arranging to call me at 3 a.m. I had no special fears for Lady Carmichael; I was too taken up with my fantastic impossible theory. I told myself it was impossible—but my mind returned to it, fascinated.

And then suddenly the stillness of the night was disturbed. Settle's voice rose in a shout, calling me. I rushed out into the corridor.

He was hammering and pounding with all his might on Lady Carmichael's door.

" Devil take the woman!" he cried. " She's locked it!"

" But——"

" *It's* in there, man! In with her! Can't you hear it?"

From behind the locked door a long-drawn cat yowl sounded fiercely. And then following it a horrible scream—and another. . . . I recognised Lady Carmichael's voice.

" The door!" I yelled. " We must break it in. In another minute we shall be too late."

We set our shoulders against it, and heaved with all

our might. It gave with a crash—and we almost fell into the room.

Lady Carmichael lay on the bed bathed in blood. I have seldom seen a more horrible sight. Her heart was still beating, but her injuries were terrible, for the skin of the throat was all ripped and torn. . . . Shuddering, I whispered: " The Claws . . ." A thrill of superstitious horror ran over me.

I dressed and bandaged the wounds carefully and suggested to Settle that the exact nature of the injuries had better be kept secret, especially from Miss Patterson. I wrote out a telegram for a hospital nurse to be despatched as soon as the telegraph office was open.

The dawn was now stealing in at the window. I looked out on the lawn below.

" Get dressed and come out," I said abruptly to Settle. " Lady Carmichael will be all right now."

He was soon ready, and we went out into the garden together.

" What are you going to do?"

" Dig up the cat's body," I said briefly. " I must be sure——"

I found a spade in a tool-shed and we set to work beneath the large copper beech tree. At last our digging was rewarded. It was not a pleasant job. The animal had been dead a week. But I saw what I wanted to see.

" That's the cat," I said. " The identical cat I saw the first day I came here."

Settle sniffed. An odour of bitter almonds was still perceptible.

" Prussic acid," he said.

I nodded.

" What are you thinking?" he asked curiously.

" What you think too!"

My surmise was no new one to him—it had passed through his brain also, I could see.

" It's impossible," he murmured. " Impossible! It's against all science—all nature. . . ." His voice tailed off in a shudder. " That mouse last night," he said. " But—oh! it couldn't be!"

" Lady Carmichael," I said, " is a very strange woman. She has occult powers—hypnotic powers. Her forbears came from the East. Can we know what use she might have made of these powers over a weak lovable nature such as Arthur Carmichael's? And remember, Settle, if Arthur Carmichael remains a hopeless imbecile, devoted to her, the whole property is practically hers and her son's—whom you have told me she adores. And Arthur was going to be married!"

" But what are we going to do, Carstairs?"

" There's nothing to be done," I said. " We'll do our best though to stand between Lady Carmichael and vengeance."

Lady Carmichael improved slowly. Her injuries healed themselves as well as could be expected—the scars of that terrible assault she would probably bear to the end of her life.

I had never felt more helpless. The power that defeated us was still at large, undefeated, and though quiescent for the minute we could hardly regard as doing otherwise than biding its time. I was determined upon one thing. As soon as Lady Carmichael was well enough to be moved she must be taken away from Wolden. There was just a chance that the terrible manifestation might be unable to follow her. So the days went on.

I had fixed September 18th as the date of Lady Carmichael's removal. It was on the morning of the 14th when the unexpected crisis arose.

I was in the library discussing details of Lady Carmichael's case with Settle when an agitated housemaid rushed into the room.

"Oh! sir," she cried. "Be quick! Mr. Arthur—he's fallen into the pond. He stepped on the punt and it pushed off with him, and he overbalanced and fell in! I saw it from the window."

I waited for no more, but ran straight out of the room followed by Settle. Phyllis was just outside and had heard the maid's story. She ran with us.

"But you needn't be afraid," she cried. "Arthur is a magnificent swimmer."

I felt forebodings, however, and redoubled my pace. The surface of the pond was unruffled. The empty punt floated lazily about—but of Arthur there was no sign.

Settle pulled off his coat and his boots. "I'm going in," he said. "You take the boat-hook and fish about from the other punt. It's not very deep."

Very long the time seemed as we searched vainly. Minute followed minute. And then, just as we were despairing, we found him, and bore the apparently lifeless body of Arthur Carmichael to shore.

As long as I live I shall never forget the hopeless agony of Phyllis's face.

"Not—not——" her lips refused to frame the dreadful word.

"No, no, my dear," I cried. "We'll bring him round, never fear."

But inwardly I had little hope. He had been under water for half an hour. I sent off Settle to the house for hot blankets and other necessaries, and began myself to apply artificial respiration.

We worked vigorously with him for over an hour but there was no sign of life. I motioned to Settle to take my place again, and I approached Phyllis.

"I'm afraid," I said gently, "that it is no good. Arthur is beyond our help."

She stayed quite still for a moment and then suddenly flung herself down on the lifeless body.

"Arthur!" she cried desperately. "Arthur! Come back to me! Arthur—come back—come back!"

Her voice echoed away into silence. Suddenly I touched Settle's arm. "Look!" I said.

A faint tinge of colour had crept into the drowned man's face. I felt his heart.

"Go on with the respiration," I cried. "He's coming round!"

The moments seemed to fly now. In a marvellously short time his eyes opened.

Then suddenly I realised a difference. *These were intelligent eyes, human eyes. . . .*

They rested on Phyllis.

"Hallo! Phil," he said weakly. "Is it you? I thought you weren't coming until to-morrow."

She could not yet trust herself to speak but she smiled at him. He looked round with increasing bewilderment.

"But, I say, where am I? And—how rotten I feel! What's the matter with me? Hallo, Dr. Settle!"

"You've been nearly drowned—that's what's the matter," returned Settle grimly.

Sir Arthur made a grimace.

"I've always heard it was beastly coming back afterwards! But how did it happen? Was I walking in my sleep?"

Settle shook his head.

"We must get him to the house," I said, stepping forward.

He stared at me, and Phyllis introduced me. "Dr. Carstairs, who is staying here."

We supported him between us and started for the

house. He looked up suddenly as though struck by an idea.

" I say, doctor, this won't knock me up for the 12th, will it?"

" The 12th?" I said slowly, " you mean the 12th of August?"

" Yes—next Friday."

" To-day is the 14th of September," said Settle abruptly.

His bewilderment was evident.

" But—but I thought it was the 8th of August? I must have been ill then?"

Phyllis interposed rather quickly in her gentle voice.

" Yes," she said, " you've been very ill."

He frowned. " I can't understand it. I was perfectly all right when I went to bed last night—at least of course it wasn't really last night. I had dreams though, I remember, dreams. . . ." His brow furrowed itself still more as he strove to remember. " Something—what was it?—scmething dreadful—someone had done it to me—and I was angry—desperate. . . . And then I dreamed I was a cat—yes, a cat! Funny, wasn't it? But it wasn't a funny dream. It was more—horrible! But I can't remember. It all goes when I think."

I laid my hand on his shoulder. " Don't try to think, Sir Arthur," I said gravely. " Be content—to forget."

He looked at me in a puzzled way and nodded. I heard Phyllis draw a breath of relief. We had reached the house.

" By the way," said Sir Arthur suddenly, " where's the mater?"

" She has been—ill," said Phyllis after a momentary pause.

" Oh! poor old mater!" His voice rang with genuine concern. " Where is she? In her room?"

" Yes," I said, " but you had better not disturb——"

The words froze on my lips. The door of the drawing-room opened and Lady Carmichael, wrapped in a dressing-gown, came out into the hall.

Her eyes were fixed on Arthur, and if ever I have seen a look of absolute guilt-stricken terror I saw it then. Her face was hardly human in its frenzied terror. Her hand went to her throat.

Arthur advanced towards her with boyish affection.

" Hallo, mater! So you've been knocked up too? I say, I'm awfully sorry."

She shrank back before him, her eyes dilating. Then suddenly, with the shriek of a doomed soul, she fell backwards through the open door.

I rushed and bent over her, then beckoned to Settle.

" Hush," I said. " Take him upstairs quietly and then come down again. Lady Carmichael is dead."

He returned in a few minutes.

" What was it?" he asked. " What caused it?"

" Shock," I said grimly. " The shock of seeing Arthur Carmichael, the *real* Arthur Carmichael, restored to life! Or you may call it, as I prefer to, the judgment of God!"

" You mean——" he hesitated.

I looked at him in the eyes so that he understood.

" A life for a life," I said significantly.

" But——"

" Oh! I know that a strange and unforeseen accident permitted the spirit of Arthur Carmichael to return to his body. But, nevertheless, Arthur Carmichael was murdered."

He looked at me half fearfully. " With prussic acid?" he asked in a low tone.

" Yes," I answered. " With prussic acid."

Settle and I have never spoken of our belief. It is not one likely to be credited. According to the orthodox point of view Arthur Carmichael merely suffered from loss of memory, Lady Carmichael lacerated her own throat in a temporary fit of mania, and the apparition of the Grey Cat was mere imagination.

But there are two facts that to my mind are unmistakable. One is the ripped chair in the corridor. The other is even more significant. A catalogue of the library was found, and after exhaustive search it was proved that the missing volume was an ancient and curious work on the possibilities of the metamorphosis of human beings into animals!

One thing more. I am thankful to say that Arthur knows nothing. Phyllis has locked the secret of those weeks in her own heart, and she will never, I am sure, reveal them to the husband she loves so dearly, and who came back across the barrier of the grave at the call of her voice.

THE CALL OF WINGS

I

SILAS HAMER heard it first on a wintry night in February. He and Dick Borrow had walked from a dinner given by Bernard Selden, the nerve specialist. Borrow had been unusually silent, and Silas Hamer asked him with some curiosity what he was thinking about. Borrow's answer was unexpected.

"I was thinking, that of all these men to-night, only two amongst them could lay claim to happiness. And that these two, strangely enough, were you and I!"

The word "strangely" was apposite, for no two men could be more dissimilar than Richard Borrow, the hard-working east-end parson, and Silas Hamer, the sleek complacent man whose millions were a matter of household knowledge.

"It's odd, you know," mused Borrow, "I believe you're the only contented millionaire I've ever met."

Hamer was silent a moment. When he spoke his tone had altered.

"I used to be a wretched shivering little newspaper boy. I wanted then—what I've got now!—the comfort and the luxury of money, not its power. I wanted money, not to wield as a force, but to spend lavishly—on myself! I'm frank about it, you see. Money can't buy everything, they say. Very true. But it can buy everything I want—therefore I'm satisfied. I'm a materialist, Borrow, out and out a materialist!"

The broad glare of the lighted thoroughfare confirmed this confession of faith. The sleek lines of Silas Hamer's body were amplified by the heavy fur-lined coat, and the white light emphasised the thick rolls of flesh beneath his chin. In contrast to him walked Dick Borrow, with the thin ascetic face and the star-gazing fanatical eyes.

" It's *you*," said Hamer with emphasis, " that I can't understand."

Borrow smiled.

" I live in the midst of misery, want, starvation—all the ills of the flesh! And a predominant Vision upholds me. It's not easy to understand unless you believe in Visions, which I gather you don't."

" I don't believe," said Silas Hamer stolidly, " in anything I can't see and hear and touch."

" Quite so. That's the difference between us. Well, good-bye, the earth now swallows me up!"

They had reached the doorway of a lighted tube station, which was Borrow's route home.

Hamer proceeded alone. He was glad he had sent away the car to-night and elected to walk home. The air was keen and frosty, his senses were delightfully conscious of the enveloping warmth of the fur-lined coat.

He paused for an instant on the curbstone before crossing the road. A great motor 'bus was heavily ploughing its way towards him. Hamer, with the feeling of infinite leisure, waited for it to pass. If he were to cross in front of it he would have to hurry—and hurry was distasteful to him.

By his side a battered derelict of the human race rolled drunkenly off the pavement. Hamer was aware of a shout, an ineffectual swerve of the motor 'bus, and then—he was looking stupidly, with a gradually awakening horror, at a limp inert heap of rags in the middle of the road.

A crowd gathered magically, with a couple of policemen and the 'bus driver as its nucleus. But Hamer's eyes were riveted in horrified fascination on that lifeless

bundle that had once been a man—a man like himself!
He shuddered as at some menace.

" Dahn't yer blime yerself, guv'nor," remarked a
rough-looking man at his side. " Yer couldn't 'a done
nothin'. 'E was done for anyways."

Hamer stared at him. The idea that it was possible
in any way to save the man had quite honestly never
occurred to him. He scouted the notion now as an ab-
surdity. Why, if he had been so foolish, he might at
this moment . . . His thoughts broke off abruptly, and
he walked away from the crowd. He felt himself shaking with a nameless unquenchable dread. He was
forced to admit to himself that he was *afraid*—horribly
afraid—of Death. . . . Death that came with dreadful
swiftness and remorseless certainty to rich and poor
alike. . . .

He walked faster, but the new fear was still with him,
enveloping him in its cold and chilling grasp.

He wondered at himself, for he knew that by nature
he was no coward. Five years ago, he reflected, this
fear would not have attacked him. For then Life had
not been so sweet. . . . Yes, that was it; love of Life
was the key to the mystery. The zest of living was at
its height for him; it knew but one menace, Death, the
destroyer!

He turned out of the lighted thoroughfare. A narrow
passageway, between high walls, offered a short-cut to
the Square where his house, famous for its art treasures,
was situated.

The noise of the streets behind him lessened and
faded, the soft thud of his own footsteps was the only
sound to be heard.

And then out of the gloom in front of him came another sound. Sitting against the wall was a man playing
the flute. One of the enormous tribe of street musicians,
of course, but why had he chosen such a peculiar spot?

Surely at this time of night the police—— Hamer's reflections were interrupted suddenly as he realised with a shock that the man had no legs. A pair of crutches rested against the wall beside him. Hamer saw now that it was not a flute he was playing but a strange instrument whose notes were much higher and clearer than those of a flute.

The man played on. He took no notice of Hamer's approach. His head was flung far back on his shoulders, as though uplifted in the joy of his own music, and the notes poured out clearly and joyously, rising higher and higher. . . .

It was a strange tune—strictly speaking, it was not a tune at all, but a single phrase, not unlike the slow turn given out by the violins of *Rienzi*, repeated again and again, passing from key to key, from harmony to harmony, but always rising and attaining each time to a greater and more boundless freedom.

It was unlike anything Hamer had ever heard. There was something strange about it, something inspiring— and uplifting . . . it . . . He caught frantically with both hands to a projection in the wall beside him. He was conscious of one thing only—*that he must keep down*—at all costs he must *keep down*. . . .

He suddenly realised that the music had stopped. The legless man was reaching out for his crutches. And here was he, Silas Hamer, clutching like a lunatic at a stone buttress, for the simple reason that he had had the utterly preposterous notion—absurd on the face of it!— that he was rising from the ground—that the music was carrying him upwards. . . .

He laughed. What a wholly mad idea! Of course his feet had never left the earth for a moment, but what a strange hallucination! The quick tap-tapping of wood on the pavement told him that the cripple was moving away. He looked after him until the man's figure was swallowed up in the gloom. An odd fellow!

He proceeded on his way more slowly; he could not efface from his mind the memory of that strange impossible sensation when the ground had failed beneath his feet. . . .

And then on an impulse he turned and followed hurriedly in the direction the other had taken. The man could not have gone far—he would soon overtake him.

He shouted as soon as he caught sight of the maimed figure swinging itself slowly along.

" Hi! One minute."

The man stopped and stood motionless until Hamer came abreast of him. A lamp burned just over his head and revealed every feature. Silas Hamer caught his breath in involuntary surprise. The man possessed the most singularly beautiful head he had ever seen. He might have been any age; assuredly he was not a boy, yet youth was the most predominant characteristic—youth and vigour in passionate intensity!

Hamer found an odd difficulty in beginning his conversation.

" Look here," he said awkwardly, " I want to know —what was that thing you were playing just now?"

The man smiled. . . . With his smile the world seemed suddenly to leap into joyousness. . . .

" It was an old tune—a very old tune. . . . Years old—centuries old."

He spoke with an odd purity and distinctness of enunciation, giving equal value to each syllable. He was clearly not an Englishman, yet Hamer was puzzled as to his nationality.

" You're not English? Where do you come from?"

Again the broad joyful smile.

" From over the sea, sir. I came—a long time ago— a very long time ago."

" You must have had a bad accident. Was it lately?"

" Some time now, sir."

" Rough luck to lose both legs."

" It was well," said the man very calmly. He turned his eyes with a strange solemnity on his interlocutor. " They were evil."

Hamer dropped a shilling in his hand and turned away. He was puzzled and vaguely disquieted. " They were evil!" What a strange thing to say! Evidently an operation for some form of disease, but—how odd it had sounded.

Hamer went home thoughtful. He tried in vain to dismiss the incident from his mind. Lying in bed, with the first incipient sensation of drowsiness stealing over him, he heard a neighbouring clock strike one. One clear stroke and then silence—silence that was broken by a faint familiar sound. . . . Recognition came leaping. Hamer felt his heart beating quickly. It was the man in the passageway playing, somewhere not far distant. . . .

The notes came gladly, the slow turn with its joyful call, the same haunting little phrase. . . . " It's uncanny," murmured Hamer, " it's uncanny. It's got wings to it. . . ."

Clearer and clearer, higher and higher—each wave rising above the last, and catching *him* up with it. This time he did not struggle, he let himself go. . . . Up—up. . . . The waves of sound were carrying him higher and higher. . . . Triumphant and free, they swept on.

Higher and higher. . . . They had passed the limits of human sound now, but they still continued—rising, ever rising. . . . Would they reach the final goal, the full perfection of height?

Rising . . .

Something was pulling—pulling him downwards. Something big and heavy and insistent. It pulled remorselessly—pulled him back, and down . . . down. . . .

He lay in bed gazing at the window opposite. Then, breathing heavily and painfully, he stretched an arm out of bed. The movement seemed curiously cumbrous to him. The softness of the bed was oppressive, oppressive too were the heavy curtains over the window that blocked out light and air. The ceiling seemed to press down upon him. He felt stifled and choked. He moved slightly under the bed clothes, and the weight of his body seemed to him the most oppressive of all. . . .

2

" I want your advice, Seldon."

Seldon pushed back his chair an inch or so from the
table. He had been wondering what was the object of
this tête-à-tête dinner. He had seen little of Hamer since
the winter, and he was aware to-night of some indefinable change in his friend.

" It's just this," said the millionaire. " I'm worried
about myself."

Seldon smiled as he looked across the table.

" You're looking in the pink of condition."

" It's not that." Hamer paused a minute, then added
quietly, " I'm afraid I'm going mad."

The nerve specialist glanced up with a sudden keen
interest. He poured himself out a glass of port with a
rather slow movement, and then said quietly, but with
a sharp glance at the other man : " What makes you
think that?"

" Something that's happened to me. Something
inexplicable, unbelievable. It can't be true, so I must
be going mad."

" Take your time," said Seldon, " and tell me about
it."

" I don't believe in the supernatural," began Hamer.
" I never have. But this thing . . . Well, I'd better
tell you the whole story from the beginning. It began
last winter one evening after I had dined with you."

Then briefly and concisely he narrated the events of
his walk home and the strange sequel.

" That was the beginning of it all. I can't explain it
to you properly—the feeling, I mean—but it was wonderful! Unlike anything I've ever felt or dreamed. Well,
it's gone on ever since. Not every night, just now and

then. The music, the feeling of being uplifted, the soaring flight . . . and then the terrible drag, the pull back to earth, and afterwards the pain, the actual physical pain of the awakening. It's like coming down from a high mountain—you know the pains in the ears one gets? Well, this is the same thing, but intensified—and with it goes the awful sense of *weight*—of being hemmed in, stifled. . . ."

He broke off and there was a pause.

" Already the servants think I'm mad. I couldn't bear the roof and the walls—I've had a place arranged up at the top of the house, open to the sky, with no furniture or carpets, or any stifling things. . . . But even then the houses all round are nearly as bad. It's open country I want. somewhere where one can breathe. . . ." He looked across at Seldon. " Well, what do you say? Can you explain it?"

" H'm," said Seldon. " Plenty of explanations. You've been hypnotised, or you've hypnotised yourself. Your nerves have gone wrong. Or it may be merely a dream."

Hamer shook his head. " None of those explanations will do."

" And there are others," said Seldon slowly, " but they're not generally admitted."

" *You* are prepared to admit them?"

" On the whole, yes! There's a great deal we can't understand which can't possibly be explained normally. We've any amount to find out still, and I for one believe in keeping an open mind."

" What do you advise me to do?" asked Hamer after a silence.

Seldon leaned forward briskly. " One of several things. Go away from London, seek out your ' open country.' The dreams may cease."

" I can't do that," said Hamer quickly. " It's come

to this that I can't do without them. I don't want to do without them."

"Ah! I guessed as much. Another alternative, find this fellow, this cripple. You're endowing him now with all sorts of supernatural attributes. Talk to him. Break the spell."

Hamer shook his head again.

"Why not?"

"I'm afraid," said Hamer simply.

Seldon made a gesture of impatience. "Don't believe in it all so blindly! This tune now, the medium that starts it all, what is it like?"

Hamer hummed it, and Seldon listened with a puzzled frown.

"Rather like a bit out of the Overture to *Rienzi*. There *is* something uplifting about it—it had wings. But I'm not carried off the earth! Now, these flights of yours, are they all exactly the same?"

"No, no." Hamer leaned forward eagerly. "They develop. Each time I see a little more. It's difficult to explain. You see, I'm always conscious of reaching a certain point—the music carried me there—not direct, but by a succession of *waves*, each reaching higher than the last, until the highest point where one can go no further. I stay there until I'm dragged back. It isn't a place, it's more a *state*. Well, not just at first, but after a little while, I began to understand that there were other things all round me waiting until I was able to perceive them. Think of a kitten. It has eyes, but at first it can't see with them. It's blind and had to learn to see. Well, that was what it was to me. Mortal eyes and ears were no good to me, but there was something corresponding to them that hadn't yet been developed —something that wasn't *bodily* at all. And little by little that grew . . . there were sensations of light . . . then of sound . . . then of colour. . . . All very vague and unformulated. It was more the knowledge of things than seeing or hearing them. First it was light, a light that grew stronger and clearer . . . then sand, great stretches of reddish sand . . . and here and there straight long lines of water like canals——"

Seldon drew in his breath sharply. "*Canals*! That's interesting. Go on."

"But these things didn't matter—they didn't count any longer. The real things were the things I couldn't see yet—but I heard them. . . . It was a sound like the rushing of wings . . . somehow, I can't explain why, it was glorious! There's nothing like it here. And then came another glory—*I saw them*—the Wings! Oh, Seldon, the Wings!"

"But what were they? Men—angels—birds?"

"I don't know. I couldn't see—not yet. But the colour of them! *Wing colour*—we haven't got it here—it's a wonderful colour."

"Wing colour?" repeated Seldon. "What's it like?"

Hamer flung up his hand impatiently. "How can I tell you? Explain the colour blue to a blind person! It's a colour you've never seen—Wing colour!"

"Well?"

"Well? That's all. That's as far as I've got. But each time the coming back has been worse—more painful. I can't understand that. I'm convinced my body never leaves the bed. In this place I get to I'm convinced I've got no *physical* presence. Why should it hurt so confoundedly then?"

Seldon shook his head in silence.

"It's something awful—the coming back. The *pull* of it—then the pain, pain in every limb and every nerve, and my ears feel as though they were bursting. Then everything *presses* so, the weight of it all, the dreadful sense of imprisonment. I want light, air, space—above all *space* to breathe in! And I want freedom."

" And what," asked Seldon, " of all the other things that used to mean so much to you?"

" That's the worst of it. I care for them still as much as, if not more than, ever. And these things, comfort, luxury, pleasure, seem to pull opposite ways to the Wings. It's a perpetual struggle between them—and I can't see how it's going to end."

Seldon sat silent. The strange tale he had been listening to was fantastic enough in all truth. Was it all a delusion, a wild hallucination—or could it by any possibility be true? And if so, why *Hamer*, of all men . . .? Surely the materialist, the man who loved the flesh and denied the spirit, was the last man to see the sights of another world.

Across the table Hamer watched him anxiously.

" I suppose," said Seldon slowly, " that you can only wait. Wait and see what happens."

" I can't! I tell you I can't! Your saying that shows you don't understand. It's tearing me in two, this awful struggle—this killing long-drawn-out fight between—between——" He hesitated.

" The flesh and the spirit?" suggested Seldon.

Hamer stared heavily in front of him. " I suppose one might call it that. Anyway, it's unbearable. . . . I can't get free. . . ."

Again Bernard Seldon shook his head. He was caught up in the grip of the inexplicable. He made one more suggestion.

" If I were you," he advised, " I would get hold of that cripple."

But as he went home he muttered to himself: " *Canals* —I wonder."

3

Silas Hamer went out of the house the following morning with a new determination in his step.   He had
decided to take Seldon's advice and find the legless man.
Yet inwardly he was convinced that his search would be
in vain and that the man would have vanished as completely as though the earth had swallowed him up.

The dark buildings on either side of the passageway
shut out the sunlight and left it dark and mysterious.
Only in one place, half-way up it, there was a break in
the wall, and through it there fell a shaft of golden light
that illuminated with radiance a figure sitting on the
ground.   A figure—yes, it was the man!

The instrument of pipes leaned against the wall beside
his crutches, and he was covering the paving stones with
designs in coloured chalk.   Two were completed, sylvan
scenes of marvellous beauty and delicacy, swaying trees
and a leaping brook that seemed alive.

And again Hamer doubted.   Was this man a mere
street musician, a pavement artist?   Or was he something more . . .

Suddenly the millionaire's self-control broke down,
and he cried fiercely and angrily: " Who are you? For
God's sake, who are you?"

The man's eyes met his, smiling.

" Why don't you answer? Speak, man, speak!"

Then he noticed that the man was drawing with incredible rapidity on a bare slab of stone.   Hamer
followed the movement with his eyes. . . . A few bold
strokes, and giant trees took form.   Then, seated on a
boulder . . . a man . . . playing an instrument of
pipes.   A man with a strangely beautiful face—*and
goat's legs.* . . .

The cripple's hand made a swift movement. The man still sat on the rock, but the goat's legs were gone. Again his eyes met Hamer's.

" They were evil," he said.

Hamer stared, fascinated. For the face before him was the face of the picture, but strangely and incredibly beautified. . . . Purified from all but an intense and exquisite joy of living.

Hamer turned and almost fled down the passageway into the bright sunlight, repeating to himself incessantly: " It's impossible. Impossible. . . . I'm mad—dreaming!" But the face haunted him—the face of Pan. . . .

He went into the Park and sat on a chair. It was a deserted hour. A few nursemaids with their charges sat in the shade of the trees, and dotted here and there in the stretches of green, like islands in a sea, lay the recumbent forms of men. . . .

The words " a wretched tramp " were to Hamer an epitome of misery. But suddenly, to-day, he envied them. . . .

They seemed to him of all created beings the only free ones. The earth beneath them, the sky above them, the world to wander in . . . they were not hemmed in or chained.

Like a flash it came to him that that which bound him so remorselessly was the thing he had worshipped and prized above all others—wealth! He had thought it the strongest thing on earth, and now, wrapped round by its golden strength, he saw the truth of his words. It was his money that held him in bondage. . . .

But was it? Was that really it? Was there a deeper and more pointed truth that he had not seen? Was it the money or was it his own love of the money? He was bound in fetters of his own making; not wealth itself, but love of wealth was the chain.

He knew now clearly the two forces that were tearing

at him, the warm composite strength of materialism that enclosed and surrounded him, and, opposed to it, the clear imperative call—he named it to himself the Call of the Wings.

And while the one fought and clung the other scorned war and would not stoop to struggle. It only called—called unceasingly. . . . He heard it so clearly that it almost spoke in words.

" You cannot make terms with Me," it seemed to say. " For I am above all other things. If you follow my call you must give up all else and cut away the forces that hold you. For only the Free shall follow where I lead. . . ."

" I can't," cried Hamer. " I can't. . . ."

A few people turned to look at the big man who sat talking to himself.

So sacrifice was being asked of him, the sacrifice of that which was most dear to him, that which was part of himself.

Part of himself—he remembered the man without legs. . . .

4

"What in the name of Fortune brings you here?" asked Borrow.

Indeed the east-end mission was an unfamiliar background to Hamer.

"I've listened to a good many sermons," said the millionaire, "all saying what could be done if you people had funds. I've just come to tell you this: you can have the funds."

"Very good of you," answered Borrow, with some surprise. "A big subscription, eh?"

Hamer smiled dryly. "I should say so. Just every penny I've got."

"*What?*"

Hamer rapped out details in a brisk businesslike manner. Borrow's head was whirling.

"You—you mean to say that you're making over your entire fortune to be devoted to the relief of the poor in the East-End, with myself appointed as trustee?"

"That's it."

"But why—*why?*"

"I can't explain," said Hamer slowly. "Remember our talk about visions last February? Well, a vision has got hold of me."

"It's splendid!" Borrow leaned forward, his eyes gleaming.

"There's nothing particularly splendid about it," said Hamer grimly. "I don't care a button about poverty in the East-End. All they want is grit! *I* was poor enough—and I got out of it. But I've got to get rid of the money, and these tom-fool societies shan't get hold of it. You're a man I can trust. Feed bodies or souls with it—preferably the former. I've been hungry, but you can do as you like."

"There's never been such a thing known," stammered Borrow.

"The whole thing's done and finished with," continued Hamer. "The lawyers have fixed it up at last, and I've signed everything. I can tell you I've been busy this last fortnight. It's almost as difficult getting rid of a fortune as making one."

"But you—you've kept *something?*"

"Not a penny," said Hamer cheerfully. "At least—that's not quite true. I've just twopence in my pocket." He laughed.

He said good-bye to his bewildered friend, and walked out of the mission into the narrow evil-smelling streets. The words he had said so gaily just now came back to him with an aching sense of loss. "Not a penny!" Of all his vast wealth he had kept nothing. He was afraid now—afraid of poverty and hunger and cold. Sacrifice had no sweetness for him.

Yet behind it all he was conscious that the weight and menace of things had lifted, he was no longer oppressed and bound down. The severing of the chain had seared and torn him, but the vision of freedom was there to strengthen him. His material needs might dim the Call, but they could not deaden it, for he knew it to be a thing of immortality that could not die.

There was a touch of autumn in the air, and the wind blew chill. He felt the cold and shivered, and then, too, he was hungry—he had forgotten to have any lunch. It brought the future very near to him. It was incredible that he should have given it all up; the ease, the comfort, the warmth! His body cried out impotently. . . . And then once again there came to him a glad and uplifting sense of freedom.

Hamer hesitated. He was near a Tube station. He

had twopence in his pocket. The idea came to him to journey by it to the Park where he had watched the recumbent idlers a fortnight ago. Beyond this whim he did not plan for the future. He believed honestly enough now that he was mad—sane people did not act as he had done. Yet, if so, madness was a wonderful and amazing thing.

Yes, he would go now to the open country of the Park, and there was a special significance to him in reaching it by Tube. For the Tube represented to him all the horrors of buried, shut-in life. . . . He would ascend from its imprisonment free to the wide green and the trees that concealed the menace of the pressing houses.

The lift bore him swiftly and relentlessly downward. The air was heavy and lifeless. He stood at the extreme end of the platform, away from the mass of people. On his left was the opening of the tunnel from which the train, snakelike, would presently emerge. He felt the whole place to be subtly evil. There was no one near him but a hunched-up lad sitting on a seat, sunk, it seemed, in a drunken stupor.

In the distance came the faint menacing roar of the train. The lad rose from his seat and shuffled unsteadily to Hamer's side, where he stood on the edge of the platform peering into the tunnel.

Then—it happened so quickly as to be almost incredible—he lost his balance and fell. . . .

A hundred thoughts rushed simultaneously to Hamer's brain. He saw a huddled heap run over by a motor 'bus, and heard a hoarse voice saying: " Dahn't yer blime yerself, guv'nor. Yer couldn't 'a done nothin'.'' And with that came the knowledge that *this* life could only be saved, if it were saved, by himself. There was no one else near, and the train was close. . . . It all passed through his mind with lightning rapidity. He experienced a curious calm lucidity of thought.

He had one short second in which to decide, and he knew in that moment that his fear of Death was unabated. He was horribly afraid. And then—was it not a forlorn hope? A useless throwing away of two lives?

To the terrified spectators at the other end of the platform there seemed no gap between the boy's fall and the man's jump after him—and then the train, rushing round the curve of the tunnel, powerless to pull up in time.

Swiftly Hamer caught up the lad in his arms. No natural gallant impulse swayed him, his shivering flesh was but obeying the command of the alien spirit that called for sacrifice. With a last effort he flung the lad forward on to the platform, falling himself. . . .

Then suddenly his Fear died. The material world held him down no longer. He was free of his shackles. He fancied for a moment that he heard the joyous piping of Pan. Then—nearer and louder—swallowing up all else—came the glad rushing of innumerable Wings . . . enveloping and encircling him. . . .

THE LAST SEANCE

RAOUL DAUBREUIL crossed the Seine humming a little tune to himself. He was a good-looking young Frenchman of about thirty-two, with a fresh-coloured face and a little black moustache. By profession he was an engineer. In due course he reached the Cardonet and turned in at the door of No. 17. The concierge looked out from her lair and gave him a grudging "Good-morning," to which he replied cheerfully. Then he mounted the stairs to the apartment on the third floor. As he stood there waiting for his ring at the bell to be answered he hummed once more his little tune. Raoul Daubreuil was feeling particularly cheerful this morning. The door was opened by an elderly Frenchwoman, whose wrinkled face broke into smiles when she saw who the visitor was.

"Good-morning, Monsieur."

"Good-morning, Elise," said Raoul.

He passed into the vestibule, pulling off his gloves as he did so.

"Madame expects me, does she not?" he asked over his shoulder.

"Ah, yes, indeed, Monsieur."

Elise shut the front door and turned towards him.

"If Monsieur will pass into the little *salon*, Madame will be with him in a few minutes. At the moment she reposes herself."

Raoul looked up sharply.

"Is she not well?"

"*Well!*"

Elise gave a snort. She passed in front of Raoul and opened the door of the little *salon* for him. He went in and she followed him.

"*Well!*" she continued. "How should she be well, poor lamb? *Séances, Séances,* and always *Séances!* It is not right—not natural, not what the good God intended for us. For me, I say straight out, it is trafficking with the devil."

Raoul patted her on the shoulder reassuringly.

"There, there, Elise," he said soothingly, "do not excite yourself, and do not be too ready to see the devil in everything you do not understand."

Elise shook her head doubtingly.

"Ah, well," she grumbled under her breath, "Monsieur may say what he pleases, I don't like it. Look at Madame, every day she gets whiter and thinner, and the headaches!"

She held up her hands.

"Ah, no, it is not good, all this spirit business. Spirits indeed! All the good spirits are in Paradise, and the others are in Purgatory."

"Your view of the life after death is refreshingly simple, Elise," said Raoul as he dropped into a chair.

The old woman drew herself up.

"I am a good Catholic, Monsieur."

She crossed herself, went towards the door, then paused, her hand on the handle.

"Afterwards when you are married, Monsieur," she said pleadingly, "it will not continue—all this?"

Raoul smiled at her affectionately.

"You are a good faithful creature, Elise," he said, "and devoted to your mistress. Have no fear, once she is my wife, all this ' spirit business ' as you call it, will cease. For Madame Daubreuil there will be no more Séances."

Elise's face broke into smiles.

" Is it true what you say?" she asked eagerly.

The other nodded gravely.

" Yes," he said, speaking almost more to himself than to her. " Yes, all this must end. Simone has a wonderful gift and she has used it freely, but now she has done her part. As you have justly observed, Elise, day by day she gets whiter and thinner. The life of a medium is a particularly trying and arduous one, involving a terrible nervous strain. All the same, Elise, your mistress is the most wonderful medium in Paris—more, in France. People from all over the world come to her because they know that with her there is no trickery, no deceit."

Elise gave a snort of contempt.

" Deceit! Ah, no, indeed. Madame could not deceive a new-born babe if she tried."

" She is an angel," said the young Frenchman with fervour. " And I—I shall do everything a man can to make her happy. You believe that?"

Elise drew herself up, and spoke with a certain simple dignity.

" I have served Madame for many years, Monsieur. With all respect I may say that I love her. If I did not believe that you adored her as she deserves to be adored —eh bien, Monsieur! I should be willing to tear you limb from limb."

Raoul laughed.

" Bravo, Elise! You are a faithful friend, and you must approve of me now that I have told you Madame is going to give up the spirits."

He expected the old woman to receive this pleasantry with a laugh, but somewhat to his surprise she remained grave.

" Supposing, Monsieur," she said hesitatingly, " the spirits will not give her up?"

Raoul stared at her.

" Eh! What do you mean?"

" I said," repeated Elise, " supposing the spirits will not give *her* up?"

" I thought you didn't believe in the spirits, Elise?"

" No more I do," said Elise stubbornly. " It is foolish to believe in them. All the same——"

" Well?"

" It is difficult for me to explain, Monsieur. You see, me, I always thought that these mediums, as they call themselves, were just clever cheats who imposed on the poor souls who had lost their dear ones. But Madame is not like that. Madame is good. Madame is honest, and——"

She lowered her voice and spoke in a tone of awe.

" *Things happen.* It is not trickery, things happen, and that is why I am afraid. For I am sure of this, Monsieur, it is not right. It is against nature and le bon Dieu, and *somebody will have to pay.*"

Raoul got up from his chair and came and patted her on the shoulder.

" Calm yourself, my good Elise," he said, smiling. " See, I will give you some good news. To-day is the last of these Séances; after to-day there will be no more."

" There *is* one to-day then?" asked the old woman suspiciously.

" The last, Elise, the last."

Elise shook her head disconsolately.

" Madame is not fit——" she began.

But her words were interrupted, the door opened and a tall, fair woman came in. She was slender and graceful, with the face of a Botticelli Madonna. Raoul's face lighted up, and Elise withdrew quickly and discreetly.

" Simone!"

He took both her long, white hands in his and kissed each in turn. She murmured his name very softly.

" Raoul, my dear one."

Again he kissed her hands and then looked intently into her face.

" Simone, how pale you are! Elise told me you were resting; you are not ill, my well-beloved?"

" No, not ill——" she hesitated.

He led her over to the sofa and sat down on it beside her.

" But tell me then."

The medium smiled faintly.

" You will think me foolish," she murmured.

" I? Think you foolish? Never."

Simone withdrew her hand from his grasp. She sat perfectly still for a moment or two gazing down at the carpet. Then she spoke in a low, hurried voice

" I am afraid, Raoul."

He waited for a minute or two expecting her to go on, but as she did not he said encouragingly:

" Yes, afraid of what?"

" Just afraid—that is all."

" But——"

He looked at her in perplexity, and she answered the look quickly.

" Yes, it is absurd, isn't it, and yet I feel just that. Afraid, nothing more. I don't know what of, or why, but all the time I am possessed with the idea that some-thing terrible—terrible, is going to happen to me." . . .

She stared out in front of her. Raoul put an arm gently round her.

" My dearest," he said, " come, you must not give way. I know what it is, the strain, Simone, the strain of a medium's life. All you need is rest—rest and quiet."

She looked at him gratefully.

" Yes, Raoul, you are right. That is what I need, rest and quiet."

She closed her eyes and leant back a little against his arm.

" And happiness," murmured Raoul in her ear.

His arm drew her closer. Simone, her eyes still closed, drew a deep breath.

" Yes," she murmured, " yes. When your arms are round me I feel safe. I forget my life—the terrible life —of a medium. You know much, Raoul, but even you do not know all it means."

He felt her body grow rigid in his embrace. Her eyes opened again, staring in front of her.

" One sits in the cabinet in the darkness, waiting, and the darkness is terrible, Raoul, for it is the darkness of emptiness, of nothingness. Deliberately one gives oneself up to be lost in it. After that one knows nothing, one feels nothing, but at last there comes the slow, painful return, the awakening out of sleep, but so tired —so terribly tired."

" I know," murmured Raoul, " I know."

" So tired," murmured Simone again.

Her whole body seemed to droop as she repeated the words.

" But you are wonderful, Simone."

He took her hands in his, trying to rouse her to share his enthusiasm.

" You are unique—the greatest medium the world has ever known."

She shook her head, smiling a little at that.

" Yes, yes," Raoul insisted.

He drew two letters from his pocket.

" See here, from Professor Roche of the *Salpêtrière*, and this one from Dr. Genir at Nancy, both imploring that you will continue to sit for them occasionally."

" Ah, no!"

Simone sprang suddenly to her feet.

" I will not, I will not. It is to be all finished—all done with. You promised me, Raoul."

Raoul stared at her in astonishment as she stood wavering, facing him almost like a creature at bay. He got up and took her hand.

" Yes, yes," he said. " Certainly it is finished, that is understood. But I am so proud of you, Simone, that is why I mentioned those letters."

She threw him a swift sideways glance of suspicion.

" It is not that you will ever want me to sit again?"

" No, no," said Raoul, " unless perhaps you yourself would care to, just occasionally for these old friends——"

But she interrupted him, speaking excitedly.

" No, no, never again. There is danger. I tell you. I can feel it, great danger."

She clasped her hands on her forehead a minute, then walked across to the window.

" Promise me never again," she said in a quieter voice over her shoulder.

Raoul followed her and put his arms round her shoulders.

" My dear one," he said tenderly, " I promise you after to-day you shall never sit again."

He felt the sudden start she gave.

" To-day," she murmured. " Ah, yes—I had forgotten Madame Exe."

Raoul looked at his watch.

" She is due any minute now; but perhaps, Simone, if you do not feel well——"

Simone hardly seemed to be listening to him; she was following out her own train of thought.

" She is—a strange woman, Raoul, a very strange woman. Do you know I—I have almost a horror of her."

" Simone !''

There was reproach in his voice, and she was quick to feel it.

'' Yes, yes, I know, you are like all Frenchmen, Raoul. To you a mother is sacred and it is unkind of me to feel like that about her when she grieves so for her lost child. But—I cannot explain it, she is so big and black, and her hands—have you ever noticed her hands, Raoul? Great big strong hands, as strong as a man's. Ah!''

She gave a little shiver and closed her eyes. Raoul withdrew his arm and spoke almost coldly.

'' I really cannot understand you, Simone. Surely you, a woman, should have nothing but sympathy for another woman, a mother bereft of her only child.''

Simone made a gesture of impatience.

'' Ah, it is you who do not understand, my friend ! One cannot help these things. The first moment I saw her I felt——''

She flung her hands out.

'' *Fear!* You remember, it was a long time before I would consent to sit for her? I felt sure in some way she would bring me misfortune.''

Raoul shrugged his shoulders.

'' Whereas, in actual fact, she brought you the exact opposite,'' he said drily. '' All the sittings have been attended with marked success. The spirit of the little Amelie was able to control you at once, and the materialisations have really been striking. Professor Roche ought really to have been present at the last one.''

'' Materialisations,'' said Simone in a low voice. '' Tell me, Raoul (you know that I know nothing of what takes place while I am in the trance), are the materialisations really so wonderful?''

He nodded enthusiastically.

" At the first few sittings the figure of the child was visible in a kind of nebulous haze," he explained, " but at the last séance——"

" Yes?"

He spoke very softly.

" Simone, the child that stood there was an actual living child of flesh and blood. I even touched her—but seeing that the touch was acutely painful to you, I would not permit Madame Exe to do the same. I was afraid that her self-control might break down, and that some harm to you might result."

Simone turned away again towards the window.

" I was terribly exhausted when I woke," she murmured. " Raoul, are you sure—are you really sure that all this is *right?* You know what dear old Elise thinks, that I am trafficking with the devil?"

She laughed rather uncertainly.

" You know what I believe," said Raoul gravely. " In the handling of the unknown there must always be danger, but the cause is a noble one, for it is the cause of Science. All over the world there have been martyrs to Science, pioneers who have paid the price so that others may follow safely in their footsteps. For ten years now you have worked for Science at the cost of a terrific nervous strain. Now your part is done, from to-day onward you are free to be happy."

She smiled at him affectionately, her calm restored. Then she glanced quickly up at the clock.

" Madame Exe is late," she murmured. " She may not come."

" I think she will," said Raoul. " Your clock is a little fast, Simone."

Simone moved about the room, rearranging an ornament here and there.

" I wonder who she is, this Madame Exe?" she observed. " Where she comes from, who her people are? It is strange that we know nothing about her."

Raoul shrugged his shoulders.

" Most people remain incognito if possible when they come to a medium," he observed. " It is an elementary precaution."

" I suppose so," agreed Simone listlessly.

A little china vase she was holding slipped from her fingers and broke to pieces on the tiles of the fireplace. She turned sharply on Raoul.

" You see," she murmured, " I am not myself. Raoul, would you think me very—very cowardly if I told Madame Exe I could not sit to-day?"

His look of pained astonishment made her redden.

" You promised, Simone——" he began gently.

She backed against the wall.

" I won't do it, Raoul. I won't do it."

And again that glance of his, tenderly reproachful, made her wince.

" It is not of the money I am thinking, Simone, though you must realise that the money this woman has offered you for a last sitting is enormous—simply enormous."

She interrupted him defiantly.

" There are things that matter more than money."

" Certainly there are," he agreed warmly. " That is just what I am saying. Consider—this woman is a mother, a mother who has lost her only child. If you are not really ill, if it is only a whim on your part—you can deny a rich woman a caprice, can you deny a mother one last sight of her child?"

The medium flung her hands out despairingly in front of her.

" Oh, you torture me," she murmured. " All the

same you are right. I will do as you wish, but I know now what I am afraid of—it is the word ' mother.' "

" Simone ! "

" There are certain primitive elementary forces, Raoul. Most of them have been destroyed by civilisation, but motherhood stands where it stood at the beginning. Animals—human beings, they are all the same. A mother's love for her child is like nothing else in the world. It knows no law, no pity, it dares all things and crushes down remorselessly all that stands in its path."

She stopped, panting a little, then turned to him with a quick, disarming smile.

" I am foolish to-day, Raoul. I know it."

He took her hand in his.

" Lie down for a minute or two," he urged. " Rest till she comes."

" Very well." She smiled at him and left the room.

Raoul remained for a minute or two lost in thought, then he strode to the door, opened it, and crossed the little hall. He went into a room the other side of it, a sitting-room very much like the one he had left, but at one end was an alcove with a big arm-chair set in it. Heavy black velvet curtains were arranged so as to pull across the alcove. Elise was busy arranging the room. Close to the alcove she had set two chairs and a small round table. On the table was a tambourine, a horn, and some paper and pencils.

" The last time," murmured Elise with grim satisfaction. " Ah, Monsieur, I wish it were over and done with."

The sharp ting of an electric bell sounded.

" There she is, that great gendarme of a woman," continued the old servant. " Why can't she go and pray decently for her little one's soul in a church, and burn a candle to Our Blessed Lady? Does not the good God know what is best for us?"

"Answer the bell, Elise," said Raoul peremptorily.

She threw him a look, but obeyed. In a minute or two she returned ushering in the visitor.

"I will tell my mistress you are here, Madame."

Raoul came forward to shake hands with Madame Exe. Simone's words floated back to his memory.

"So big and so black."

She *was* a big woman, and the heavy black of French mourning seemed almost exaggerated in her case. Her voice when she spoke was very deep.

"I fear I am a little late, Monsieur."

"A few minutes only," said Raoul, smiling. "Madame Simone is lying down. I am sorry to say she is far from well, very nervous and overwrought."

Her hand, which she was just withdrawing, closed on his suddenly like a vice.

"But she will sit?" she demanded sharply.

"Oh, yes, Madame."

Madame Exe gave a sigh of relief, and sank into a chair, loosening one of the heavy black veils that floated round her.

"Ah, Monsieur!" she murmured, "you cannot imagine, you cannot conceive the wonder and the joy of these Séances to me! My little one! My Amelie! To see her, to hear her, even—perhaps—yes, perhaps to be even able to—stretch out my hand and touch her."

Raoul spoke quickly and peremptorily.

"Madame Exe—how can I explain?—on no account must you do anything except under my express directions, otherwise there is the gravest danger."

"Danger to me?"

"No, Madame," said Raoul, "to the medium. You must understand that the phenomena that occur are explained by Science in a certain way. I will put the matter very simply, using no technical terms. A spirit, to manifest itself, has to use the actual physical substance of the medium. You have seen the vapour of fluid issuing from the lips of the medium. This finally condenses and is built up into the physical semblance of the spirit's dead body. But this ectoplasm we believe to be the actual substance of the medium. We hope to prove this some day by careful weighing and testing— but the great difficulty is the danger and pain which attends the medium on any handling of the phenomena. Were anyone to seize hold of the materialisation roughly, the death of the medium might result."

Madame Exe had listened to him with close attention.

" That is very interesting, Monsieur. Tell me, shall not a time come when the materialisation shall advance so far that it shall be capable of detachment from its parent, the medium?"

" That is a fantastic speculation, Madame?"

She persisted.

" But, on the facts, not impossible?"

" Quite impossible to-day."

" But perhaps in the future?"

He was saved from answering, for at that moment Simone entered. She looked languid and pale, but had evidently regained entire control of herself. She came forward and shook hands with Madame Exe, though Raoul noticed the faint shiver that passed through her as she did so.

" I regret, Madame, to hear that you are indisposed," said Madame Exe.

" It is nothing," said Simone rather brusquely. " Shall we begin?"

She went to the alcove and sat down in the armchair. Suddenly Raoul in his turn felt a wave of fear pass over him.

" You are not strong enough," he exclaimed. " We had better cancel the Séance. Madame Exe will understand."

" Monsieur !"

Madame Exe rose indignantly.

" Yes, yes, it is better not, I am sure of it."

" Madame Simone promised me one last sitting."

" That is so," agreed Simone quietly, " and I am prepared to carry out my promise."

" I hold you to it, Madame," said the other woman.

" I do not break my word," said Simone coldly. " Do not fear, Raoul," she added gently, " after all, it is for the last time—the last time, thank God."

At a sign from her Raoul drew the heavy black curtains across the alcove. He also pulled the curtains of the window so that the room was in semi-obscurity. He indicated one of the chairs to Madame Exe and prepared himself to take the other. Madame Exe, however, hesitated.

" You will pardon me, Monsieur, but—you understand I believe absolutely in your integrity and in that of Madame Simone. All the same, so that my testimony may be the more valuable, I took the liberty of bringing this with me."

From her handbag she drew a length of fine cord.

" Madame !" cried Raoul. " This is an insult !"

" A precaution."

" I repeat it is an insult."

" I don't understand your objection, Monsieur," said Madame Exe coldly. " If there is no trickery you have nothing to fear."

Raoul laughed scornfully.

" I can assure you that I have nothing to fear, Madame. Bind me hand and foot if you will."

His speech did not produce the effect he hoped, for Madame Exe merely murmured unemotionally :

H.D.   P

" Thank you, Monsieur," and advanced upon him with her roll of cord.

Suddenly Simone from behind the curtain gave a cry. " No, no, Raoul, don't let her do it."

Madame Exe laughed derisively.

" Madame is afraid," she observed sarcastically.

" Yes, I am afraid."

" Remember what you are saying, Simone," cried Raoul. " Madame Exe is apparently under the impression that we are charlatans."

" I must make sure," said Madame Exe grimly.

She went methodically about her task, binding Raoul securely to his chair.

" I must congratulate you on your knots, Madame," he observed ironically when she had finished " Are you satisfied now?"

Madame Exe did not reply. She walked round the room examining the panelling of the walls closely. Then she locked the door leading into the hall, and, removing the key, returned to her chair.

" Now," she said in an indescribable voice, " I am ready."

The minutes passed. From behind the curtain the sound of Simone's breathing became heavier and more stertorous. Then it died away altogether. to be succeeded by a series of moans. Then again there was silence for a little while, broken by the sudden clattering of the tambourine. The horn was caught up from the table and dashed to the ground. Ironic laughter was heard The curtains of the alcove seemed to have been pulled back a little, the medium's figure was just visible through the opening, her head fallen forward on her breast. Suddenly Madame Exe drew in her breath sharply. A ribbon-like stream of mist was issuing from the medium's mouth. It condensed and began gradually to assume a shape, the shape of a little child.

" Amelie! My little Amelie!"

The hoarse whisper came from Madame Exe. The hazy figure condensed still further. Raoul stared almost incredulously. Never had there been a more successful materialisation. Now, surely it was a real child, a real flesh and blood child standing there.

" *Maman!*"

The soft childish voice spoke.

" My child!" cried Madame Exe. " My child!"

She half-rose from her seat.

" Be careful, Madame," cried Raoul warningly.

The materialisation came hesitatingly through the curtains. It was a child. She stood there, her arms held out.

" *Maman!*"

" Ah!" cried Madame Exe.

Again she half-rose from her seat.

" Madame," cried Raoul, alarmed, " the medium——"

" I must touch her," cried Madame Exe hoarsely.

She moved a step forward.

" For God's sake, Madame, control yourself," cried Raoul.

He was really alarmed now.

" Sit down at once."

" My little one, I must touch her."

" Madame, I command you, sit down!"

He was writhing desperately with his bonds, but Madame Exe had done her work well; he was helpless. A terrible sense of impending disaster swept over him.

" In the name of God, Madame, sit down!" he shouted. " Remember the medium."

Madame Exe paid no attention to him. She was like a woman transformed. Ecstasy and delight showed plainly in her face. Her outstretched hand touched the little figure that stood in the opening of the curtains. A terrible moan came from the medium.

" My God!" cried Raoul. " My God! This is terrible. The medium——"

Madame Exe turned on him with a harsh laugh.

" What do I care for your medium?" she cried. " I want my child."

" You are mad!"

" My child, I tell you. Mine! My own! My own flesh and blood! My little one come back to me from the dead, alive and breathing."

Raoul opened his lips, but no words would come. She was terrible, this woman! Remorseless, savage, absorbed by her own passion. The baby lips parted, and for the third time the same word echoed:

" *Maman!*"

" Come then, my little one," cried Madame Exe.

With a sharp gesture she caught up the child in her arms. From behind the curtains came a long-drawn scream of utter anguish.

" Simone!" cried Raoul. " Simone!"

He was aware vaguely of Madame Exe rushing past him, of the unlocking of the door, of retreating footsteps down the stairs.

From behind the curtain there still sounded the terrible high long-drawn scream—such a scream as Raoul had never heard. It died away in a horrible kind of gurgle. Then there came the thud of a body falling. . . .

Raoul was working like a maniac to free himself from his bonds. In his frenzy he accomplished the impossible, snapping the rope by sheer strength. As he struggled to his feet, Elise rushed in, crying " Madame!"

" Simone!" cried Raoul.

Together they rushed forward and pulled the curtain. Raoul staggered back.

" My God!" he murmured. " Red—all red. . . ."

Elise's voice came beside him harsh and shaking.

" So Madame is dead. It is ended. But tell me, Monsieur, what has happened. *Why is Madame all shrunken away—why is she half her usual size? What has been happening here?*"

" I do not know," said Raoul.

His voice rose to a scream.

" I do not know. I do not know. But I think—I am going mad. . . . Simone! Simone!"

S.O.S.

I

"AH!" said Mr. Dinsmead appreciatively.

He stepped back and surveyed the round table with approval. The firelight gleamed on the coarse white tablecloth, the knives and forks, and the other table appointments.

"Is—is everything ready?" asked Mrs. Dinsmead hesitatingly. She was a little faded woman, with a colourless face, meagre hair scraped back from her forehead, and a perpetually nervous manner.

"Everything's ready," said her husband with a kind of ferocious geniality.

He was a big man, with stooping shoulders, and a broad red face. He had little pig's eyes that twinkled under his bushy brows, and a big jowl devoid of hair.

"Lemonade?" suggested Mrs. Dinsmead, almost in a whisper.

Her husband shook his head.

"Tea. Much better in every way. Look at the weather, streaming and blowing. A nice cup of hot tea is what's needed for supper on an evening like this."

He winked facetiously, then fell to surveying the table again.

"A good dish of eggs, cold corned beef, and bread and cheese. That's my order for supper. So come along and get it ready, mother. Charlotte's in the kitchen waiting to give you a hand."

Mrs. Dinsmead rose, carefully winding up the ball of her knitting.

"She's grown a very good-looking girl," she murmured. "Sweetly pretty, I say."

226

" Ah!" said Mr. Dinsmead. " The mortal image of her Ma! So go along with you, and don't let's waste any more time."

He strolled about the room humming to himself for a minute or two. Once he approached the window and looked out.

" Wild weather," he murmured to himself. " Not much likelihood of our having visitors to-night."

Then he too left the room.

About ten minutes later Mrs. Dinsmead entered bearing a dish of fried eggs. Her two daughters followed, bringing in the rest of the provisions. Mr. Dinsmead and his son Johnnie brought up the rear. The former seated himself at the head of the table.

" And for what we are to receive, etcetera," he remarked humorously. " And blessings on the man who first thought of tinned foods. What would we do, I should like to know, miles from anywhere, if we hadn't a tin now and then to fall back upon when the butcher forgets his weekly call?"

He proceeded to carve corned beef dexterously.

" I wonder who ever thought of building a house like this, miles from anywhere," said his daughter Magdalen pettishly. " We never see a soul."

" No," said her father. " Never a soul."

" I can't think what made you take it, father," said Charlotte.

" Can't you, my girl? Well, I had my reasons—I had my reasons."

His eyes sought his wife's furtively, but she frowned.

" And haunted too," said Charlotte. " I wouldn't sleep alone here for anything."

" Pack of nonsense," said her father. " Never seen anything, have you? Come now."

" Not *seen* anything perhaps, but——"

" But what?"

Charlotte did not reply, but she shivered a little. A
great surge of rain came driving against the window-
pane, and Mrs. Dinsmead dropped a spoon with a tinkle
on the tray.

"Not nervous, are you, mother?" said Mr. Dinsmead. "It's a wild night, that's all. Don't you worry,
we're safe here by our fireside, and not a soul from outside likely to disturb us. Why, it would be a miracle if
anyone did. And miracles don't happen. No," he
added as though to himself, with a kind of peculiar
satisfaction. "Miracles don't happen."

As the words left his lips there came a sudden knock-
ing at the door. Mr. Dinsmead stayed as though
petrified.

"Whatever's that?" he muttered. His jaw fell.

Mrs. Dinsmead gave a little whimpering cry and pulled
her shawl up round her. The colour came into Magdalen's face and she leant forward and spoke to her
father.

"The miracle has happened," she said. "You'd
better go and let whoever it is in."

2

Twenty minutes earlier Mortimer Cleveland had stood in the driving rain and mist surveying his car. It was really cursed bad luck. Two punctures within ten minutes of each other, and here he was, stranded, miles from anywhere, in the midst of these bare Wiltshire downs with night coming on, and no prospect of shelter. Serve him right for trying to take a short-cut. If only he had stuck to the main road! Now he was lost on what seemed a mere cart-track on the hillside, with no possibility of getting the car further, and with no idea if there were even a village anywhere near.

He looked round him perplexedly, and his eye was caught by a gleam of light on the hillside above him. A second later the mist obscured it once more, but, waiting patiently, he presently got a second glimpse of it. After a moment's cogitation, he left the car and struck up the side of the hill.

Soon he was out of the mist, and he recognised the light as shining from the lighted window of a small cottage. Here, at any rate, was shelter. Mortimer Cleveland quickened his pace, bending his head to meet the furious onslaught of wind and rain which seemed to be trying its best to drive him back.

Cleveland was in his own way something of a celebrity though doubtless the majority of folks would have displayed complete ignorance of his name and achievements. He was an authority on mental science and had written two excellent text books on the subconscious. He was also a member of the Psychical Research Society and a student of the occult in so far as it affected his own conclusions and line of research.

He was by nature peculiarly susceptible to atmosphere, and by deliberate training he had increased his own natural gift. When he had at last reached the cottage and rapped at the door, he was conscious of an excitement, a quickening of interest, as though all his faculties had suddenly been sharpened.

The murmur of voices within had been plainly audible to him. Upon his knock there came a sudden silence, then the sound of a chair being pushed back along the floor. In another minute the door was flung open by a boy of about fifteen. Cleveland could look straight over his shoulder upon the scene within.

It reminded him of an interior by some Dutch Master. A round table spread for a meal, a family party sitting round it, one or two flickering candles and the firelight's glow over all. The father, a big man, sat one side of the table, a little grey woman with a frightened face sat opposite him. Facing the door, looking straight at Cleveland, was a girl. Her startled eyes looked straight into his, her hand with a cup in it was arrested half-way to her lips.

She was, Cleveland saw at once, a beautiful girl of an extremely uncommon type. Her hair, red gold, stood out round her face like a mist, her eyes, very far apart, were a pure grey. She had the mouth and chin of an early Italian Madonna.

There was a moment's dead silence. Then Cleveland stepped into the room and explained his predicament. He brought his trite story to a close, and there was another pause harder to understand. At last, as though with an effort, the father rose.

" Come in, sir—Mr. Cleveland, did you say?"

" That is my name," said Mortimer, smiling.

" Ah! yes. Come in, Mr. Cleveland. Not weather for a dog outside, is it? Come in by the fire. Shut the door, can't you, Johnnie? Don't stand there half the night."

Cleveland came forward and sat on a wooden stool by the fire. The boy Johnnie shut the door.

" Dinsmead, that's my name," said the other man. He was all geniality now. " This is the Missus, and these are my two daughters, Charlotte and Magdalen."

For the first time, Cleveland saw the face of the girl who had been sitting with her back to him, and saw that, in a totally different way, she was quite as beautiful as her sister. Very dark, with a face of marble pallor, a delicate aquiline nose, and a grave mouth. It was a kind of frozen beauty, austere and almost forbidding. She acknowledged her father's introduction by bending her head, and she looked at him with an intent gaze that was searching in character. It was as though she were summing him up, weighing him in the balance of her clear young judgment.

" A drop of something to drink, eh, Mr. Cleveland?"

" Thank you," said Mortimer. " A cup of tea will meet the case admirably."

Mr. Dinsmead hesitated a minute, then he picked up the five cups, one after another, from the table and emptied them into the slop bowl.

" This tea's cold," he said brusquely. " Make us some more, will you, Mother?"

Mrs. Dinsmead got up quickly and hurried off with the teapot. Mortimer had an idea that she was glad to get out of the room.

The fresh tea soon came, and the unexpected guest was plied with viands.

Mr. Dinsmead talked and talked. He was expansive, genial, loquacious. He told the stranger all about himself. He'd lately retired from the building trade— yes, made quite a good thing out of it. He and the Missus thought they'd like a bit of country air—never lived in the country before. Wrong time of year to choose, of course, October and November, but they didn't want to wait. "Life's uncertain, you know, sir." So they had taken this cottage. Eight miles from anywhere, and nineteen miles from anything you could call a town. No, they didn't complain. The girls found it a bit dull, but he and mother enjoyed the quiet.

So he talked on, leaving Mortimer almost hypnotised by the easy flow. Nothing here, surely, but rather commonplace domesticity. And yet, at that first glimpse of the interior, he had diagnosed something else, some tension, some strain, emanating from one of those four people—he didn't know which. Mere foolishness, his nerves were all awry! They were startled by his sudden appearance—that was all.

He broached the question of a night's lodging, and was met with a ready response.

"You'll have to stop with us, Mr. Cleveland. Nothing else for miles round. We can give you a bedroom, and though my pyjamas may be a bit roomy, why, they're better than nothing, and your own clothes will be dry by morning."

"It's very good of you.'

"Not at all," said the other genially. "As I said just now, one couldn't turn away a dog on a night like this. Magdalen, Charlotte, go up and see to the room."

The two girls left the room. Presently Mortimer heard them moving about overhead.

"I can quite understand that two attractive young ladies like your daughters might find it dull here," said Cleveland.

"Good lookers, aren't they?" said Mr. Dinsmead with fatherly pride. "Not much like their mother or myself. We're a homely pair, but much attached to each other, I'll tell you that, Mr. Cleveland. Eh, Maggie, isn't that so?"

Mrs. Dinsmead smiled primly. She had started knitting again. The needles clicked busily. She was a fast knitter.

Presently the room was announced ready, and Mortimer, expressing thanks once more, declared his intention of turning in.

" Did you put a hot water-bottle in the bed?" demanded Mrs. Dinsmead, suddenly mindful of her house pride.

" Yes, Mother, two."

" That's right," said Dinsmead. " Go up with him, girls, and see that there's nothing else he wants."

Magdalen preceded him up the staircase, her candle held aloft. Charlotte came behind.

The room was quite a pleasant one, small and with a sloping roof, but the bed looked comfortable, and the few pieces of somewhat dusty furniture were of old mahogany. A large can of hot water stood in the basin, a pair of pink pyjamas of ample proportions were laid over a chair, and the bed was made and turned down.

Magdalen went over to the window and saw that the fastenings were secure. Charlotte cast a final eye over the washstand appointments. Then they both lingered by the door.

" Good-night, Mr. Cleveland. You are sure there is everything?"

" Yes, thank you, Miss Magdalen. I am ashamed to have given you both so much trouble. Good-night."

" Good-night."

They went out, shutting the door behind them. Mortimer Cleveland was alone. He undressed slowly and thoughtfully. When he had donned Mr. Dinsmead's pink pyjamas, he gathered up his own wet clothes and put them outside the door as his host had bade him. From downstairs he could hear the rumble of Dinsmead's voice.

What a talker the man was! Altogether an odd personality—but indeed there was something odd about the whole family, or was it his imagination?

He went slowly back into his room and shut the door. He stood by the bed lost in thought. And then he started——

The mahogany table by the bed was smothered in dust. Written in the dust were three letters, clearly visible. *S.O.S.*

Mortimer stared as if he could hardly believe his eyes. It was a confirmation of all his vague surmises and forebodings. He was right, then. Something was wrong in this house.

S.O.S. A call for help. But whose finger had written it in the dust? Magdalen's or Charlotte's? They had both stood there, he remembered, for a moment or two, before going out of the room. Whose hand had secretly dropped to the table and traced out those three letters?

The faces of the two girls came up before him. Magdalen's, dark and aloof, and Charlotte's, as he had seen it first, wide-eyed, startled, with an unfathomable something in her glance. . . .

He went again to the door and opened it. The boom of Mr. Dinsmead's voice was no longer to be heard. The house was silent.

He thought to himself.

" I can do nothing to-night. To-morrow—well. we shall see."

3

Cleveland woke early. He went down through the living-room, and out into the garden. The morning was fresh and beautiful after the rain. Someone else was up early, too. At the bottom of the garden, Charlotte was leaning on the fence staring out over the Downs. His pulses quickened a little as he went down to join her. All along he had been secretly convinced that it was Charlotte who had written the message. As he came up to her, she turned and wished him " Good-morning." Her eyes were direct and childlike, with no hint of a secret understanding in them.

" A very good morning," said Mortimer, smiling. " The weather this morning is a contrast to last night."

" It is indeed."

Mortimer broke off a twig from a tree near by. With it he began idly to draw on the smooth, sandy patch at his feet. He traced an S, then an O, then an S, watching the girl narrowly as he did so. But again he could detect no gleam of comprehension.

" Do you know what these letters represent?" he said abruptly.

Charlotte frowned a little. " Aren't they what boats —liners, send out when they are in distress?" she asked.

Mortimer nodded. " Someone wrote that on the table by my bed last night," he said quietly. " I thought perhaps *you* might have done so."

She looked at him in wide-eyed astonishment.

" I? Oh, no."

He was wrong then. A sharp pang of disappointment shot through him. He had been so sure—so sure. It was not often that his intuitions led him astray.

" You are quite certain?" he persisted.

" Oh, yes."

They turned and went slowly together toward the house. Charlotte seemed preoccupied about something. She replied at random to the few observations he made. Suddenly she burst out in a low, hurried voice:

" It—it's odd your asking that about those letters, S.O.S. I didn't write them, of course, but—I so easily might have done."

He stopped and looked at her, and she went on quickly:

" It sounds silly, I know, but I have been so frightened, so dreadfully frightened, and when you came in last night, it seemed like an—an answer to something."

" What are you frightened of?" he asked quickly.

" I don't know."

" You don't know."

" I think—it's the house. Ever since we came here it has been growing and growing. Everyone seems different somehow. Father, Mother, and Magdalen, they all seem different."

Mortimer did not speak at once, and before he could do so, Charlotte went on again.

" You know this house is supposed to be haunted?"

" What?" All his interest was quickened.

" Yes, a man murdered his wife in it, oh, some years ago now. We only found out about it after we got here. Father says ghosts are all nonsense, but I—don't know."

Mortimer was thinking rapidly.

" Tell me," he said in a businesslike tone, " was this murder committed in the room I had last night?"

" I don't know anything about that," said Charlotte.

" I wonder now," said Mortimer half to himself, " yes, that may be it."

Charlotte looked at him uncomprehendingly.

" Miss Dinsmead," said Mortimer, gently, " have you ever had any reason to believe that you are mediumistic?"

She stared at him.

" I think you know that you *did* write S.O.S. last night," he said quietly. " Oh! quite unconsciously, of course. A crime stains the atmosphere, so to speak. A sensitive mind such as yours might be acted upon in such a manner. You have been reproducing the sensations and impressions of the victim. Many years ago *she* may have written S.O.S. on that table, and you unconsciously reproduced her act last night."

Charlotte's face brightened.

" I see," she said. " You think that is the explanation?"

A voice called her from the house, and she went in, leaving Mortimer to pace up and down the garden paths. Was he satisfied with his own explanation? Did it cover the facts as he knew them? Did it account for the tension he had felt on entering the house last night?

Perhaps, and yet he still had the odd feeling that his sudden appearance had produced something very like consternation, he thought to himself:

" I must not be carried away by the psychic explanation, it might account for Charlotte—but not for the others. My coming as I did upset them horribly, all except Johnnie. Whatever it is that's the matter, Johnnie is out of it."

He was quite sure of that, strange that he should be so positive, but there it was.

At that minute, Johnnie himself came out of the cottage and aproached the guest.

" Breakfast's ready," he said awkwardly.   " Will you come in?"

Mortimer noticed that the lad's fingers were much stained. Johnnie felt his glance and laughed ruefully.

" I'm always messing about with chemicals, you know," he said. " It makes Dad awfully wild sometimes. He wants me to go into the building, but I want to do chemistry and research work."

Mr. Dinsmead apeared at the window ahead of them, broad, jovial, smiling, and at sight of him all Mortimer's distrust and antagonism re-awakened. Mrs. Dinsmead was already seated at the table. She wished him " Good-morning " in her colourless voice, and he had again the impression that for some reason or other, she was afraid of him.

Magdalen came in last. She gave him a brief nod and took her seat opposite him.

" Did you sleep well?" she asked abruptly. " Was your bed comfortable?"

She looked at him very earnestly, and when he replied courteously in the affirmative he noticed something very like a flicker of disappointment pass over her face. What had she expected him to say, he wondered?

He turned to his host.

" This lad of yours is interested in chemistry, it seems!" he said pleasantly.

There was a crash. Mrs. Dinsmead had dropped her tea cup.

" Now then, Maggie, now then," said her husband.

It seemed to Mortimer that there was admonition, warning, in his voice. He turned to his guest and spoke fluently of the advantages of the building trade, and of not letting young boys get above themselves.

After breakfast, he went out in the garden by himself, and smoked. The time was clearly at hand when he must leave the cottage. A night's shelter was one thing, to prolong it was difficult without an excuse, and what possible excuse could he offer? And yet he was singularly loath to depart.

Turning the thing over and over in his mind, he took

a path that led round the other side of the house. His shoes were soled with crêpe rubber, and made little or no noise. He was passing the kitchen window, when he heard Dinsmead's words from within, and the words attracted his attention immediately.

" It's a fair lump of money, it is."

Mrs. Dinsmead's voice answered. It was too faint in tone for Mortimer to hear the words, but Dinsmead replied :

" Nigh on £60,000, the lawyer said."

Mortimer had no intention of eavesdroping, but he retraced his steps very thoughtfully. The mention of money seemed to crystallise the situation. Somewhere or other there was a question of £60,000—it made the thing clearer—and uglier.

Magdalen came out of the house, but her father's voice called her almost immediately, and she went in again. Presently Dinsmead himself joined his guest.

" Rare good morning," he said genially.

" I hope your car will be none the worse."

" Wants to find out when I'm going," thought Mortimer to himself.

Aloud he thanked Mr. Dinsmead once more for his timely hospitality.

" Not at all, not at all," said the other.

Magdalen and Charlotte came together out of the house, and strolled arm in arm to a rustic seat some little distance away. The dark head and the golden one made a pleasant contrast together, and on an impulse Mortimer said :

" Your daughters are very unlike, Mr. Dinsmead."

The other who was just lighting his pipe gave a sharp jerk of the wrist, and dropped the match.

" Do you think so?" he asked. " Yes, well, I suppose they are."

Mortimer had a flash of intuition.

" But of course they are not both your daughters,"
he said smoothly.

He saw Dinsmead look at him, hesitate for a moment,
and then make up his mind.

" That's very clever of you, sir," he said. " No, one
of them is a foundling, we took her in as a baby and we
have brought her up as our own. She herself has not
the least idea of the truth, but she'll have to know soon."
He sighed.

" A question of inheritance?" suggested Mortimer
quietly.

The other flashed a suspicious look at him.

Then he seemed to decide that frankness was best;
his manner became almost aggressively frank and open.

" It's odd that you should say that, sir."

" A case of telepathy, eh?" said Mortimer, and
smiled.

" It is like this, sir. We took her in to oblige the
mother—for a consideration, as at the time I was just
starting in the building trade. A few months ago I
noticed an advertisement in the papers, and it seemed
to me that the child in question must be our Magdalen.
I went to see the lawyers, and there has been a lot of
talk one way and another. They were suspicious—
naturally, as you might say, but everything is cleared up
now. I am taking the girl herself to London next week:
she doesn't know anything about it so far. Her father,
it seems, was one of these rich Jewish gentlemen. He
only learnt of the child's existence a few months before
his death. He set agents on to try and trace her, and
left all his money to her when she should be found."

Mortimer listened with close attention. He had no
reason to doubt Mr. Dinsmead's story. It explained
Magdalen's dark beauty; explained too, perhaps, her
aloof manner. Nevertheless, though the story itself
might be true, something lay behind it undivulged.

But Mortimer had no intention of rousing the other's suspicions. Instead, he must go out of his way to allay them.

" A very interesting story, Mr. Dinsmead," he said. " I congratulate Miss Magdalen. An heiress and a beauty, she has a great time ahead of her."

" She has that," agreed her father warmly, " and she's a rare good girl too, Mr. Cleveland."

There was every evidence of hearty warmth in his manner.

" Well," said Mortimer, " I must be pushing along now, I suppose. I have got to thank you once more, Mr. Dinsmead, for your singularly well-timed hospitality."

Accompanied by his host, he went into the house to bid farewell to Mrs. Dinsmead. She was standing by the window with her back to them, and did not hear them enter. At her husband's jovial: " Here's Mr. Cleveland come to say good-bye," she started nervously and swung round, dropping something which she held in her hand. Mortimer picked it up for her. It was a miniature of Charlotte done in the style of some twenty-five years ago. Mortimer repeated to her the thanks he had already proffered to her husband. He noticed again her look of fear and the furtive glances that she shot at him from beneath her eyelids.

The two girls were not in evidence, but it was not part of Mortimer's policy to seem anxious to see them; also he had his own idea, which was shortly to prove correct.

He had gone about half a mile from the house on his way down to where he had left the car the night before, when the bushes on one side of the path were thrust aside, and Magdalen came out on the track ahead of him.

" I had to see you," she said.

" I expected you," said Mortimer. " It was you who

wrote S.O.S. on the table in my room last night, wasn't
it?''

Magdalen nodded.

'' Why?'' asked Mortimer gently.

The girl turned aside and began pulling off leaves
from a bush.

'' I don't know,'' she said, '' honestly, I don't
know.''

'' Tell me,'' said Mortimer.

Magdalen drew a deep breath.

'' I am a practical person,'' she said, '' not the kind
of person who imagines things or fancies them. You, I
know, believe in ghosts and spirits. I don't, and when
I tell you that there is something very wrong in that
house,'' she pointed up the hill, '' I mean that there is
something tangibly wrong; it's not just an echo of the
past.   It has been coming on ever since we've been
there.   Every day it grows worse, father is different,
mother is different, Charlotte is different.''

Mortimer interposed.   '' Is Johnnie different?'' he
asked.

Magdalen looked at him, a dawning appreciation in
her eyes. '' No,'' she said, '' now I come to think of it,
Johnnie is not different. He is the only one who's—
who's untouched by it all. He was untouched last night
at tea.''

'' And you?'' asked Mortimer.

'' I was afraid—horribly afraid, just like a child—
without knowing what it was I was afraid of. And father
was—queer, there's no other word for it, queer.   He
talked about miracles and then I prayed—actually
prayed for a miracle, and *you* knocked on the door.''

She stopped abruptly, staring at him.

'' I seem mad to you, I suppose,'' she said defiantly.

' No,'' said Mortimer, '' on the contrary you seem

extremely sane. All sane people have a premonition of danger if it is near them.''

" You don't understand," said Magdalen. " I was not afraid—for myself.''

" For whom, then?''

But again Magdalen shook her head in a puzzled fashion. " I don't know.''

She went on:

" I wrote S.O.S. on an impulse. I had an idea—absurd, no doubt, that they would not let me speak to you —the rest of them, I mean. I don't know what it was I meant to ask you to do. I don't know now.''

" Never mind," said Mortimer. " I shall do it.''

" What can you do?''

Mortimer smiled a little.

" I can think.''

She looked at him doubtfully.

" Yes," said Mortimer, " a lot can be done that way, more than you would ever believe. Tell me, was there any chance word or phrase that attracted your attention just before that meal last evening?''

Magdalen frowned. " I don't think so," she said. " At least I heard father say something to mother about Charlotte being the living image of her, and he laughed in a very queer way, but—there's nothing odd in that, is there?''

" No," said Mortimer slowly, " except that Charlotte is not like your mother.''

He remained lost in thought for a minute or two, then looked up to find Magdalen watching him uncertainly.

" Go home, child," he said, " and don't worry; leave it in my hands.''

She went obediently up the path towards the cottage. Mortimer strolled on a little further, then threw himself down on the green turf. He closed his eyes, detached himself from conscious thought or effort, and let a series of pictures flit at will across the surface of his mind.

Johnnie! He always came back to Johnnie. Johnnie, completely innocent, utterly free from all the network of suspicion and intrigue, but nevertheless the pivot round which everything turned. He remembered the crash of Mrs. Dinsmead's cup on her saucer at breakfast that morning. What had caused her agitation? A chance reference on his part to the lad's fondness for chemicals? At the moment he had not been conscious of Mr. Dinsmead, but he saw him now clearly, as he sat, his teacup poised half-way to his lips.

That took him back to Charlotte, as he had seen her when the door opened last night. She had sat so staring at him over the rim of her teacup. And swiftly on that followed another memory. Mr. Dinsmead emptying teacups one after the other, and saying " this tea is cold."

He remembered the steam that went up. Surely the tea had not been so very cold after all?

Something began to stir in his brain. A memory of something read not so very long ago, within a month perhaps. Some account of a whole family poisoned by a lad's carelessness. A packet of arsenic left in the larder had all dripped through on the bread below. He had read it in the paper. Probably Mr. Dinsmead had read it too.

Things began to grow clearer. . . .

Half an hour later, Mortimer Cleveland rose briskly to his feet.

4

It was evening once more in the cottage. The eggs were poached to-night and there was a tin of brawn. Presently Mrs. Dinsmead came in from the kitchen bearing the big teapot. The family took their places round the table.

" A contrast to last night's weather," said Mrs. Dinsmead, glancing towards the window.

" Yes," said Mr. Dinsmead, " it's so still to-night that you could hear a pin drop. Now then, Mother, pour out, will you?"

Mrs. Dinsmead filled the cups and handed them round the table. Then, as she put the teapot down, she gave a sudden little cry and pressed her hand to her heart. Mr. Dinsmead swung round in his chair, following the direction of her terrified eyes. Mortimer Cleveland was standing in the doorway.

He came forward. His manner was pleasant and apologetic.

" I'm afraid I startled you," he said. " I had to come back for something."

" Back for something," cried Mr. Dinsmead. His face was purple, his veins swelling. " Back for what, I should like to know?"

" Some tea," said Mortimer.

With a swift gesture he took something from his pocket, and, taking up one of the teacups from the table, emptied some of its contents into a little test-tube he held in his left hand.

" What—what are you doing?" gasped Mr. Dinsmead. His face had gone chalky-white, the purple dying out as if by magic. Mrs. Dinsmead gave a thin, high, frightened cry.

" You read the papers, I think, Mr. Dinsmead? I am sure you do. Sometimes one reads accounts of a whole family being poisoned, some of them recover, some do not. In this case, *one would not*. The first explanation would be the tinned brawn you were eating, but supposing the doctor to be a suspicious man, not easily taken in by the tinned food theory? There is a packet of arsenic in your larder. On the shelf below it is a packet of tea. There is a convenient hole in the top shelf, what more natural to suppose then that the arsenic found its way into the tea by accident? Your son Johnnie might be blamed for carelessness, nothing more."

" I—I don't know what you mean," gasped Dinsmead.

" I think you do." Mortimer took up a second teacup and filled a second test-tube. He fixed a red label to one and a blue label to the other.

" The red-labelled one," he said, " contains tea from your daughter Charlotte's cup, the other from your daughter Magdalen's. I am prepared to swear that in the first I shall find four or five times the amount of arsenic than in the latter."

" You are mad," said Dinsmead.

" Oh! dear me, no. I am nothing of the kind. You told me to-day, Mr. Dinsmead, that Magdalen was not your own daughter. You lied to me. Magdalen *is* your daughter. Charlotte was the child you adopted, the child who was so like her mother that when I held a miniature of that mother in my hand to-day I mistook it for one of Charlotte herself. Your own daughter was to inherit the fortune, and since it might be impossible to keep your supposed own daughter Charlotte out of sight, and someone who knew the mother might have realised the truth of the resemblance, you decided on, well—a pinch of white arsenic at the bottom of a tea-cup."

Mrs. Dinsmead gave a sudden high cackle, rocking herself to and fro in violent hysterics.

" Tea," she squeaked, " that's what he said, tea, not lemonade."

" Hold your tongue, can't you?" roared her husband wrathfully.

Mortimer saw Charlotte looking at him, wide-eyed, wondering, across the table. Then he felt a hand on his arm, and Magdalen dragged him out of earshot.

" Those," she pointed at the phials—" Daddy. You won't——"

Mortimer laid his hand on her shoulder. " My child," he said, " you don't believe in the past. I do. I believe in the atmosphere of this house. If he had not come to it, perhaps—I say *perhaps*—your father might not have conceived the plan he did. I keep these two test-tubes to safeguard Charlotte now and in the future. Apart from that, I shall do nothing, in gratitude, if you will, to that hand that wrote S.O.S."